THE LOST ART OF REVERIE

AVELINE BOOK ONE

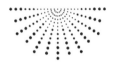

RAE WALSH

SMALL SEED PRESS

PROLOGUE

"Katie... Katie!"

Katie pulled herself back from her daydreams, back to the hill beside Lake Aveline on a sunny summer afternoon. She was ten years old and her friend, Sammy, stood waving his hands in front of her face.

"Hmmm?" she said.

"Where did you go?" he asked, laughing. "You're always dreaming."

"I was imagining the perfect kitchen."

"A kitchen?" Sammy screwed up his face. "Why?"

"A *huge* kitchen with everything you could ever need for cooking." She stood up and put her hands on her hips, imagining. "I'm going to be a chef when I grow up!" she announced.

Sammy continued to look puzzled, his hair sticking up all over his head and his brow furrowed as though he couldn't imagine why anyone would daydream about something as mundane as a kitchen. Katie laughed at his look and jumped to her feet, brushing off her shorts. "Last one to the rope swing has to wait forever!" She took off running before he started, but he got there first, his skinny arms and legs scissoring across the rocky hill. She pulled up behind him at the rope swing.

"Forever, huh?" he asked, holding on to the rope, laughing and out of breath. He was twelve this year. Next year he would be thirteen. A teenager! It seemed impossible. She thought fast. How could she get the swing away from him? He was only two years older than her, but he was scrappy and strong.

But then he handed it to her, with a funny little bow.

"For you, Chef Katie. You can take the first swing."

She smiled and took it. Sometimes Sammy hesitated before jumping, taking time to drum up his courage. But Katie never hesitated. She pulled the rope back away from the cliff edge, as far as it would go, then ran with it and jumped onto the big knot in the cord, red hair streaming behind her, only letting go when the swing stretched all the way over the glittering lake. Then she was flying, shrieking, into the blue water, the sun warm on her skin until she plunged into the cool water. She loved these summer days that stretched on forever. She loved the bright air, the smell of the forest, and the sound of Sammy's yells as he didn't bother waiting for the rope swing and jumped straight off the edge of the cliff, landing in the water beside her.

KATIE FELT the blood drain from her face, and she clutched the phone tighter to her. "What?"

"It's going to be okay, sweetheart," Katie's Nana's voice was calm. "They say it's operable and that I should be able to recover."

"Cancer?" Katie repeated dully. She was twelve. "But what will you do? You're all alone there." Her heart hurt at the thought of her Nana alone in the big house in Aveline, trying to deal with cancer alone. "I know! I can move to Aveline and take care of you."

Her grandmother laughed. "That's sweet of you, Katie girl. But I'm going to move in with you and your parents in L.A."

"You are? But what about the house?"

"I'll rent it out. It will just be for a short time while I recover. I'm thinking that this old lady needs to come and live with her family. How do you feel about that?"

Katie shook herself. She couldn't say the thoughts that were going through her mind. *What about the lake? What about summers? What about Sammy?* Katie didn't know how to have a summer that wasn't at the lake in Aveline, where she swam every day and practically lived outdoors.

But it didn't matter. All that mattered now was that Nana got better.

"I feel wonderful about that," she said. "I want you to live with us." She brightened. "I'll cook for you! I'll cook feel-better food."

"Of course you will, sweetheart," Katie's grandmother said, and Katie put the aching part of her heart, the part that waited all year for summers in Aveline, to one side. It was time to help Nana.

~

"KATIE! WHY ARE YOU LEAVING?"

Twenty-two-year-old Katie could hardly see for tears. She walked quickly, ignoring the question tossed casually by a classmate who didn't actually care, her backpack slung over one shoulder, heart aching. What would she do now? Culinary school had been her dream for as long as she could remember. But Katie had failed spectacularly, and there was no resurrecting her vision. If only she had been paying attention.

It was her own fault. All of it had been too good to be true. The acceptance letter and the move across the country to New York City. The shiny knives and countertops in the beautiful kitchen. Fresh vegetables and markets in the early mornings. Cooking all day long.

She should have learned how to disappear. She should have learned how not to draw attention, to fade into the background and not stand out.

She felt a splinter of anger. *Is it really your fault, though?* she asked herself. *He should have been more professional. He shouldn't have lied.*

The injustice pricked at her.

She was at the front door of the school, getting ready to walk away.

It didn't matter whose fault it was. The result was the same: Katie was leaving, her dream crushed. She was the only one paying for this particular failure. She took one last look at the school as she stood on the sidewalk, remembering how large and luminous her hope had been when she arrived. The memory hurt, and she turned away, walking along the busy street, head down to hide her tears.

"Hurry up, Katie!" Ed's voice was sharp, as though he was already annoyed.

Katie finished applying her lipstick and called back to him. "Just a minute!"

"We're going to be late!" he called back.

She sat and quickly strapped her high heels on, adjusting her skirt as she stood, then grabbed her briefcase and joined Ed at the door to their little Los Angeles bungalow. It was hers, actually, but Ed had moved in a year ago when she turned twenty-six. She guessed that made it theirs.

Ed was looking at his watch. "Let's go," he said.

"Wait a minute," she said. She kissed him and smiled into his handsome face. "Good morning," she said.

He sighed. "You know I don't like those shoes. They make you taller than me."

Her face fell.

"That's the problem with you, Katie," he said, as they climbed into the car. "You don't pay attention. You make us late when you space out."

Resentment bubbled inside Katie as she listened to his tirade. Ed got like this when he was stressed. Sometimes she wondered why she stayed with him, but Katie was loyal, and

Ed wasn't like this all the time. Katie had worked hard to be where she was, resurrecting herself from the crash of her first career choice, finding a new space in the world. And he was right—though Katie worked hard, she still daydreamed too much. But if Ed had any idea how much Katie forced herself to stay in the present, to do her job cheerfully and with precision, maybe he would give her some credit. Compared to the child she had been, Katie was hardly a dreamer anymore.

They arrived on time, but Ed didn't apologize. Instead, he linked arms with her and swept into the offices like a king, smiling at everyone he saw. Katie walked beside him, wondering about the show he was putting on.

She didn't dwell on it, though, her mind already flitting ahead to all the work she had laid out for her today: A meeting with her boss—Philip—an intake of a new employee, and other usual meetings of the company's human resources representative.

Working in human resources had not been part of Katie's vision for her life. Turned out she was good at it, though, and everyone had to do something.

Sometimes Katie remembered a long-buried part of herself. The brave girl with wild red hair who jumped into lakes in the sunshine and spent the afternoons lost in reverie. Those days were long past. After Nana had finished treatment for her cancer and gone into remission, she had never moved back to Aveline. Katie's parents visited the lake occasionally, but these days Katie was always too busy, and Ed liked to vacation in big cities or on the beach. He had no time for a small lakeside town.

"Katie!"

Katie turned toward her boss, pulling her arm out of Ed's grip.

"Good morning, Philip," she said.

"The meeting's moved up," he told her, looking handsome in his suit, as he always did. "Come join us as soon as you can."

Katie nodded an affirmative, gathering her things from her desk and heading toward the boardroom. As she passed Ed, though, she saw the strangest expression on his face. Jealousy, maybe? But Katie had always been a star at their company, practically family at Philip's house, invited to exclusive parties usually reserved for the officers. Ed had never seemed jealous about it before. He grabbed her arm for a quick kiss, and his hand wasn't gentle. Then he was gone. She stood there for a minute, waiting until her heart was ready, then walked to join the meeting.

"THE DEFENDANT HAS CALLED you a traitor, Ms. Grace. What's your response?"

Katie held a hand in front of her face, trying to shield herself from the cameras in front of the courthouse. Reporters called out questions, and she flinched away from them, hating the attention, hating the fact that things had come to this.

"People are saying you can't be trusted, that you listened to the wrong person. Do you have any comments?"

No comment. No comment. No comment.

She stumbled as she tried to push by, and when her shoe fell off, she just left it there in her hurry to get to her car. Her grandmother's funeral had barely been over when the situation at work blew up. In the best of times, all of it would be too much, but overwhelmed by grief and aware that one person who loved her without condition had left the world, it was unbearable. Katie couldn't hold it together to talk to reporters. All she could do was show up and try to tell the truth.

"You weren't paying attention," Ed told her at the breakfast table the next day, holding out the newspaper. It featured a courtroom illustration of Katie gazing off into the air as though she was trying to think of what to say next. Ed was right—she didn't look very believable.

"Why am I the one they are focusing on?" Katie asked. "I'm just H.R. Just another witness." Her mild attempt to stick up for herself sounded pitiful, even to her.

"I tried to warn you about what would happen to you if you pursued this, but you didn't listen to me. I'm sorry. Obviously, I want to help you, but I don't think I can. And I'm not going down with you."

When Ed was gone, Katie stared at the spaces his books had left on the shelves. Eight years, she thought. Finished like that. Because she didn't pay attention. She closed her eyes and laid her head on the table. Red hair flashing in the sun. Wind on her skin. A plucky kid with dreams. Katie didn't recognize herself anymore.

"Katie, honestly. It's just lunch. Everyone eats lunch. There's no reason for a panic attack."

Katie sat on the curb, shaking, desperately trying to breathe. How had she forgotten how lungs worked? If she could breathe, she could tell her mother that scolding someone for a panic attack *when they were in the middle of a panic attack* wasn't helpful. In the month since the court case and Ed leaving, simple things had grown more and more difficult, until Katie barely left the house. At her mother's insistence, she had come out for lunch today. It had not been a success.

How could her mother have known a group of her old colleagues would be eating lunch at the restaurant she'd chosen, Ed at the center of the group, laughing and sure of himself? Had they seen her? Katie was terrified that they might have seen her.

She couldn't get the air in. Panic washed over her in waves. Her face was wet with tears. She was going to throw up.

"Katie, answer me. Answer me."

There was nothing left. Katie had disappeared. She was a shell of a person now.

When her mother had left her at home with some toast and juice, Katie curled on her side in bed, thankful to be alone and in a darkened room. She idly flipped through the mail her mother had brought in. Her mother had removed the hate mail, which was just one more side effect from her testimony in court.

One letter looked interesting. It had the return address of a law firm called Jackson & Jackson in Aveline. Katie's mother had told her that something from her grandmother's estate should be arriving soon.

Katie felt a familiar stab of grief. She didn't want any silver cutlery or jewelry. She wanted Nana back. The sadness for Nana felt clean, so Katie let it rush over her. It was different than the choking tentacles of shame that had imprisoned her since the trial. Since the accusations of "attention seeker," "traitor," and "money grabber," had settled around her neck.

She felt the sadness of missing Nana, and also a tiny fizz of curiosity. Maybe she would get Nana's extensive collection of hats. She was pretty sure her parents were getting the bulk of Nana's estate.

Katie unfolded the crisp, thick paper and scanned it. After a moment she clutched it, reading more closely. The letter did not inform Katie that she had inherited the hats, or even a few thousand dollars, which would have helped pay of the bills that had been accumulating while she spent days in bed. The letter told her that she had inherited Nana's large Victorian house in Aveline, as well as the profits of the last seventeen years of renting the house out to students. Katie dropped the paper.

Nana's house. She could leave. The single thought crashed over her, draining the blood from her face.

Katie could leave this city and all its memories. She could go back to Aveline, to the lake of her childhood, the trees outlined in light. If she went to Aveline, Katie would never have to see an ex-colleague again, or fear that she would see one.

Suddenly Katie wanted Nana so much she ached. Nana had a fierce faith in God, and she had always made everything seem possible, as though any magical thing could happen because God was there and big and able to do anything. Katie had believed her. She found that she couldn't muster up the belief by herself. Nana had made all the ordinary things in life seem like a game, like everything was fun and playful. She had always teased Katie about her seriousness about career and job. Katie didn't know how to find that lightness when Nana wasn't there to offer it. Maybe being in Nana's house would be something like being with her.

Katie wanted to go back to feeling like life was expansive and full of possibility. She wanted Nana, but maybe the house was the next best thing.

CHAPTER ONE

On the sixth of May, three months after she received the letter, Katie tightened her fingers on the steering wheel of her car and held her breath. The viewpoint for Aveline should be just around this curve. There it was. She pulled the car over to the side of the road, heart pattering like a rabbit's, her hands shaking. She ignored the fear and carefully opened the door of her Subaru, stepping into the bright spring sunshine.

The scent of warm redwoods rose as the fallen needles were crushed under her flip-flops. She gazed at the town cradled between the hill and the lake in the little valley, tears pricking behind her eyes as she remembered stopping here when she was eight years old, knobby-kneed and snaggle-toothed, reading in the back seat on the long drive to her grandmother's house in the summers. Back then she hadn't really seen how beautiful the town was. She hadn't known how scarce true beauty could be. She breathed deeply. After the winter rains, everything was green and the air was fresh.

A mixture of oaks and firs and the occasional giant redwood swept down the hill to a perfect oval of sapphire blue. Lake Aveline was nestled in the hills of Los Padres National Forest like a secret jewel. Houses dotted the valley and the university campus spread like a fan on one side of the lake.

It was so familiar, as though nothing had changed in the nineteen years since she had last driven down to the lake. Nineteen years! She hadn't stayed away on purpose, but time had passed when she wasn't paying attention. She had been caught up, she supposed, entangled, enmeshed in so many more important things—high school, a career that had come to nothing, a life that had crashed down around her. She breathed in sharply. Nope. She was not going down the spiral of shame.

She ran sweaty palms down the legs of her jeans and took deep breaths, imagining herself in a circle where nothing bad could touch her. Katie's new therapist had told her to imagine a perfect place when she felt so close to panic. For three months, Katie had visualized this very lake. And now she was here. Everything she cared about was in the back of her Subaru. She had dropped the rest at Goodwill. Her life in Los Angeles was over. Good riddance.

Your problem, Katie, is that you dream too much. You're always daydreaming, not paying enough attention.

Her spine went rigid as Ed's words replayed in her head. She growled and banished them, going back to breathing and gazing at the jewel-like lake. What was wrong with daydreaming anyway?

It was nice simply to stand there, watching the wind ruffle the tops of the trees. Learning to walk, eat, and breathe again had taken a lot of work, and she was definitely pushing it with the move. It had to be worth it. It would be worth it if some of Nana's strength came with the house. When she finally stopped trembling she got back in her car and kept driving.

The sun flashed through the trees as she wound down the hill. Driving into town as a kid, this golden light through green leaves was the signal that the spacious doors of summer had been thrown open. Her heart would lift with happiness because soon she would see her grandmother, kick off her shoes, and not put them back on for the whole summer. That young, wild girl had been so brave, with no idea what life would bring, no idea about the toxic effects of shame and guilt.

She frowned at the McDonald's that had sprung up at the edge of town since she had gone away. There was a Target, as well, clumsy and out of place, looming over the little taqueria next door. Changes pushing at the boundaries. She kept driving toward the main street that ran through the heart of town, with a row of local shops that led to the park at the lake. There it was. Oak Street.

She drove slowly, gazing at the stores she passed, lost in memories. Someone in the truck behind her honked, impatient with her slow pace. Tears sprang to her eyes at the reprimand, and she wiped them away quickly, angry with herself for being so fragile. She refused to look at the big truck as it passed her and sped away, but out of the corner of her eye she saw a man shaking his fist. Goodness. He didn't seem like he was from around here. She took a shaky breath and continued along the street that was named for the large black oaks that lined it, limbs drifting toward one another over the wide street.

The Aveline Diner was gone. Katie blinked and looked around. No, it was definitely gone. Darn. Her daydreams about moving back had featured eating breakfast at the old town diner, listening to gossip from a corner booth, but it had disappeared and there was a pizza shop in its place. The hardware store was still there, though, flashing sales for inner tubes—summer was coming. And Greens, the small grocery store. Katie was glad to see it was still on Oak Street; shopping close to home would make life easier. It had changed since she was a kid, though. It looked far more hip, with blue European-style awnings and a sign that proclaimed "Organic avocados! Specialle extraordinaire! 99 cents a piece!" in elaborate chalk art. Katie smiled.

There was the law firm, Jackson & Jackson PC, run by Mercy and George Jackson, an African American couple who had moved to Aveline from L.A. twelve years earlier. Katie had never met them in person, but she'd been writing back and forth to Mercy for the past few months. She had an appointment to discuss Nana's estate with the lawyers later in the week. It was nice that the office was so close. Next to Jackson & Jackson was the post office, and on the other side of the street was a line of boutiques and one coffee shop, the Aveline Bean. Everything was upgraded and more refined than her memories.

Katie needed to park soon and find the real estate office. She clenched and unclenched her hands on the steering wheel, taking deep breaths to keep the panic down. She hadn't been out of the house this long in months. Her mother had wanted to come help today but Katie knew she needed to be alone. She wanted to sink into her new life by herself, without discussion, especially when she arrived at her new home for the first time.

Finally she arrived at the Oak Street Real Estate office. She parked her car, getting it parallel to the curb on the seventeenth try, then let herself out and plugged the meter with a couple of quarters. There weren't parking meters in the Aveline of her childhood either.

She glanced at her reflection in the back car window. Her waist length hair was wild from the drive, so she gathered it in a fist and shook it behind her, trying to smooth it down. It evaded her, vaulting in every direction. Oh well. She took another deep breath and stood up straighter, squaring her shoulders, exhausted from the effort of being out in public for so long. But this was it—just this one stop, and then she could hide away for days if she felt like it.

It had taken time to settle everything so she could actually take ownership. Her mother wanted her to sell the house and stay in L.A. But Katie knew what she wanted. She would never go back to her old career. She was a ghost of the sunny, confident person she had been and she didn't know if she would ever have her old self back. But she had Nana's house, and Nana's lake. She wanted them with a ferocity that surprised her.

Aveline was the right place, close to Nana and the love that had surrounded her and her old self. And besides, there weren't any better options. Katie still cried for hours every day. She didn't know who she was. She was sad and overwhelmed and couldn't muster enthusiasm for getting dressed most days, but when she remembered the house, she could picture the beauty of the oaks and almost feel the safety of being with her grandmother. She felt as though she was being pulled to something hopeful. If there was safety in the world, if there was anything like a true home in the harsh universe, it would be at Nana's house.

CHAPTER TWO

She walked up to the front door of the real estate office and pulled it open quickly before she could change her mind. In a glance, she took in the small, tidy room with a woman at a reception desk. Every wall was hung with paintings of whales: whales jumping, whales swimming underwater, whales with babies. Katie moved closer to one of the paintings to get a better look.

"Our daughter is an artist," the woman at the desk said. "She went through a whale phase recently. They're all for sale if you want one. We double as an art gallery for her work." This was said with a hint of dry humor.

"Really?" Katie asked, wondering if the woman was joking.

"Really," the woman answered. She stood and held out a hand. "I'm Juanita," she said. "I'm going to assume you're Kate."

"Katie," she corrected, taking the woman's hand. It was about half the size of her own. Juanita barely skimmed her shoulder. Katie shook the small hand carefully. "But how did you know?"

"We don't get all that many people off the street," Juanita replied, in the same dry tone. "I know this town looks like it has a huge turnover rate, but looks can be deceiving." Katie grinned, surprising herself. Juanita smiled back at her.

"Is she here?" came an enormous, raspy voice from beyond a doorway in the back. Katie braced herself for the person who owned it and she wasn't disappointed. The man who walked into the front room was a giant, several inches taller than Katie's six feet, and wide. His clothes weren't anything she might have thought of as office clothes—a flannel shirt and jeans. He looked like he had Mexican roots, like Juanita, but with a beard that brushed his chest. Katie blinked as he came closer. He stuck his hand out and she shook it. This time she didn't have to be careful. His hand easily enveloped her own.

"Kate. Hi. Carlo. It's so good to finally meet you," he said. "And you've met my wife, Juanita."

"She goes by Katie," Juanita said.

Katie had a brief, insane moment of wondering how they kissed. Did Juanita have to stand on a chair? "Nice to meet you too," she murmured, though she hadn't thought much about who he actually was. He had just been a cloudy form on the other end of her emails about the house.

Carlo jumped right to business. "My company has cleaned the place, but you'll see that it still looks like it needs a lot of work." He shook his head. "It's the way with students. They're not the most careful of tenants. I also brought a lot of furniture out of storage. Your grandmother wanted some of it stored, so it's been closed away all these years. We tried to put it back exactly as it was in the house before."

"Oh!" Juanita exclaimed. Katie and Carlo looked at her. "That reminds me..." She went to her desk and rummaged through it, emerging with an envelope in one hand. "This is from your grandmother. She told me, years ago, to give it to you when you came to take the house."

Katie's heart sped up, and she took the precious envelope out of Juanita's hand.

"Thank you," she said, feeling speechless. A last letter from her grandmother. It felt like gold.

Carlo crossed his arms over his chest and regarded her. "This is quite a moment for me," he said. "I've been caring for this place for more than half my career. And here you are to take it off my hands."

Katie had been only half listening, absorbed by the feeling of the piece of paper she held in her hand and mesmerized by the way Carlo's beard rose and fell with his words, tapping at his chest like it was alive, but she felt a splinter of alarm at the look in his eyes. He looked...gleeful. Was it glee over the prospect of not taking care of the house anymore? Was the house a monster? Katie remembered Nana's home as a large Victorian with high ceilings and a wraparound porch. Simple, though, right? Not too much to take care of, surely. Was her memory faulty?

"Thanks for taking care of it," she said finally, forcing the words out through a tight throat. Her pet anxiety dragon was getting riled up. Her therapist had told her it was a reaction to the trauma of the court cases and all the ensuing mail and hatred, to the threat of accusal. Her body had unfortunately decided that she was open for accusation at any moment, so it flooded her with flight or fight hormones, even in friendly situations. She closed her eyes for a moment, then opened them.

Both of them were staring at her in concern.

"Are you okay?" Juanita asked. "Do you need to sit down?"

"I'll be fine," she said. "I've been... a bit sick recently. I'd really just like to get settled in. Do you have the keys for me?"

"Are you sure she's up for the house?" Juanita asked Carlo in an audible whisper.

"I'd like to accompany you if that's okay," Carlo said, ignoring Juanita. "Take you through quickly. We can do a more thorough survey later."

"THAT'S FINE," Katie said, closing her hands into fists and squeezing tight. She waited as Carlo hurried back to the office to retrieve the keys, then followed her out to her car. Carlo paused as they got close to the car. Katie's passenger seat was piled high with books, the back seat packed tight. There was no room for him.

"I can meet you there," he said, waving at a bicycle chained to the rack in front of the office. Katie looked from the bike to Carlo. Her eyes widened as she imagined the large man riding the medium-sized bicycle.

"Do you remember how to get there?" he asked.

"I have a pin on my phone. But actually...I do think I remember."

"It's so close I could probably jump over there," he said, "so it's not like you could get lost. See you in a few."

Katie climbed into her car and waited as Carlo unlocked the bike, thinking that it was only polite not to speed off before he was ready, and he had the keys to the house anyway.

As she watched, another man walked over to join Carlo. He thumped Carlo on the shoulder, pointing his chin toward the bike and saying something Katie couldn't hear. The man was tall and broad-shouldered, easy in his posture, wearing a threadbare T-shirt and jeans. Carlo pointed at Katie's car, and the man turned and looked directly at her. Katie felt a jolt like missing a stair. He seemed so familiar, quiet and tall, with messy hair and blue eyes framed by black eyelashes, days of beard growth on his face. She turned away quickly, flustered, and turned her car on, maneuvering it out of the parking spot. She could meet Carlo at the house. Did she know that man? Why did he look so familiar?

Jeez, Louise, her heart was hammering. The panic again. This was why she needed to move. Her emotions were all over the map when she was in public. Chance encounters with strangers could have her in tears. Also normal after her experience, her therapist had assured her. But Katie knew she needed a place to hide, to be quiet, to figure out why her belief in goodness had disappeared.

Two blocks before the lake, the GPS directed her to turn right. She turned her car onto a wide street lined with trees. Oaks and jacaranda laced together overhead, forming a canopy that cast dancing shadows on the smooth asphalt. She saw the big Victorian right away, set back from the road on the corner lot, two stories tall. Her eyes widened. It was much larger than she remembered.

"Well, you said you wanted space, Katie," she murmured, pulling the car into the driveway and turning it off. "Seems to be enough." She stepped out of the car, hearing the click of the door as she shut it. The sound echoed on the quiet street.

The house was beautiful, though it did look worn around the edges. The pale yellow paint was fading, and parts of the intricate lacework were falling off. But it still had the diamond-paned windows she had always loved. When she was really small, she had pretended that she could see a different world through each diamond, spending hours putting an eye to each one, whispering to herself.

No one can stop me from daydreaming now, Ed, she told her ex-boyfriend in her mind. There was room with its bay windows and view of the lake, the enormous trees she had climbed, the wide, wraparound porch with its swing. She frowned at the swing. It hung drunkenly, only one rope connecting it to the ceiling. She walked carefully up the steps to the house, noting the uneven boards, and waited at the front door for Carlo. After a few minutes, he rode up and wheeled his bicycle to the porch, leaning it against the railing. He leapt up the stairs with much more energy than she would have expected for someone of his age and size, smiling before he handed her the keys.

"You open it," he said.

It might have been a perfect moment, if not for the fact that her heart was beating wildly with unnecessary fear, she was well past exhausted, and the key wouldn't open the door. She pushed and tugged, then finally sighed and turned to

Carlo, who struggled with the key, swearing under his breath. After what seemed like forever, the lock gave way, and Carlo swung the door open.

The smell of the old house greeted her first, and even after all these years, it brought tears to her eyes. It smelled like wood and sunshine. It smelled like her grandmother. Like summer, eucalyptus, old books, old furniture. She put a hand on her chest and walked inside. The stairs to the second floor were off to the right. Straight ahead was a hallway that led to the kitchen and rooms at the back of the house. On either side of the corridor were large rooms with tall doorways. The curtains were all drawn, and the wood floors were dark in the dim light.

She turned to Carlo. "Can we do the survey tomorrow?" she asked. "I need to rest."

He nodded. "Are you sure you'll be okay?" he asked.

"I'm fine," she answered, not meeting his eyes. "I drove a long way today, and I'm exhausted."

He gave a few more instructions that she barely registered, and then he was gone. She was blissfully alone in the large house. She walked around, tugging heavy curtains open. The light was fading, filtering through the trees and the wavy glass of the old windows. It was calm, gentle light, and she stood in it for a few moments, letting it bathe her hands and face.

She unloaded her overnight case and a bag of groceries from her car, brushed her teeth in the downstairs bathroom, then walked upstairs. She found the smallest bedroom, the one she had slept in as a child, and spread one of her sheets on top of the mattress, finally collapsing onto the bed with a sigh. She lay on her side, curled in a ball, staring at the play of light and shadows on her wall as the sun started to set. Grief, self-doubt, and fear swirled inside her, patterns that were becoming familiar. She felt ugly and unloved, and horribly ashamed.

She remembered the letter, and rummaged through her bag to find it. She opened the white envelope gingerly to find a piece of paper covered with her grandmother's careful writing. Tears sprang to her eyes.

Dear one, it read.

I can imagine that you are surprised by my gift. You are so successful where you are, so busy, so capable. But I see you, Katie girl, and this city eats at you. Aveline was always kind to me. A spacious place, a place to dream. You always dreamed when you were a girl. I hope you find time to dream again. Here is my house, my gift to you. I hope it is good to you as it was to me.

All my love,

Nana

Katie wept and clutched the paper. Deep inside her, a seed of something new came to life. Katie grasped it and held onto it. Comfort. The memory of feeling loved. The letter and the old house had welcomed her the way she had hoped. They had reminded her of the Katie she used to be.

CHAPTER THREE

S am opened his eyes and glanced at his phone. It was five-thirty exactly. He was awake right on time, thanks to his internal alarm clock. Through the window he saw a sliver of light above the hills. Dawn was coming.

He stood and stretched, then made his way into the kitchen in his boxer shorts, flicking on lights as he went. He scooped the last of the coffee grounds from the coffee jar into the filter of the coffee maker, then turned it on, reaching into a cupboard under the counter to pull out a new bag of coffee. He snipped the bag open, poured it into the jar, then pulled out his phone and wrote "coffee" on his grocery list.

While he waited for the coffee, he poured himself a bowl of cereal and sat on a stool at the bar counter that overlooked the street. He ran his hand over the wood, admiring his work. There was only one stool. No one ever joined him at this counter. He liked it that way. He did have two chairs at the kitchen table, and a couple of couches in his rarely used living room, but the breakfast counter was his own and a second chair was unnecessary. He flicked through articles on his phone, spooning oat bran flakes into his mouth and listening for the click that would mean the coffee was ready. He jumped up when he heard it, poured a cup of coffee and sat down again, scrolling through more articles.

He read about the refugee crisis and the rate of unemployment, scrolling past an article (after he took a quick look) of a dog and a lion who were friends. Then he switched over to his daily Bible verse, from Psalm 73 today. The familiar words echoed inside him, easing his mind and heart.

My flesh and my heart may fail, but God is the strength of my heart and my portion forever.

Sam set his phone on the counter and leaned back to look out on the street below, feeling a familiar sense of contentment. He loved his life of routine. Each day was the same; he ate the same thing, wore T-shirts and jeans like a uniform, worked in the hardware store that he owned. He did his books, he built furniture, and sometimes he did custom carpentry orders for clients. He talked to his neighbors on the street. In his life, there was no room for drama, no place for spiky, sharp emotions that wrecked him and filled his dreams with pain. He had worked hard to get to a place where his days were stable, smooth, and easy. Work each day, maybe go out on the lake on Saturday, and on Friday, backyard night, he would meet with George, Carlo, Sheldon, and Reverend Francisco to grill and drink beers in Frankie's garden, talking and praying together as they had for years.

Life hadn't always been this way. At one time he had been an emotional man with wild highs and desperate lows, back when he was young and hadn't learned to guard himself. The woman he loved had accepted his love and then betrayed him. It hurt so badly that Sam floundered, until he found friends and later, God, learning to look within for safety rather than searching for women to help him. He made up his mind to never return to a complicated life, to never need comfort outside himself and his routines.

He had worked to clear a quiet space around himself for his friends, his service, and his work. He lived a simple, quiet life. His employees teased him, calling him Old Man Sam. His mother never let up, telling him every other day that he needed to find a woman to love. But she was easy to ignore. People—the ones who didn't know his story—were mystified, wondering why he was still single. The guys thought he was cool and tried to emulate him, but they didn't get it. His mother told him the college girls who worked for him thought he was gorgeous in an over-thirty way. They didn't know that he was meant to be alone. He had chosen stability, the life of a monk. A simple, unfettered life.

He washed his bowl and cup, setting them in the dish drainer, and went back to his bedroom to get dressed for the day. The only decoration in his room—a painting of a whale on the wall over his bed—was a necessary purchase from his good friends Carlo and Juanita. He shrugged into a T-shirt and pulled on a pair of jeans, noticing, as he brushed his teeth, that it was past time to trim his beard. He didn't have time today. Maybe tomorrow.

He loped down the stairs into his hardware store, inhaling

the familiar fragrance of his shop. He'd been just five years old when his dad opened a store that sold building and gardening supplies, and the scent was as familiar as his own face in the mirror. He couldn't even say what the smell was—maybe a mixture of sawdust and nails, paint and the herbs in the greenhouse out back. And something else that he couldn't name.

At the front counter, he opened the cash register, restocking the bills and change from the bag he carried. Then he picked up the pad of paper that was always there, and added to the list, checking what was already on the list for today. The nail guys should be arriving with more stock. And there was a shipment of paint coming in tomorrow.

He wandered around through the shelves, checking stock. He marked down the need for hoses and large plastic containers, then walked to the back to see if there were any extras in the storeroom. Nope. Time to order. His phone alarm went off, letting him know there were fifteen minutes until opening time.

He unlocked the front door, heaving a towering pile of inner tubes outside for the sidewalk display. Late spring and summer were great for selling lake paraphernalia: innertubes and life jackets, goggles and paddles for the three large kayaks he had on sale inside. This May had been the hottest in fifty years, and people were rushing to the cool waters of the lake in droves. Most of the students had left town already, their hastily discarded furniture and clothes lining the curbs of the university campus and surrounding streets. The exodus of students always made the town seem quiet, but tourists and regulars came every year for the lake, and they bought inner tubes and kick-boards, towels, and beach blankets. Sam made sure to keep them visible.

Jaylen, one of his employees, arrived as he was building a tower of sun hats.

"What's up, Old Man Sam?" she asked.

He shot her a fake glare. "I'm going to put an end to that nickname," he said. "Next one who says it gets their pay docked."

"You always say that," she said, "and you never do it."

"I need you to squeegee the windows," he said.

"Sure thing," she said, bouncing off.

"You have far too much energy, Jaylen!" he called after her. "Tone it down a little!"

"No such thing," a deep voice said. Sam turned to find his friend, the Reverend Francisco, and his daughter Rosa standing by his display. "That's crooked," Francisco said, pointing at the inner tubes.

"It will be even more crooked before long. If you can think of a way to keep toddlers and dogs from walking into my tower, let me know," Sam said. He went and clasped hands with his friend, gripping his shoulder. "How are you, Rosa?" he asked. "Managing to keep your dad under control?"

The ten-year-old giggled. "When are you going to take us out in your boat?" she asked.

"Ooh, that sounds like fun. Let's do it when the water warms up a bit."

"Coming to backyard night this week?" Francisco asked.

"Didn't we agree to call it something other than backyard night?" He grinned at his friend. "But yes, do I ever miss it?"

Francisco had arrived in Aveline ten years before, a twenty-five-year-old widower with a baby who was devout and passionate about God, love, and justice, and immediately he'd begun to upset the status quo, feeding Aveline's handful of homeless people and working on shelter and job skills. He had more energy than any of Sam's college students and led services that were biblical and subversive. He was currently working on getting permits for community gardens. Frankie insisted that the people of Aveline were a decade behind in city gardening and that they could employ a lot more people in need of jobs than they already were. He got a lot of hate mail and also a lot of mothers who wanted to set him up with their daughters. Francisco was tall, bearded, and Salvadorian, though he had grown up San Francisco, the city that bore his name. He wasn't interested in a relationship, still in mourning for his wife, living with his parents and his daughter in the craftsman style house next to the old stone church. Sam credited Frankie for his turnaround after his breakdown in college.

"George is back from the city, so he'll be there. Carlo's coming, Sheldon too. We need more men. Keep your eyes peeled, eh? Keep your mind open about the surf trip. And Rosa and I will see you on the boat soon, right Rosa?"

"Don't have time for surfing, Frankie," Sam shot back, as his friend waved and walked away, holding his daughter's hand.

Sam finished the display with a sun hat tower and went to the front counter to make a few phone calls. He had his phone in his hand but was interrupted mid-dial by a sing-song voice echoing in the store.

"Hellooo!"

He sighed and laid his phone on the counter.

"Hey, Mom," he said. "You're up early today." Sam's mother, Dorothy, wore a bright purple, knee-length dress, and had a red scarf knotted around her hair, gray curls escaping from its edges.

"Not any earlier than usual," she said. "But it's none of your business."

He crossed his arms and leaned back. "Your customers keep coming over at eleven, asking me why you're not open when the sign clearly says nine o'clock. And then I worry. And I have to explain that my mother makes rules and rebels against her own rules. Why don't you just change your hours?"

She shot him a look. "I've earned a little freedom with my hours, haven't I?" she asked. She was wearing tasseled earrings so large they brushed at her shoulders.

"I think it confuses people."

"Who? My customers? They should come in the afternoon! Who shops for baby clothes in the morning anyway? I'm not taking advice from a twenty-something boy, successful hardware store or no."

"Mom, I'm thirty-two."

"Sure, sure, I can't keep track of how old everyone is."

Sam gave up. It didn't matter anyway. His mother had started her shop five years ago, on a whim, after Sam's father passed away, and despite her confusing hours and lack of business skills, it was wildly successful.

"Okay, whatever you think!" he said, uncrossing his arms and opening his hands.

His mother smiled and leaned on the counter. "That's right." She turned to Jaylen, who was walking by holding the squeegee and bucket. "No one likes a scolder, do they Jaylen?"

Jaylen's eyes widened. She shook her head and sped up, throwing Sam a glance over her shoulder as she started washing the windows.

Sam sighed. "If you talk to my employees like that, they won't respect me, Mom."

"If they don't respect you that's your own fault, but they do respect you, and you know it. They line up to work here. Your shop is famous. I swear they put pictures of it on the university flyers to attract students. 'Besides our beautiful campus and lake view, if you choose our school it's possible that you'll get a job at the hardware store of Samuel Grant.'"

He laughed. "Come on, Mom."

"Look at Jaylen—she stayed in town just to keep working. She could be anywhere on her summer break, but she chose to stay and work for you."

"I need the money!" Jaylen called, sloshing water onto the front windows.

Sam pinched the bridge of his nose. His mother smiled up at him.

"Who else is coming to work today?" she asked.

"Larry will be by at noon. Business is slow. No one wants to do renovations in a heat wave. Why?"

"I need you to come and work for me," she said, gazing up at him with her most winning look.

He looked steadily back at her. "What do you need?"

"Shelves," she said.

"Your shelves are fine. I made them myself." He picked up a stack of flyers for their upcoming early summer sale and flipped through them.

"Of course my shelves are fine, but I want more of them, and crafty ones, like this." She pulled out her phone and scrolled to a picture of square shelf blocks with four different levels and compartments branching out around the center.

"Hmm, those are nice. What are you going to put on them?"

"Jewelry," she said.

He raised an eyebrow. "For babies?"

"No, silly, for mothers. Have you seen all that new teething jewelry? It's made of rubber so that babies can chew on it, but it looks fabulous." She tapped her fingers on the counter.

Sam frowned. Selling jewelry specifically for a baby to chew seemed very niche. But his mother knew her market well. He shrugged.

"Sure, I'll come over and do some measuring this afternoon," he said.

"Thank you, darling! And by the way, your sister called," she said. She sighed, and her eyes grew watery. "She's having such a hard time with Maddie. She doesn't know what to do with her."

Sam hadn't seen his niece since she was four years old. His sister, Theresa, had taken her off to live in Minnesota ten years earlier, right at the time that Sam was having his own issues. According to his mother, nothing had gone right ever since. Sam had always meant to visit, but the years had flown by quickly, and he never felt ready to enter the drama that was his sister's life. Without meaning to, he'd missed Maddie's whole childhood.

"That's normal, isn't it?" he asked. "Teenagers are hard to deal with, right?"

"You were both angels," his mother said. Sam gave her a skeptical look, but she just trilled a goodbye and bustled out of the store. He shook his head at her selective memory. He didn't think he had been an angel, and Theresa certainly hadn't. His older sister had been difficult, and she was pregnant by age nineteen. Sam loved Theresa, but after she moved away, the air felt lighter. She was just too much, somehow. She took up all the molecules in a room. He felt horrible for thinking of her that way. Maybe he could call her this week and see how she was doing.

CHAPTER FOUR

S am busied himself with more work, still thinking about
his sister and niece, and was shelving hammers when
Lucy came in a few hours later. As usual, he heard Lucy
before he saw her. Lucy and his mother—the two women in
town who made a movie entrance every time they entered a
room.

"Sam!" she called. "Sam!" He stood up so she could see
him over the shelves. "There you are! Thank God."

He grinned, unable to keep from smiling. Everything was
an emergency with Lucy. She was a short, plump, Thai-
American woman from San Francisco, like Frankie. She had
moved to Aveline when Sam was a boy, and he had known
her most of his life. Lucy was forty-five and a single mother,
with one grown son enrolled in the local university—Larry,
who worked for Sam.

"You don't have any more work available, do you?" she
asked him. His smile faded as he realized that she was

genuinely troubled. She had dark shadows under her eyes and was gnawing at her lip.

"For Larry? He's already working full time. Today's his only half day."

"No, for me. I haven't been able to find anything since the mattress store shut down, and I'm getting to the end of my unemployment insurance. I'm desperate, Sam. I think we'll be out on the streets soon."

Sam went to her and gave her a quick hug. "Come on, Luce, we'll never let that happen," he said. She leaned her head on his arm. He did some calculations in his head.

"I can't hire you in slow season, Luce, not without cutting back on Larry's hours."

"Well, that won't do us any good."

"Have you asked Sheldon?"

"I don't want to work for Sheldon!" she wailed. "I've heard he makes you do calisthenics in the afternoons!" Sheldon owned Green's, the grocery store down the street, and was one of Sam's best friends. He was notoriously quirky and thought group aerobics were good for employee morale.

"I think the aerobics are optional," Sam said, looking down at her frowning face and patting her on the arm. "Legally, he couldn't make them mandatory. Come on, Lucy, he's a great boss. And he's had a 'Help Wanted' sign on his window for a few days. You're a shoo-in."

"Oh, I don't know about that." She sighed. "But I'll try." She looked around the store. "I need some lightbulbs while I'm here."

He led her to the lightbulbs and waited while she took twenty minutes to choose between brands. At the counter, he charged her for two instead of the three she had in her basket. She didn't notice, just exclaimed over how they were cheaper than she had thought, and he nodded and smiled at her. She passed her son on the way out, and he look surprised and gave her a quick kiss on the cheek before she left.

"What was my mother doing here?" he asked Sam when he reached the counter.

"Buying lightbulbs. And asking for a job."

"What? Goodness, you didn't give her one, did you?"

"No, she's going to go ask Sheldon."

Larry breathed a sigh of relief that seemed to come straight from his toes. "Thank God. Can you imagine it?"

Sam tried to, and found that he didn't want to picture the two of them working together. He grinned at Larry and clapped a hand on his shoulder, then glanced at his watch.

"Whoops, I told my mom I'd come down and measure out some shelves for her. Work on the list, will you? And add garden hoses. We need all sizes."

He left in a rush, plucking his tape measure from the counter and walking out onto the sunny street. A few doors down, he spotted his friend Carlo unchaining his bike.

"Where are you off to, Carlo? Thought you were bringing lunch to work. The diet, remember?"

"Sam! What's going on, my friend?" Carlo said. He sighed, straightening. "Diet's still on. I'm heading over to the old Grace house. Katie's moving in today." He nodded at a green Subaru parked in front of his office, and Sam realized a woman was sitting in the driver's seat, her hands resting on the steering wheel.

He felt a shock go through him when he heard her name and saw her red hair. He knew Katie Grace. She used to breeze through town and out-swim everyone in the summers, bringing the excitement of races and dock jumping competitions with her. He remembered her red hair gleaming in the sun, her freckled face and green eyes, how he had always felt so empty and bored after she left for school in the fall. She was two years younger than him, and their friendship had started with their discovery that both their last names started with "Gr." They called themselves the growlers, and it helped that she had an obsession with frogs and he had a strange talent for catching them. The friendship of years culminated in a quick, closed-mouthed kiss the day before she left, the summer she was eleven and he was thirteen. The summer before her grandmother got sick and moved. He never saw her again.

She was sitting in the Subaru, biting her lip, her face sad. She looked over and met his eyes briefly, and he thought he might go say hi, but she quickly started the car and pulled away from the parking spot. It didn't seem like she recognized him.

Carlo was watching him. "Might be some work for you in that old house," he said. "It's got a lot of problems. And who knows what will happen? Romance is in the air." He laughed loudly at his own joke. Sam frowned. He had the uneasy feeling he got when he was taking too much interest in someone. He punched Carlo lightly on the arm.

"I'd love to work on that house," he said. "It's such a beauty."

"It is. And so is Katie!" Sam left Carlo chuckling to

himself and jogged across the street to reach his mother's boutique. She was standing at the window.

"Did you see that woman?" she asked, when he came in. "That must have been Katie Grace. The whole town has been talking about the transfer of her grandmother's house. Carlo leaked it, not the Jacksons, they wouldn't tell me a thing about who was getting it. Ethics. Oh, I hope she does something nice with it. Such a shame for it to be a rental for careless students. Did you see what a beauty she's turned out to be? And she must be six feet tall!"

She turned to him then, her eyes narrowed. He took a step back. He was four inches over six feet and had always used that as an excuse to veto the women his mother wanted him to date. He shrugged, irritated at the way the day was going. Too many surprises. The Grace house had been a rental for over fifteen years. Why couldn't it stay that way? He shook his head, warning his mother that he didn't want to talk about it. She held up her hands in front of her, full of innocence. He pulled his tape measure out.

"Where do you want the shelves, Mom?" he asked, all business and determined to keep it that way.

CHAPTER FIVE

Katie sat back on her heels to look at her progress, wiping her forehead with the back of her hand. One small panel of one wooden cupboard shone in the morning light. She wore rubber gloves and her oldest clothes, her hair tied up to keep it out of the grime. Getting the whole kitchen clean was going to take most of a year, but still she smiled, peace settling inside her. It felt good to work with her hands. She pulled one glove off and reached over to turn the music up. The bright kitchen filled with the brassy sounds of Miles Davis on the trumpet. She could feel the music and the scrubbing working together to ease the tightness in her lungs. Today, for the first time in two months, she had woken up without feeling as though a large cat was sitting on her chest. She believed her therapist would call this progress. It seemed that already the gift of this large, unwieldy house was having a good effect on her.

She tugged the glove back on, plunged her scrub pad in the bucket of soapy water beside her, then scrubbed at the white cupboard again. The kitchen hadn't been altered for a long time, but it was large and full of light, a special bonus in the old house. Her grandmother had installed bigger windows when she first bought the house, so the house wasn't dark like some Victorians. She had kept the diamond-paned windows and used the same trim, so the windows still looked like they belonged, but sunshine streamed through them in abundance. Katie sat back again, looking around. What the kitchen really needed was a few buckets of paint. All the scrubbing in the world wouldn't do enough, not after over twenty years of student tenants who hadn't been bothered to wash the grime away. She bit her lip. She was going to have to venture out into the world. She wasn't sure if she was ready for it.

She climbed the stairs to get dressed. This morning she had taken a brief tour of the house, shutting the doors to most of the rooms right away, overwhelmed by piles of dusty furniture and old boxes. For now, Katie decided, she would use only a few rooms: kitchen, bathroom, her bedroom, and a corner of one of the front rooms. She had slept in the small bedroom that was always hers when she visited as a kid. Katie imagined that it made more sense for her to take her grandmother's room, a lovely, spacious room with three bay windows that overlooked the street. But she found she couldn't do it. The walking stack of shame and disillusionment that Katie had become wasn't ready for a move like that. This morning, she had opened the door a crack to peek inside. She saw her grandmother's four-poster bed, back in place after Carlo had retrieved it from storage. But she shut the door again quickly. Sometime, maybe, but not now.

Instead, she was back in the tiny room of her childhood, smiling at the good memories it invoked. In the late mornings, after lazy summer breakfasts with Nana, she had run into her room to change into her swimsuit, which was her summer uniform, since she was in and out of the lake all day. The room was just large enough to fit a twin bed and a thin corridor of walking space. It had been cozy when she was a girl; it was cramped now. There was a shelf on the wall opposite the bed, a little dresser and mirror at the back of the room, and a desk beside the door. Katie unpacked her clothes now, hanging them in the closet, folding her T-shirts and jeans to fit in the dresser. Someone had carved the name Augustus in the wood on the dresser surface, but apart from that, the room was the same as she remembered. Carlo had done an excellent job of putting everything back where it belonged.

Going out to buy paint. Going out. Katie pulled a simple, light blue shirt dress from the closet. The hem brushed the tops of her knees. As she washed her face and swiped her eyelashes with a little mascara, she felt brave, noble even. Sure she was merely going out to run errands, but this was a mighty foray into her new town. She was an emissary from her own house. She grinned at her reflection. *Drama queen,* she thought at herself.

"Stand up straight, Katie," she whispered, growing serious. She flinched, reminding herself that no one here knew what had happened in L.A. To them she was simply Katie Grace, Eliza Grace's granddaughter, not Katie Grace, courtroom panic attack and human resources attention seeker, slandered to high heaven by the bigwigs at her old company.

She took her hair out of its bun and shook it around her, smoothing it with a bit of water and rose oil as it fell to her waist. She pulled some of the coppery mess back from her face, and fastened it with a little bird-shaped clip, then clasped a necklace around her neck. Her mother had given it to her on her last birthday—a large jasper stone set in silver.

She went back down to the kitchen, looking around, her eyes widening. The room was a mess, and she didn't know where to begin. She crossed her arms. She needed to eat, and she was nearly out the groceries she brought with her. She needed paint and cleaning supplies. She scribbled a quick grocery list on a piece of scrap paper and left the house, locking the front door behind her, wondering idly whether she even needed to bother with locks in this town. The lawn was overgrown. She added that to her mental list of things to do. The list kept growing.

Oak Street was only blocks away and Katie wanted to walk, but she needed a way to carry things home. After a moment of scanning the yard, she wandered over to an old shed and saw a red Radio Flyer wagon overturned on the grass to it. Perfect. She used a piece of newspaper to brush the dust away and then set out for the grocery store, pulling the wagon behind her, trying to ignore the way her stomach was churning.

～

SHE REACHED Greens and left the wagon parked outside, pausing inside the entrance as the tinkle of bells announced her arrival. Four pairs of eyes turned to look at her, and she nearly ducked back out again. But then a short, round lady with short brown hair stepped forward, holding out a hand. Katie took it, and the woman shook her hand enthusiastically before letting go.

"You must be Katie. I'm Lucy. I'm the new bag lady at Greens." She shook her head. "No, wait, that's not right. Not the bag lady. What would you call me, Sheldon?" she asked, turning to a man who stood near a large desk in the corner.

"I suppose you're the packing executive," said the man, walking out from behind the desk. He approached Katie with his hand out. "I'm Sheldon, as Lucy already said. It's nice to meet you."

Well, this was odd. Katie wasn't used to being personally greeted at the grocery stores she frequented in L.A. And Sheldon was...kind of strange. He was slightly taller than her, with dark, curly hair, black-framed glasses, and a handsome face. But it was his outfit that made Katie pause. He wore a rather stunning three-piece, vintage baby blue suit. She glanced back at the entrance, checking to make sure she was in the right place.

He spoke as though reading her mind. "We don't always greet our customers like this," he said. "Don't worry. You can pop in and out of here with only a few questions about whether you slept well, most of the time." He looked at Lucy, his face thoughtful. "Right, Lucy?" Lucy raised her eyebrows, then nodded reluctantly. Sheldon continued. "But we've heard for months that our grandest house is going to be occupied again, and we've naturally been curious."

"My house is the grandest?" Katie burst out. "What about the new mansions outside town?"

Sheldon laughed. "I said the grandest, not the ugliest." Katie couldn't help smiling at him. He gestured into the store with an open hand. "Anyway, my store is your store, be at home. Don't hesitate to sample from the bins or try a grape or two. And if you have questions, ask me or one of our brilliant cashiers." Katie glanced at the two cashiers. One of them was doing something on her phone, and the other was checking her nails. Sheldon cleared his throat, and they looked up and waved half-heartedly.

Katie found a shopping cart and pushed it farther into the shop. The grocery store smelled like cinnamon and baked goods, and it was gorgeously arranged, with quotes written on small chalkboards scattered throughout the store. She stopped to read one by C. S. Lewis.

"You are never too old to set a new goal or dream a new dream."

Nice. Katie wished it were true. She peered back at Sheldon, who was talking animatedly with a customer at the cash register. Maybe for him it was true. She tried to remember whether she had known him when she was a kid. He looked like he was a few years older than her, and she drew a blank. It was possible they hadn't met. She remembered a handful of kids from the lake, but not much more than that.

She put milk, cheese, and yogurt in her cart, as well as a loaf of fresh, crusty bread. Then she went to the produce section, and her mouth fell open. Fruits and vegetables were heaped in large piles, many of them with little signs that said, "I'm Organic!" She put a few avocados in her cart, then added tomatoes, basil, lemons, peppers, and spinach. She found some excellent looking zucchini and threw that in as well, exclaiming to herself over the shiny purple eggplant she found. Reluctantly, she decided that it was enough and wandered over to the meat section. She added a packet of chicken breasts and a lean cut of grass-fed beef to her cart, then walked into the dried goods aisle and stocked her cart with lentils, chickpeas, pintos, and a bag of brown rice. She bought a few bottles of spices and herbs and thought about the big yard at her new house. She needed to start an herb garden.

The last things Katie added to her cart were a pepper mill and a bag of peppercorns. She looked at the loaded cart. What a stash. Her heart swelled with happiness. She could cook again! She didn't have to rush meals at the end of a long day in the office. She had been so busy in the city that she hardly ever took the time to cook, but she had always loved cooking and often spent her weekends making meals for Ed. Her heart fell. Oh, Ed. She had no one to cook for now. She felt herself falter, her breath catch, her heart thud. Suddenly she was nearly ready to abandon the cart and leave the store, but she stood there, breathing until the feeling passed. Her therapist had called this the fear of follow-through. It was why she hadn't been able to eat or shower or do anything at all for so many months. Her body thought something horrible would happen, and any painful thought could make her freeze.

"You can just make friends," she whispered fiercely. "Come on, Katie, next step. Just get your butt to the cash register."

"Wow, are you, like, having a party?" asked the teenager who rang her up.

"Um, no," Katie murmured. "Just stocking my pantry."

Lucy bagged the first items. "It's a lot to move into a new place," she said. "Anything else you need? Anywhere I can direct you?"

Katie smiled at her. "I was just thinking I'd like some herbs to plant in my garden. Is there a place in town that sells plants?"

"Is there? Of course there is. Sam's got all kinds of herbs in pots."

"Sam?"

"Sam Grant. Grant's Hardware." Lucy stacked groceries in paper bags as carefully as if she was building a house.

"Oh, great, I need that place anyway. I have to pick up paint for my kitchen." Katie opened a bag and began to help. She frowned. She needed to unpack her cloth bags from the moving boxes if she didn't want to waste a million paper bags.

"Sam has almost everything you could ever need," Lucy told her. "I go to Grant's nearly every day. My son works there, too."

The cashier looked up. "I go too, but mostly just to look at Sam." She closed her eyes and sighed, then went back to her work.

Lucy snorted. "He's far too old for you, child." She looked at Katie, and her eyes glinted. "But not for you, Katie."

Katie snorted an awkward laugh, alarmed. "I'm not looking for anyone right now, old or not, but now you're making me nervous. I remember the hardware store owner as a rather pear-shaped man with thick glasses."

Lucy nodded. "Sam's dad. He passed away around five years ago."

"Oh, I'm sorry."

"Well, people die. But take a good look at Sam while you're in there. He might change your mind about whether you're in the market for a man."

Katie's eyes widened, and she shook her head.

"Not in the market for a man," she managed to say.

Lucy crossed her arms and regarded her thoughtfully. Katie thought she was preparing to say something else about this apparent dreamboat and was relieved when she changed the subject.

"Do you go to church, Katie?"

"I...did when I was growing up. I have...I got a little sidetracked by my career."

Lucy grunted. "Happens to the best of us. I meet with a few women every week to talk and connect. Sometimes we pray together. Sometimes we just sit and get all our gripes out. Do you want to join us? It may be a good way to meet some more people."

Katie was taken aback. The grocery store visit had started odd and just gotten stranger, passing from introductions to an invitation to a women's group. She had never been part of a women's group. She'd never had the time.

Lucy sensed her hesitation. "It's at Mercy's house on Saturday night, if you're interested. Do you know Mercy?"

"Mercy Jackson? The lawyer? I have an appointment with her this week."

"Oh? Great! She can give you the rest of the details then. You'll love her. And hopefully we won't scare you away. I'll do my best."

Katie nodded, swallowing. Emotions welled up inside

her. Lucy's openness had caught her off guard. In Katie's plans to move to Aveline, she had visualized the lake and the house, silence, and space. She hadn't imagined friends. She wasn't sure she could do friendship, feeling the way she did.

"Thank you," she said.

It took three trips to get all the bags into the radio flyer, and when she finished, it was full to the brim. What was she going to do with the paint she needed to buy? She stood for a minute, then shrugged. She could come back to pick it up later, but she still had energy now— she should get the next store out of the way and then go home and take a nap. Though Katie was doing better, she still needed to lie down in the dark in the afternoons, or risk falling apart. She hadn't yet christened a crying closet in this house, and she would love it if things stayed that way.

CHAPTER SIX

Walking along the sidewalk toward Grant's Hardware, Katie took a moment to look up at the large oak and jacaranda trees that lined the street. The gnarled branches of the oaks were silhouetted against the sun, the jacarandas in full purple bloom. They were stunning, and she sighed, soaking them in. When she looked down from the trees, she saw the man she had noticed yesterday, standing about fifteen feet down the sidewalk, in front of the hardware store, watching her with his arms crossed over his chest. He stood with the stillness of a pond, or a clear sky. She drew in a breath. As she got nearer, she saw that he had blue, deep-set eyes, fringed with dark eyelashes. He was very tall, wide-shouldered, with short brown hair and a scruffy, days-old beard on his face, and built lean, like a runner. He wore an apron over worn jeans and a T-shirt, and with a shock, Katie realized she must be looking at Sam Grant.

The cashier's comments made sense now. Of course the

girl came to the hardware store to stare at Sam Grant. Anyone would. With that, Katie realized she was staring at him, so she set forward again, pulling her wagon behind her, feeling foolish and like she'd really rather head back to her house. It was too late, though. He had seen her. Pulling a wagon U-turn would be humiliating.

"Hi, where can I—um—"she stood there looking down at the wagon for a minute, "park this?" she asked when she finally reached him. He had turned away while she walked, wiping what looked like a toddler faceprint off the large window. He glanced up as she spoke. Katie watched in fascination as a blush grew from his beard to the crinkles at the corners of his eyes. He was a blusher, like her. She wasn't sure that she had seen a man blush before.

He looked down at the wagon. "I've never had anyone park a wagon before," he said. "I suppose here in the shade is as good a place as any. I don't think anyone will take off with your tomatoes."

"But what about my cheese?" she said. "That's what I'm really worried about. It's a nice Gruyére."

He smiled. "I'll take full responsibility for your Gruyére," he said.

She moved the wagon to the spot where he pointed, then stood, unsure of where to look.

"What can I help you with today?" he asked. His voice was soft but slightly gravelly.

"Well," she said, looking down at the crumpled list she clutched in her hand. "I just moved into my new-old house, and I probably need every cleaning solution ever invented." He smiled, raising his eyebrows. She went on. "Also, some paint, but I'm not sure what color. And some lavender and potted herbs—do you have them? Lucy, from Green's, said you might."

His smile grew wider, and smile lines radiated from the outer corners of his eyes. Katie's heart was fluttering away. She mentally cursed the cashier. It was all her fault. Katie wouldn't have even noticed this man if she and Lucy hadn't been rambling away about him.

"So you've met Lucy, have you?" he said. "She's right. I do have a lot of plants."

He gestured for her to go first. She walked ahead of him into the store, which was cool after the hot sun on the sidewalk. She took a deep breath. It smelled like fresh wood and lemons, like a piece of her childhood.

"Oh, it's nearly the same," she said. She turned to him. "I used to come to Aveline during the summers when I was a girl, but I haven't been here in twenty years."

"I remember you, Katie Grace," he said, and his eyes creased at the edges again. He went past her to walk to the back of the shop, and she followed. He knew her? Who was he? She cast her memory back to the summers she had been in Aveline, the long evenings, the feeling of sand and sun at the lake, and then it struck her. He was her friend, Sammy. They had played as children, they had been best summer friends even, but he had been skinny as a kid. He didn't look like this, although she remembered that he had always been a blusher. And with a shock, she also recalled that the beautiful man walking ahead of her to the back of the shop had been her first kiss, back when she was only eleven.

"Sammy," she said, and he looked back and grinned at her as they walked into the garden room.

"Took you long enough."

"I can't help it that you look so different."

"Whereas you," he reached back and poked at one of her wild red curls, "look exactly the same."

He picked up a basket, handing it to her and nodding at one section of the greenhouse. "That's the herb section. Call if you need any help."

She watched as he walked back toward the front of the store, then turned to the herbs eagerly.

A few minutes later, she had the lavender she wanted, as well as thyme, rosemary, sage, basil, oregano, and mint in her basket. She hauled it to the front of the store and heaved it onto the counter. Sam's eyes grew wide.

"Starting small, are you?"

"I never start small," she said. She went back to the shelves to find cleaning supplies, feeling like she had told a lie. It was true that the old Katie had never started small—didn't even know what it meant to start small—but the Katie she had become was different. Even now, she could feel the panic waking inside of her skin. She needed to get back to the comfort of her little room and lie down in the dark before she found herself curled up on the sidewalk in the fetal position. She grabbed floor and window cleaner from the shelves, as well as an industrial-sized mop. One part of her mind was thankful that Sam carried ecologically safe brands, and the other part was beating the drums of doom. *I hate myself, I hate myself,* the drone started in her head.

"How are you going to get all this home?" Sam asked as

she took another trip to the front. "Your wagon is already full."

She looked at the collection of goods on the counter. "I haven't figured that part out yet. Can I leave them here? I also need paint, but now that I'm here, I don't even know what color I want."

"I could make a delivery when my second employee gets here," he said, ringing up the pots of herbs. "I do a little renovation work here and there, so I can also give you color advice if you want. I'll bring some color chips, and you can make an order." He laughed at the look on her face. "A bonus of living in a small town."

"Would you?" She asked. Her heart was racing with unwarranted fear. Away, get away, it said. Katie struggled to appear normal. "I could really use the help. It's such a big job, and I'm kind of overwhelmed."

He shrugged a shoulder. "I'd love to. I love that house, and I've only been inside a couple of times. I'd be happy for the chance to see it again."

"Okay, I'll be home. See you. I need to go. I'm not feeling so well." He gave her a concerned look. "Nothing big, just tired," she said quickly.

"I could come in a couple of hours—give you some time to rest."

Katie thought. She could lie down for an hour and watch a sitcom. Hopefully, by the time Sam came over, she would feel better.

"Sounds good," she said.

She walked home as fast as she could, hauling the wagon behind her, watching the branches of the trees pass overhead, counting the steps. Panic had come on quickly. At home, she collapsed in the hallway and lay on the ground for a long while, breathing in the warm wood smell of the house. When she could think again, she actually felt proud of herself. She had shopped at two stores and made it home before anything happened. This was progress.

CHAPTER SEVEN

Sam pulled his truck into the driveway and turned it off, leaning back in his seat to look up at the old Grace house. Such a beautiful structure. It could certainly use a coat of paint. Currently, it was faded blue with peeling white trim, a columned porch, and large bay windows on both floors. The wooden lace trim needed work, but the porch was the real shining star. Twice as wide as any other porch he had seen in this town, it wrapped all the way around the house.

He opened the truck door and jumped down, walking around to pull Katie's plants and cleaning supplies out of the truck bed. On his way to the porch, he reached in through the open passenger side window and grabbed a handful of paint chips from the dashboard.

He was nervous, his stomach rumbling uneasily. He laughed at himself. Sam was absolutely not interested in Katie. He was just thrown off by the way the past and the future were coming together in a house that he had always secretly longed to own. Or, that was what he tried to tell himself, as he felt a traitorous blush rise into his face while he climbed the stairs to the front door. The main door was open, the screen door closed. Sam heard faint music coming from farther back in the house. He lifted his hand and knocked on the doorpost.

"Hello?" he called.

"Sam?" he heard Katie answer from another room. "Come in! I'm in the kitchen! Just head straight back."

He set the plants on the porch and opened the screen door, which screeched in protest. "Better fix that," he muttered. He carried Katie's cleaning supplies in one hand: a mop, some natural floor cleaner, other bottles of soaps and sprays, and about twenty sponges. The floors were hardwood. He squatted to touch them, marveling at how good they looked after so many years. They were scuffed, but they glowed with the richness of the old wood, and the marks didn't detract from their beauty. The walls were severely in need of paint, flaking in places, grimy from years of neglect. He noted several broken spindles in the staircase railing. The house would be a massive project for Katie. He felt a tingle of challenge on the back of his neck, but he shrugged it off. It wasn't his house.

The kitchen was at the rear of the house. He paused in the doorway, looking in. It was bright and warm, with open windows and squares of sunshine falling across the wooden cupboards and white tile countertops. Katie stood at the stove, stirring something in a pot. She was barefoot, and she had twisted her hair up into a topknot. She was still wearing the light blue dress from earlier, now with an apron tied over it. This morning, as he had seen her standing on the street, looking up at the trees, he had realized with a sudden certainty that he had never before seen anyone as beautiful to him as Katie Grace. She looked so much like she had when they were younger and he would have sworn he was in love with her. He didn't know if she was beautiful in an objective sense. Were women who were six feet tall with wild, copper hair, freckled faces, and startling black eyebrows considered beautiful? But oh, she was beautiful to him. Of course she was. She was the one who had taught him not only to love green eyes but to be brave, daring the biggest rope swing, back when they were kids. He cleared his throat. This line of thought was no good.

"I brought your things," he said.

"Thank you so much," she said, turning back to the stove. "I'm making us lunch. I hope you didn't eat."

"I didn't," he said. "But I don't think I can stay."

"Didn't you say your employee was taking care of the store?" she asked.

"Yes, Larry's there, but..."

"Please stay, I've already made it, and I'll get depressed if I have to eat on my own."

"Well...in that case..." he shrugged, but she missed it as she used a wooden spoon to taste whatever was in the pot, gazing out into space for a full minute. She smiled.

"Perfect," she said, waving the spoon in his direction. "Let's carry one of the little tables to the porch."

She led the way to a room with a closed door. All the rooms in the Victorian house had doors that closed, which meant Carlo had been able to rent it to a good number of students—even the living room could be rented out as a bedroom. Sam blinked as Katie opened the door. The front living room was so full of furniture and boxes that it was unusable. It was a sharp contrast to the bright, mostly clean kitchen behind them. She wrinkled her nose at the look on his face.

"I'm working on one room at a time," she said, frowning at the towers of junk. "Clearly, I have a lot of work ahead of me."

Sam nodded slowly, raising his eyebrows. He glanced at her arms. She looked strong, but there was a lot of solid antique furniture in here. She would need help. She found what she wanted under a blocky, massive television that was so old it had dials instead of buttons. Together they hauled the table out to the porch.

"I saw some chairs in there," Sam said. "I'll get them."

"Thanks," Katie said. "I'll clean this off."

By the time he got back with the chairs, she had wiped the table (surprisingly lovely under all the dust) and brought out two plates of salad. She hurried back to the kitchen and came back with bowls of soup.

"It's cream of wild mushroom," she said, sitting. "I found the most excellent mushrooms in the woods after I got home. Well, first, I lay at the foot of the stairs for a while, then I got up and doused my head in water, then I went exploring and found the mushrooms."

He blinked at her, unsure of what to tackle first. "Are you sure they're edible?"

"Absolutely. My Nana taught me how to recognize edible mushrooms beyond a shadow of a doubt." She paused, and her face grew so sad that he almost put a hand on hers.

"I'm sorry about your grandmother," he said, as she picked up a spoon. "I remember her. She was fierce."

"Oh, well, people die," she said, putting the spoon down again.

"You sound like Lucy."

"Yeah, that's what she said today. It's not how I really feel. I feel like no one should die, ever." She was silent for a moment. "I'm sorry about your father as well. I remember him, as well as I remember anything from being a kid."

"Which isn't so well, considering how long it took you to remember me this morning," he teased. "But thank you. I miss him. People do die, and we avoid remembering that everyone will die, though all evidence points to the contrary." She met his eyes then. He tried to ignore the shock he felt in his chest.

"Bon Appetit," she said.

He put a spoonful of soup in his mouth and closed his eyes. "What is this?" he asked, shocked.

"What do you mean? Is it bad?"

"No, it's incredible! What did you do?"

"I told you," she said, laughing. "I made mushroom soup."

He stared at her. "Are you a chef?" he asked. "Because there is a clear divide in my life now. Before I tasted this soup, and after I tasted this soup. Nothing will ever be the same."

She put a hand to her mouth to hide her laughter. "Not at all. I was a human resources manager," she said. "But not anymore." She looked down at her plate, growing serious, fiddling with her spoon, and he felt sure that there was more to that story. There was also the part where she said she had been lying at the foot of the stairs, but he couldn't talk anymore because he needed to focus on the soup. It was mild and nutty, creamy and peppery. He felt as though he had never eaten soup until this moment. He speared some of the salad, eyes widening at the mixture of flavors in the first forkful.

"I put the gruyére in it," she said, looking at him expectantly. Yes, there was cheese, but there were also nuts, fresh vegetables, and the brightest, best dressing he'd ever had, citrus and smoke, tart, yet mellow.

"Do you know how good this is?"

She shook her head, her lovely mouth drawn into a smile. "People used to make a big deal about my cooking," she said, "but I got busy with my career, and it became rare for me to cook. It'll be nice to have more time for food."

Sam finished and looked sadly at his bowl and plate, wondering if it would be too off-putting if he licked them clean. Fortunately for his dignity, she took the bowls and plates away into the house. He pulled the handful of paint chips out of his pocket while he waited for her to come back. Katie came back out of the house, holding two glasses of water with slices of lemon floating inside, her hair down now. She was beautiful, a vision of summer. He shook his head, hard, staring at the paint chips. This was not going well. He was so suggestible. Carlo must have really gotten under his skin yesterday, not to mention his mother with her eternal tricks.

"Oh, I love that one," Katie said, pointing to one of his own favorite colors; a creamy white with a hint of sunshine, a color that would brighten the kitchen beautifully.

"Yeah, that one's great," he said, gratefully turning his attention to color, "and I was thinking of the trim being something like this." He showed her a deep red. It wasn't a conventional choice, but it would be striking. They bent their heads together, talking quietly about color choices. She flipped through the selections, finally settling on the cream for the walls, and light blue for the trim, a softer contrast. All the while they talked about colors, Sam was half involved in the world of paint and half trying to ignore the way her knee occasionally bumped his under the table. Another, happier part of him recognized the friendship of their childhood as they got reacquainted. At moments, Katie was strikingly similar to the girl he remembered, all grins and hyperactivity, plans bigger than either of them could tackle. He had been the shy kid, the one who reluctantly trailed behind her whirlwind. But at other times, she seemed so different. What had happened to her?

CHAPTER EIGHT

O nce they had settled on the colors for the kitchen, Sam asked what parts of the house she thought needed to be fixed.

"What doesn't?" Katie asked, laughing. "But I do have a list, let me go find it." Sam, looking around, agreed with her. Maybe they should make a list of the few things that weren't broken or peeling and then work through the rest.

Katie came back carrying a thick, black book, stuffed with extra pages, and as she flipped through it, looking for her list, a sheet of paper escaped and drifted to the floor. Sam stooped to pick it up and couldn't help noticing the large block letters at the top of the page: IDEAS FOR WORK.

"What's this?" he said, holding it up so she could see it. She blushed, and he stared at the color spreading across her face. He had always hated the fact that he was a blusher, but on Katie, blushes looked pretty. She plucked the paper from his hand.

"I need to talk with the bank about what my options are

with the money my grandmother left me, but one thing is certain: if I'm going to get this house in decent shape, it'll take a lot of money, and I'll have to start working again."

"In human resources?"

She sat back and shook her head. "I'll never work in HR again," she said, her voice hard.

He waited, but she didn't say anything else. "Let's see your list," he said, holding his hand out for it. After a moment, she gave it to him. "Real estate. Well, unless you want to do it in Billers, that's out. I'm pretty sure we have enough of those." She looked at him for a moment, then crossed it off the list, a sudden smile crossing her face.

"Perfect," she said. "You can help me narrow my list."

"Okay," he said, smiling back at her. "Let's go. Artist? Have you ever made art?"

"I could learn," she said. She leaned close and drew a star beside the word artist. He moved along.

"Work at the bank? I guess that's possible."

She was shaking her head. "I don't know why I wrote that down. Too close to HR—offices and stuff."

"Okay, no offices. Window washer? Now you're reaching."

"I heard there was good money in it," she said, laughing.

"Maybe in a place where people actually hire people to wash their windows because the buildings are more than two stories tall," he said.

She tipped her head back and laughed, then drew a thick black line through "window washer."

He sat back in his chair and stared at her, struck by a

thought. "Katie? Have you ever thought about cooking for a living?"

She frowned. "I have... but where? There's nothing in town but a pizza place, a Greek restaurant, that weird family restaurant, and a bunch of coffee shops. Some taquerias, too. I guess I could work at a taqueria, though my Spanish isn't great."

"No, no." He shook his head and crossed his arms, leaning back in his chair. "I mean, open a restaurant."

"Open a restaurant? Me?" She laughed. "What? How? Where?"

"Why not here?" he asked, sweeping his arm to indicate the porch and house, glowing in the afternoon light. "You could live upstairs. There's far more room here than one person needs. Look. You even have a view of the lake."

"That is not a view," she said, smiling again. "I believe that's called a glimpse." She gazed off toward the little bit of lake that they could see, her face knitted in thought. The lake was two blocks away, separated from them by the tree-filled park. Sam could see slightly more than a glimpse of it sparkling in the distance, an alluring blue.

She spoke again. "Maybe you're right. This could be a great location for a restaurant, so close to the center of town." Her eyes came back to focus on him. "Not many people know this about me, but I was in culinary school for two years before I moved to human resources."

"Really? What made you switch?"

She looked down at the table between them, rubbing a fingertip into a sharp groove in the wood. It looked like someone had taken a knife to the surface of the table. "I don't talk about that. But the restaurant idea...I guess I'm just saying it's not as wild a thought as you might imagine. I always thought, back then, that I would run a restaurant. Talk me through it, Sam." She leaned forward. "What would I have to do?"

A little breeze whipped up and blew her hair around her face. She brushed it away, impatiently, pulling it back in her hands and dropping it behind her. Sam watched, fascinated.

"I don't know anything about the business side of things," he said slowly. "But with the structure, I think you'd want to open up the rooms downstairs to make one big open space for the indoor dining room and let it spill out onto the porch and maybe even into the garden."

She nodded, swiveling to look into the house. "I see it... that would be beautiful. It could work. Any money I put into the house would be an investment in my new business. It would pay off eventually. But I'd need staff..." she frowned, biting her lip.

"You could keep it small if you wanted. But yes, I think you would want at least a few employees."

She nodded again and took a breath, still looking around at the porch and the garden, her gaze finally settling on his face. "Would you have time for the renovation?" she asked.

The question took Sam by surprise. He had been talking as though it was a foregone conclusion that he'd be working for Katie, but now he considered what that would mean. For a moment, he had been swept up in the idea of a big project, more ambitious than any he'd done since he took over the store, and in a house he had always loved. But it would mean spending days and days with this woman, endangering his commitment to a simple life. Was it worth it? It all seemed so momentous—the two of them on the porch, the new idea, their old friendship somehow intact. He hadn't really been missing Katie, all these years, besides the first two when he thought he would never get over her, but he realized she was a welcome familiarity. Their friendship had always been effortless. Would it really risk his peace of mind? His monk life? He looked at the antique diamond-paned windows beside him, the worn boards of the porch, and it suddenly seemed like his dream job. He could do this. He was an adult. And as for making time? He could steal Lucy from Sheldon and put her to work in his store. Hopefully, she and Larry wouldn't kill each other, and he could work full time on the renovation.

"I can do it," he said. "I want to write some ideas out. Can you spare some paper?" She pulled a few sheets out of the notebook, and they bent over them together while he drew. She pointed out several places where he could adjust something to make it better, and each time she was right. He looked at her, surprised. She was different from the force of nature he remembered. She seemed... hurt. Quiet. Deeply tired. But she was as smart as ever, and he saw that the old Katie Grace was in there somewhere.

They wandered through the house as the light turned golden, looking at walls and doorways, even going upstairs for a quick peek. Sam was startled to find that Katie was sleeping in a tiny room at the back of the house.

"What's this about?" he asked, and then blushed at how personal his question was. Today was the first time they had seen each other in over twenty years. Katie shut the door to the room, and it closed with a sharp crack.

"Just not ready yet," she said, and he realized that she was in hiding. Hurt and making a den for herself.

"Are you sure you're up for a project like this?" he asked. She looked back at him, crossing her arms over her stomach. "You just got here. I don't want to start some big project if you're not ready."

"As long as we take it slowly," she said. "You're right. Things have been horrible lately. But if I'm the boss, I can pause if I need to. We can start renovating and...see where it goes."

Sam's phone dinged, and he pulled it out of his pocket. His eyes widened at Larry's text.

Old Man Sam? R U going to close up shop? Cash register + me = no clue.

"It's nearly six o'clock," he said, his mouth dropping open. "I've been here all day."

"And we finished with a lot more than paint colors," she said and laughed, then she sighed and twisted her hands in front of herself.

He looked at her thoughtfully. "Sleep on it," he said. "Make sure you're really sure."

CHAPTER NINE

Maddie sat with her arms crossed, staring dully at a poster of a cop putting a man in handcuffs. Bright red words read, "Shoplifting is a crime." How ironic. She clenched her fists inside her sleeves, listening to her mother in the next room talking with the two police officers who had apprehended Maddie at Walgreen's.

"It's only a bottle of nail polish," she heard her mother say. Maddie tried to shrink into the trench coat with the large pockets, the piece of clothing she had bought partly because she liked the way it enveloped her and partly because she could drop things in the pockets almost without moving. Tonight, though, the pharmacist had seen her, and though Maddie had protested that the nail polish was hers, neither the store employees or the cops believed her.

The police officers hadn't cuffed her, despite the image on the poster. Were cops allowed to put handcuffs on four-teen-year-olds? The nail polish in question had been a deep, shiny purple, so alluring that it almost asked to be taken.

Maddie could see her mobile phone sitting on the desk where the woman cop had dropped it when she pulled Maddie in here and told her to sit down and not move a muscle. Maddie eyed the phone, wondering what they would do to her if she took it back.

She didn't find out, because the cops came back, and there was Maddie's mother, her eyes red and wet. Maddie looked away. She hadn't meant for her mother to get pulled into this. Her mom had too much to think about, and Maddie tried not to do more to worry her. But lately, things were backfiring. All the undone schoolwork had started to reveal itself, and now even her stealing was out into the open. She was making her mother's difficult life even harder. Maddie scowled, feeling a deep pang of shame at the tears on her mother's face. This kind of guilt only felt better if she could steal something. It was an endless loop.

"We're letting you go, for now, Maddie," the man cop said. He was the nicer cop. Maddie glared at both of them. "You'll be back once we have the terms of your community service worked out."

"Community service?" her mother asked. "What will that look like?"

"Probably cleaning up litter or something," the woman cop said, as though she really couldn't be bothered with Maddie's mother's emotional questions, and then Maddie hated her almost as much as she hated herself for making her mother sad.

On the way out of the office, she took a pen from the desk and dropped it in her pocket. Immediately, she felt better.

· · ·

She was silent in the car on the way home. Her mother ranted and cried, wiping her face with the backs of her hands as tears rolled continually down her cheeks.

"What happened? We used to be so close Maddie. I don't know you anymore. Stealing? Nail polish?"

Yes, Maddie thought. Nail polish, magazines, toy cars that felt nice in her hand, sometimes just one egg out of a carton, a tube of mascara, endless candy bars. The trees passed swiftly on her side of the car, then opened into the fields she loved, just before they got to their boring suburb.

"This is it, Maddie. You won't even talk to me and you know I'm not strong. I've just gotten stable again. I'm going to have to make a change." She gulped.

Maddie turned to look at her, frowning. This wasn't her mother's usual rant. The lights from passing cars illuminated her mother's tear-streaked face. She was still beautiful.

"After you finish with your community service," her mother continued, "I'm sending you to your grandmother to live."

"What?" Maddie said, but the word fell out of her mouth like a stone, sounding less like a question and more like a grunt.

"Oh, now you'll talk. Yes. I'm not going to tell her why, so you don't either. Even your grandmother would struggle to keep her cool if she knew you had been arrested. Actually, you know what? We're just going to put you on a plane, and I'll tell her that you're coming when you're halfway there."

Only Maddie's mother would think a cracked idea like that was worth anything. Maddie glanced over at her mother again, worried. Had she pushed her too far? Maddie knew her mother's mental stability was a flexible, fragile thing. She thought about her grandmother, who had come to visit two years before. She thought about the little town in California where she lived. It could be okay, she thought. Maybe it really would do her mother good if she was gone. She made sure to turn her face farther toward the window so her mom wouldn't see the tears that began to fall down her cheeks.

CHAPTER TEN

Katie poured the last of the hot water into the pour-over coffee filter and waited. After the water seeped through, she lifted the ceramic cone away and picked up her mug, holding her face over it, breathing in the scent of freshly brewed coffee. She poured a dollop of cream into the coffee, then carried it and her notebook to a table she had cleaned and set by one of the large windows. Outside, branches waved in a chilly spring rain, but Katie wrapped her hands around the cup, and it warmed her. She took a sip and closed her eyes. Oh, coffee. It was perfect.

She opened her notebook to the current page, smoothing it with her hand, glancing down at the long list of things to do. Her eyes kept flicking back to the first two items. They were starred and underlined. *This is very, very important, Katie,* she told herself. *You have to go.* It was a big step for someone who only recently had remembered how to eat real food, and she felt dread swirling in her stomach.

Bank

Meeting with lawyer

She laughed at herself, but it didn't sound genuine. How ridiculous could she get? She was scared of going to the bank. But these appointments would change her life, change everything. Was she ready for a restaurant? She thought of what she had told Sam. One step at a time. Money was the first step. After all, she needed to find out what was in the bank account. There could be nothing, and then her decision would be made for her!

She had woven her hair into one long braid, and she wore a sea-green vintage dress that reached to mid-calf. She was even wearing lip gloss. This visit to the bank was serious business. She looked outside again. The rain had stopped, and the sun had come out.

"Come on, Katie girl," she said, using her Nana's nickname for her. "No time like the present."

She walked everywhere these days, and it didn't take her long to reach the bank that was halfway down Oak street, across from Sam's store and next to a boutique that carried baby clothes. She paused in front of the display window for a moment, transfixed by tiny shoes, arranged as though they were walking up a flight of stairs. She pulled herself away and kept going until she was standing in front of the bank. Her knees felt wobbly and weak as she climbed the stairs, flames of panic stirring as she entered the air-conditioned room with its fluorescent lighting. It was too familiar—corporate, too much like her old job.

For a moment she was blindsided by memories: the disappointment in Ed's face, the sneer as he had walked out that last time. All the yelling from her bosses at the office. Waiting too long and still managing to mess it up. Misplaced trust. Packing her things while she sobbed.

She took a deep breath and shoved the images far back in her mind, then moved forward as though in a dream, standing in line behind a man who reeked cologne. This is a bank, she told herself, digging her nails into her palms. Not your job, silly. You're nowhere near L.A.

"Ma'am?" the teller asked. She blinked. She was next. The teller was a medium-sized man with a kind face. Her breath came back. He was just a person. Not a judge, not a corporation or a boss, not Ed.

She went to stand at the counter in front of him. "I wanted to talk to someone about my bank account. It's a joint high-interest savings account with my grandmother," she said.

The man took her bank book and typed a few things into the computer.

"It seems that it's now a single account, due to the death of the other account holder. Your grandmother. I'm sorry for your loss."

Katie nodded, pressing her lips together into a line. "Can I see the balance?" she asked. "I've never received a balance statement. My grandmother kept the account a secret until her death. To be honest, I didn't even know she had put my name on the account. She did it with my mom when I was still underage..." She was babbling.

He raised an eyebrow. "Well, that's a nice surprise," he said. "I can print a statement out for you." After a few taps on the computer, the printer behind him spit out a few sheets of paper, and he handed them to her.

Katie looked at the statement, her eyes growing wide. It showed that a significant amount of money had been deposited into the account every month until very recently. There were years of deposits represented on the paper in front of her, and the balance took her breath away. She looked up at the teller, stunned. He smiled at her. She said goodbye vaguely and left the bank.

Katie sank onto a bench under a tree on the sidewalk and stared at the document in front of her. Had Nana always planned to give her house and all this money to Katie? How had she kept it a secret? Katie looked away from the paper, finally, still not really comprehending what had happened.

A little girl wandered by, trailing after her mother, showering crumbs from the muffin she was eating. Delighted sparrows fluttered down to hop behind her, snatching at the crumbs she left in her wake as she picked chocolate chips out of the muffin delicately.

Katie watched the sparrows and the girl, watched the mother lean over and kiss her daughter on the head. She felt shaky, as though she had run a long distance. Her life was changing very quickly. She did some quick calculations in her head. She would have plenty of money to do the renovations really, really beautifully, and even after that, some to spare. Money she could live on. She wouldn't need to work for a few years. She actually didn't even need to start a restaurant right now. She let her eyes glaze over as she turned her face to the dappled sunlight that came through the tree's branches. Beyond the tree, the sky was very blue.

She twisted her hands in her skirt. Could she rest and do nothing? No renovations, no dreams? When she tried to imagine it, all she could see was her bed in her old house, rumpled and covered in crumbs. A lot of spare time to think didn't seem like a good option for Katie. Did she want to start a restaurant, even if she didn't need the money yet? It was a smart move. If she wasn't desperate for money, the restaurant would have time to grow. She tried to imagine it. Cooking in a fixed-up kitchen, with people in the garden and on the porch, eating her food. It still seemed like a dream that she had a house! Her own house. And money to fix it.

Whenever she had thought of other ways to live her life, Ed had rolled his eyes. "The problem with you, Katie, is that you dream too much. No one succeeds at things like that anymore. Those days are gone. Stay where you are. You've worked hard to be here."

He was gone. Katie let herself daydream, leaning into a full reverie of her very own house, her very own—filled with fragrant food, people eating and chatting, dishes clinking, and music playing. It gave her a thrill of joy. When she thought of the house staying empty, she felt her heart drop with disappointment. She looked down at her hands, still clutching her dress, white-knuckled. She let go, smoothing the crumpled material. The sunlight dazzled her eyes. This was the first time she had wanted something for a very long time. How had Sam come up with something so crazy and yet so perfect? Katie was going to do it. She was actually going to try something this big; she was going to build a restaurant. The panic stirred, but Katie shushed it down.

CHAPTER ELEVEN

O n her way to the law office, Katie stopped at the window display of the baby shop again, smiling at the tiny pairs of shoes, but she was startled by the sight of a familiar pair of jeans and threadbare T-shirt. Sam stood holding a complicated set of shelves against the wall with one hand, and a drill with the other. Without putting much thought into it, Katie walked into the little shop, noticing within moments that a woman was standing behind the counter, talking to Sam.

"Not there, no. Up and to the left."

"Are you sure?" Sam's voice was exasperated. "That's where I had it before, and I've already got one screw in."

"One screw won't take nearly as much time to undo as twenty-five, or however many you've got to put in."

"You've got a screw loose," Sam muttered as he drilled the screw out of the shelves, and set them on the ground, swinging his arms and moving his neck from side to side. He turned around and caught sight of Katie. His eyebrows shot up, then he smiled.

The woman, who had short gray hair, black-framed glasses, and long, swinging earrings, had already been watching Katie for a minute or so. Now her gaze swiveled to Sam, who blushed. Once again, Katie was fascinated by the color that rushed to his cheeks. The color stayed in his cheeks and jaw, rather than rushing over his forehead and chest, as her blushes did. Her breath caught in her throat as she remembered the humiliation of blushing the entire time she was testifying. The defense lawyer had tried to say it was her lies that made her blush.

"Hi," Sam said. Katie blinked. She was here, safe. Not in court on the witness stand.

"I'm sorry," she said. "I didn't realize you were working. I just remembered when I saw you that I don't have your phone number..."

Sam's eyes grew wide. He turned his head and frowned at the older woman. She smiled back at him, twirling an earring with the fingers of her right hand. Katie had walked into something, but she had no idea what it was.

"I'm not working," Sam said. "Just putting some shelves up for my mother." The woman held out a hand, and Katie walked closer to take it. She was Sammy's mother, Katie saw, as she looked at the woman more closely. She looked very, very different from the plainly dressed woman who had made them sandwiches and mopped the house after they ran out of the lake and trailed water everywhere.

"I'm very pleased to meet you," Sam's mother said. "I'm Dorothy, and I've been waiting with bated breath to acquaint myself with the young, tall woman who has moved into the Grace house."

"All right, that's it," Sam said, lunging forward to take Katie by the elbow. "Mother, you met Katie when she was a kid. You made us Kool-Aid and peanut butter and jelly sandwiches. Remember? Isn't there somewhere you needed to be right now, Katie?"

She looked at him, surprised. "Actually, I do need to get to an appointment at Jackson & Jackson."

"Great! I'll go with you," Sam said. "Back soon, Mother." He steered both of them out the door and down the sidewalk. Katie gave him a sideways look, acutely aware of his hand on her elbow. He met her eyes and dropped his hand immediately, staring at it before wiping it across his jeans. She burst out laughing.

"I don't have cooties, you know," she said. After a moment, Sam grinned.

"Here's the thing," he said, pulling out his phone and tapping until he got to his contacts. "We're going to have to be smart because certain people in this town see me as a 'project.'" He looked up at her seriously. "They're going to try to throw us together."

Looking into his eyes, Katie almost couldn't breathe. At that moment she forgot Ed and his sneers or how she had failed at everything she had worked at for ten years. All she could think of was eyes. Whoa girl, time to switch gears.

She pulled herself back slightly and saw that he was still looking at her earnestly. She thought about what he had just said and burst out laughing.

He stared at her in confusion. "What's so funny?"

"You are. It's no big deal if they try to throw us together. We're cool, right? Also, how do you have eyes like that?"

"Eyes like what?"

Whoops, she had said that out loud. "With those eyelashes," she said lightly, "Girls would kill for those."

"Yeah, well, I got teased for them plenty," he answered. He looked down at his phone.

Snap out of it, Katie, she told herself.

"What's your phone number?" he asked, typing the first letters of her name.

"Sam?" she said. He looked up. "Do you think I can do this restaurant thing?"

He rubbed at his face. "If you cook food like the other day... you'll have a line out the door," he said. "But whether or not you do it is up to you."

"I crashed pretty badly before I left L.A," she told him, not at all sure why she was confessing, but pushing on anyway. "I failed— lost everything I had worked for, the last decade of my life. I don't think I could handle something like that happening again."

"Do you think the same disaster could happen twice?" he asked. He was giving her his full attention.

"Nooo-oo, but something bad could happen."

"Something bad certainly could. Will that stop you?"

She stared at him. Why was she asking for reassurance from Sam? Was it because he was her old friend Sammy, who had invented a language called Gibroon and knew how to skip rocks for more than ten skips? Or was this like Katie and Ed all over again? She had blindly followed Ed around as he basked in the glow of her success, waiting for his approval before she did anything. He ditched her as soon as her brightness dimmed—or blinked out entirely, more like it. No, Sam was not like Ed, but she heard the words behind Sam's words, the profound question that dropped and rippled outward. She needed to stop asking others for validation and reassurance. She needed to find out what she was capable of for herself.

He went on. "Let me ask you this. Can you do the next step?"

She nodded slowly.

"And can you make an appointment for me to come over again, maybe on Monday, for more measuring?" he asked.

She nodded again, more decisively.

"Then I think you can do it. But you do need to know that for yourself. No one can do what she's meant to do five years from now, though. She can only do what she's meant to do right now." His voice was gentle, and he was still holding his phone out with his contacts page open.

"Two-oh-six," she said.

He blinked at her. "What?"

"Those are the first three numbers."

"Ah," he said, comprehension washing over his face. He added Katie's number, calling her phone.

"Save that," he said when his number appeared on her screen. "Now, you need to get to your appointment, right?"

"Yes," she said.

"Call me when you're really, really, really sure, and I'll come with all my tape measures and levels and things." He paused. "And, Katie?"

"Yeah?"

"I think it's going to be more fun than we could even imagine."

She smiled at him shyly as he left her at the door to the law office, waving as he ran back to his mother and her shelves—a man who owned a store directly across the street from his mother's boutique. Katie had never heard of such a thing. She was still thinking about his eyes as she walked into the law office, the bell tinkling overhead.

She smiled at George and Mercy Jackson as she settled into the chair across from George's desk, but Mercy came right around the desk and hugged Katie. She wore an indigo colored suit and had short, natural hair, showing off her lovely dark skin and large silver earrings. "It's so good to meet you in person. I'm sorry for the loss of your grandmother," she said. "Welcome to Aveline. Lucy told me you might come to our gathering tomorrow?"

"I was thinking about it," Katie said. "How many people usually come?"

"Oh, just a handful. Lucy, Juanita, and Dorothy, you know, Sam's mother."

"I just met her. Or, met her again. I remember her from when I was here as a kid."

"Sometimes my daughter comes," Mercy went on, "if she has time, but she's a therapist in Billers, so she's busy a lot. And Zoe—she's a professor at the university—and Ingrid, who runs the coffee shop."

"That seems like a lot of people," Katie said, unsure.

Mercy smiled. "Just think about it."

"They're a great bunch of women," George said. "Very smart and extremely kind." He wore a purple dress shirt with the sleeves rolled up, and though he had silver generously sprinkled through his hair, Katie hadn't thought of them as old enough to have grown kids.

Mercy walked back to sit in her chair, smiling at her husband. "Can you draw Katie a map to our place?" she asked. Then, "Katie, no need to even let us know if you're coming. Just drop by if you're up for it." She straightened some papers on her desk. "Now for business," she said, as George handed Katie the map he had sketched on a piece of paper.

Mercy began to talk through the final steps for Katie to receive her inheritance. Then, at Katie's request, Mercy outlined the process for renovation permits and zoning changes for her new business.

"Are you going to have a grand opening?" George asked.

Katie laughed. "I haven't got that far yet," she said.

"Well, if you do, remember our band: the Aveline Swing Band. Carlo didn't tell you?"

Katie shook her head.

"Ah, well," George said, "Carlo's lead vocalist, I'm on trumpet, Daniel on bass and the reverend on the drum kit."

"I'll remember that," Katie said. An opening with live music seemed like a lot to think about at the moment. Mercy gave George a look, and they got back to talking about next steps.

When their business was done, George brought out a pitcher of ice water and poured them all glasses. Katie drank hers thankfully, realizing that she was parched.

"What made you move to Aveline, Katie?" he asked. "Rather than selling? You could have stayed in L.A."

Mercy gave her husband a look. "A little personal, maybe?" she said.

Katie laughed. "It's okay," she said.

George smiled and shrugged. "I'm asking because we made the same move, twelve years ago. I'm always curious when people decide to move here."

Katie thought about how much to share. "The fact that my life in L.A. imploded, I guess," she answered. "I imagine choosing small-town life is easier if you struggle with anxiety." George threw Katie a sharp glance that she couldn't interpret. "What about you?" she asked. "What made you choose Aveline?"

Mercy looked down at the desk. "We struggled to decide, especially since we specialize in civil rights cases." She glanced at her husband, then seemed to make a decision. "Our son, Zion, was killed in a police shooting, thirteen years ago. He was simply in the wrong place at the wrong time."

Katie's heart seemed to stop for a moment. She barely restrained herself from reaching out to touch Mercy, realizing that although the older woman was opening up, Katie was still a stranger.

Mercy went on. "I lost myself for a time, and it became too hard for me to live there. We sought justice for a long while. The officer is still free, and we're still waiting. In the meantime, we travel to L.A. or Billers to work on bigger cases, and we work remotely, but Aveline is home. We chose it because it's peaceful like you said, but full of people from many walks of life."

"Because of the university," George added. He laid his

hand on top of Mercy's on the desk. Katie saw deep sorrow in his eyes.

"We understand anxiety," Mercy said. "If you need any help, our daughter really is an excellent therapist." She opened a desk drawer and took a card out, handing it to Katie. Katie took it and thanked them, standing to leave.

"Thank you for the invitation," she said, just before leaving. "I'll try to come tomorrow."

Back at home, she took a lot of pleasure from crossing out those daunting lines on her To-Do list. She thought for a while, then she called Sam and told him she was really, really, really sure. She made an appointment with him to come over Monday morning.

She sat on the stairs of her porch, rubbing her arms. It was Friday night, the stars were out, and she could hear the crickets starting up their night song.

She thought of the people she had met in Aveline. The sorrow in Mercy's eyes. Dorothy and her swinging earrings. Lucy. Images from the past flickered through her mind, as they often did when the day was over. Pictures of the courtroom, of Philip's wife shrieking at her, of Ed pulling his stuff out of the closet with such drama, of the knife flashing. She stared at her phone. Ed hadn't sent her even one text message since he left her. She was still shocked by what a flimsy thing his commitment had turned out to be, but sitting there, under the dark sky, Katie realized she didn't miss him. She liked her solitude. She liked being away from his strange pressure and worry about appearance. And apparently, it wasn't hard to find company when you wanted it in this town. All Katie needed to do was walk down to the grocery store. She smiled, thinking of Sheldon and his baby blue suit.

She had the weekend ahead of her before the next appointment with Sam. She could make some more food to try on Monday. She could dream as much as she wanted, about colors and food and words that reflected what she wanted in a restaurant. How long had it been since she dreamed? Even before everything crashed, the only thing she had put any energy into was her career and Ed.

They were both gone. Katie had wasted a lot of time. But she was here now, with time to dream and no one to tell her she shouldn't. She looked down at her bare feet, remembering that just five months ago, she had spent every day in a suit, squeezing her toes into tights and high heels. Now her feet were free. She laughed then, running out to her lawn and jumping around in the dark. The smell of grass and night blooming jasmine filled the night. Everything seemed possible.

"Thank you, Nana," she whispered to the stars, and she felt it with all of her heart, tears filling her eyes. How did her grandmother know what she needed? Katie wished she could thank Nana with a big hug. It felt wrong that she could only whisper her thanks into the night sky.

CHAPTER TWELVE

On Saturday, when Katie went into Green's, Sheldon was wearing a maroon velour shirt and ripped up jeans with a yellow bandana tied around one knee. Katie gazed at him with her mouth slightly open. The frames of his glasses were now a brilliant green, rather than the black from the other day.

"What does the bandana do?" she asked.

"Keeps my knee on," he replied. He was staring at a list on a clipboard in his hand, and after a moment he looked up and smiled at her. "It belonged to an ex-girlfriend. I'm trying to get over her, but every once in a while, when I want to feel lonely and miserable, I tie it on."

"That makes sense, I guess," she said.

"It doesn't, but thanks for trying to make me feel better. I probably never will."

"Feel better?"

"That too. But I'll probably never get over her."

"How long has it been since you broke up?" Katie asked, eying the vegetables in the distance, wondering if she could reach them safely if she made a break for it.

"Ten years on Saturday," he said, sighing. His whole body radiated misery. Katie moved closer and patted his arm. "I still wonder if she'll come back one day," he said.

"Oh. I'm really sorry."

"It's okay. It's been a long time."

"I have something that might cheer you up," she said.

"What's that?"

"How do you feel about taking on a medium-sized account in the not-too-distant future?" she asked.

"Who wants this account?" he asked, frowning.

"Me, of course. I'm starting a restaurant."

Sheldon's face changed, like a miracle, from misery to glee. He hugged her, then transformed into something like a tall, oddly-dressed whirlwind. He propelled her through the shop, narrowly avoiding a group of tourists conferring over a can of sardines and a pair of identical toddlers who were both tied to a shopping cart, whirling around it in a tangle, while their mother tried to stop them.

Sheldon showed Katie produce and whispered wholesale prices to her while she wrote frantically in her bulging notebook. In the end she had pages of writing, and she wearily held up a hand as he prepared to go on, seemingly ready to enumerate every item in the store. One thing had become clear. Katie needed a theme of some kind for her restaurant, because Sheldon and his groceries were going to overwhelm her. She needed to narrow it down. She left with sweet potatoes and quinoa, lamb and bell peppers, her mind spinning with ideas and scents and flavors. The panic hadn't even lifted its head.

KATIE STOOD on the sidewalk in front of Mercy's house for five straight minutes before she dared to walk up the front walk. Mercy and George lived in an old Craftsman-style house, with flowers lining the front path, and the lights in the living room glowed softly in the evening light. The sky was soft and purple. Katie was terrified. She stopped, halfway down the path, to touch a spray of calla lilies, killing time. Her stomach was in knots.

There was a time when Katie would have soared along this walk, up those steps, and into the house without a moment's hesitation. Now, however, she seemed to have paralysis of the liver, or wherever courage came from. She heard voices and turned, hoping to see Lucy.

No such luck. Katie had never met the two women who approached the house. One of the women was black, with long, impressive locks, wearing a red duster over black jeans, and a yellow scarf tied around her head. The other woman was impossibly thin and pale, with light blond hair in a top knot, and black pants and a striped T-shirt. For a moment, Katie hoped they were just walking by. They turned at the house, though, and Katie feigned intense interest in the flower. They didn't brush by her as she hoped, but stopped just behind her.

"Hello?" one of them said. Katie couldn't tell which one, because she was still gazing at the flower. Oh, for heaven's sake.

"Hi, sorry, am I in your way?" She asked. "I was just leaving."

She turned to go, but just then, the front door swung open, and Lucy called out.

"You're at the right house, Katie!"

Too late. Katie froze, then looked up at the women in resignation.

"Oh, are you Katie?" the blond woman asked. "Mercy sent an email saying a new woman was going to join us for women's circle. I'm Ingrid." She held out a slender hand. Katie shook it gently.

"I'm Zoe," said the other woman. "It's nice that you could come."

Lucy had bustled down the walk in her bare feet, and slipped her arm through Katie's, leading her up the steps and into the house. Katie looked around her, glad for the distraction from the burning in her stomach. The house was full of antique furniture and had the smell of wood polish and perfume, and something else she couldn't place.

"We're in the kitchen," Lucy said. "Come on back."

Ingrid and Zoe had already made their way past Katie and Lucy. Lucy gestured for Katie to lead the way, but she shook her head.

"You're not going to bolt, are you?"

"Depends if you're watching," Katie said with a weak grin.

Lucy looked at her. "Every woman in that kitchen has been through difficult times, one way or another. We all come from different places and backgrounds, and sometimes we find it hard to understand each other. But we are connected because of love and the kindness of God. It's a safe place, Katie. No one will hurt you."

Maybe not intentionally, Katie thought. But she followed Lucy through the hallway to the kitchen at the back of the house. The kitchen had been extensively renovated, with large, cheery windows and granite countertops, and was open to a sitting room right beside it. It was painted bright white, but the walls were covered with colorful paintings and textiles. A piano sat in the corner, with a large, loosely painted portrait of Nelson Mandela hanging on the wall above. As Katie entered the room, Dorothy called out a welcome casually, but Mercy and Juanita were too busy in conversation to notice she'd arrived. Katie relaxed slightly. She found a spot next to Lucy on the couch, and sat gingerly, hoping it was okay that she'd just come in and sit down like this. Zoe and Ingrid were in beanbag chairs, talking with Dorothy, cold glasses of sweet tea already in their hands, and Mercy came over with a drink for Katie. She handed it to her with a smile.

"Glad you could come," she said.

Eventually, they were all settled with their drinks.

"Who brought dessert tonight?" Juanita asked, after saying hello to Katie.

"I did," Dorothy said. "But Mercy cooked."

"I can cook next week," Juanita said.

"Yes, please!" Zoe said. "I miss your cooking."

"Come over any time," Juanita told her, blowing her a kiss. "I can make extra. Or Carlo can eat a little less."

The women laughed. "Is he still on his diet?" Mercy asked.

"Diet? It's hardly a diet. He's just packing lunches instead of eating pizza."

"I wish there were more healthy options in town."

"We have muffins at my shop," Ingrid said.

"Muffins aren't food!" Mercy exclaimed.

Katie shifted in her seat. Should she tell them? Mercy and Lucy exchanged looks, and then Lucy beat Katie to it.

"Katie's starting a restaurant," she said. "So we'll have that soon."

They all turned toward her, talking over one another. Katie laughed and held up a hand. "Wait, wait," she said. "I can't understand you."

"When will it be open?" Zoe asked.

"I don't know," Katie said. "We haven't even started yet."

The evening went on for a while in this way. After some time they shifted to the table and ate Mercy's macaroni and cheese casserole. She had made a salad as well, but Katie had thirds of the mac'n'cheese, groaning when she realized she'd overdone it.

"Addictive, isn't it?" Dorothy asked.

"It's the best I've ever had," Katie confessed.

"It's my mom's recipe," Mercy said. "From the South. They make it the best down there. I left out the peppers, though."

"Thank you for that."

"I'm not leaving the peppers out when I make food next week," Juanita said.

"I'll sacrifice my night's sleep for your food," Dorothy said.

"I'll bring the Pepto," said Mercy.

After some time, sitting with a glass of wine in her hand, Katie realized she felt utterly, completely relaxed. Lucy was right. It was a safe space. They talked about family, work, Zoe's classes, Ingrid's water bill. They spoke about husbands for those who had them, and exes, for those who had those. Katie shared a little of what the past weeks had been like, though she didn't go too far into the past. Lucy said she was thankful for full-time work with Sam because she could keep an eye on Larry. Katie saw Zoe and Juanita exchange glances at that and hid a smile of her own. They ate Dorothy's apple cobbler with ice cream, and once again, Katie ate too much.

It was dark when Mercy said they should pray.

"There is so much grief in the world and in our work," she said. "I need strength to keep doing this." Katie made a note to ask Mercy more about her work. They all added their prayer requests, and Katie told them she needed courage. And the permission to make decisions on her own. There were a lot of nods around the circle as she said this. And then they prayed. Mercy had opened a window, and the fragrance of the night came in quietly. Every woman had a different voice when she talked to God. Katie didn't say anything out loud, but inside her head, she sounded out two words, over and over again.

Thank you. Thank you. Thank you.

By the time Sam arrived on Monday morning, Saturday night felt far in the past, and Katie was frothing at the mouth to talk to someone. She practically attacked him on the steps, giving him a swift hug, then walking back into the house to hide her confusion. She wasn't sure whether they did hugs, but to cover up her embarrassment, she picked up her notebook and thrust it out in front of her.

"I'm excited to show you this," she said.

"Oh," he said, cool as a cucumber, but with a faint blush on his cheeks. His beard was longer, less of a scruffy look and more of a proper beard. "The notebook."

"Do you know what I've been doing this weekend?"

"I have no idea."

"Everything. I've been doing everything. I've been dreaming up menu items and names for the menu items and descriptions of the menu items."

"Lots of items."

"So many items." She crossed her arms, looking at him. "Hi. Sorry. How are you?"

"I'm fine. Tired. I'm worried about my sister, and I haven't been sleeping too well."

"Oh, and then you get here, and I attack you with my items. Is your sister okay?"

He smiled at her. "You're welcome to attack me with your items. And I think so, yes. She's just been a bit cagey on the phone lately, like she's hiding something from us. My mother wants me to fix it, but I've never been able to understand Theresa, let alone make her do anything."

"I don't remember her."

"She's a few years older, and she was obsessed with science when she was in school. Now she's an artist. Big switch."

He did look tired. Katie walked back to the kitchen, waving at him to follow her. "I know we need to measure things," she said over her shoulder, "but we're going to eat first."

"Eat? It's only ten o'clock."

She turned and eyed him. "You look like you can handle a second breakfast."

"I can always handle a second breakfast, but why now?"

"Because I can't wait a minute longer for you to taste my food!" she exclaimed. In the kitchen, she handed Sam a bowl, taking the other for herself. Katie had made a salad of quinoa and cold grilled lamb, sweet potatoes, fresh bell peppers, snap peas, and a dressing of lemon and thyme. She placed a scoop of yogurt on top and watched closely as he took a bite and closed his eyes.

"It's... what is this? It's perfect. How do you... you have the same ingredients as the rest of the world, how do you make things taste like this?"

She laughed, then took a bite, sighing as she did. She had tasted it as she was making it, but it was even better now, with Sam beside her.

They walked out to the porch and sat at the table. As Sam ate, Katie read him the theme words she had dreamed up for the restaurant: "garden, magical, fresh, whole, simple, natural."

He nodded. "That sounds exactly like what I just ate. So, how to make the house say that?"

She grinned at him. He got it. He was the perfect contractor for this work.

He patted his stomach and stood. "All right, time to measure. Where's the notebook?"

CHAPTER THIRTEEN

Sam opened his cupboard and realized, with supreme irritation, that he had forgotten to buy coffee. He didn't even have enough left for a cup, let alone a pot. How on earth? He never forgot to buy things on his list. This was the second thing out of order today. The first was sleeping in.

Sam had opened his eyes for the first time at six-thirty. For a moment, he thought his phone was broken. He lay there blinking at it until he noticed that the sun was higher than usual, and he was seeing patterns of light on his walls that he had never seen before, *never having a reason to lie around in bed until this hour.*

Sleeping in was one thing—he had been working hard. But keeping groceries stocked was a long time habit, and forgetting was inexcusable. Was he getting sick? Losing his memory?

He grumbled as he pulled on clothes for an early morning visit to Green's. This coffee incident was going to throw off his whole day. He glanced at his watch. Ten minutes to seven. Well, Sheldon would have to make an exception.

The air was fresh and bright, surprisingly pleasant. When he got to Green's, Sam pounded on the locked door, waiting five minutes between each new barrage on the large pane of glass. Finally, Sheldon shuffled into view, his face a thundercloud. When he saw Sam, though, he turned white.

"Is everyone okay?" he gasped as he threw the door open.

"Yeah, of course," Sam said. "Everything's fine."

"Nothing is wrong," Sheldon stated in a flat voice, staring at Sam for a full minute before the explosion. "What made you like this?" he growled. "Why on earth would you interrupt a man's morning exercises without an emergency?"

Sam pushed by his friend. "I'm out of coffee," he said over his shoulder. In the coffee aisle, he picked up two bags of his regular blend, then went back to Sheldon, who was still standing by the door with a strange expression on his face.

"You forgot to buy coffee?" he whispered, his eyes wide.

"Oh, shut up," Sam said, pulling a twenty out of his wallet and holding it out.

"What am I supposed to do with that?" Sheldon asked. "The register's not open."

"Take care of it after—I don't care what you do with it. Come on, Sheldon, you act like an old grandma sometimes."

"I am an old grandma, compared to you. I'm thirty-five years old next week."

"Three years older than me, old man." Sam kept holding the bill out until Sheldon took it, then he turned to go.

"How could you forget to buy coffee?" Sheldon said. "I

could set my clock by your habits. Do you think maybe you're... distracted?"

Sam swiveled to look at him hard. "What's that supposed to mean?"

"I heard about your new project. I approve, but I don't think our life goals do."

Sam shook his head. He remembered the day that he had outlined his life plan to Frankie and Sheldon: to be a modern monk, devoted to God and his store, to never get in a relationship again, to never again allow things to become complicated. Frankie was skeptical, but Sheldon had latched onto the idea, and he and Sam declared the intention of having a life free of the distraction of romantic relationships, a practice that Sheldon seemed to be embracing a little too enthusiastically, Sam thought, eyeing the striped shirt and overalls that his friend was wearing.

"It's just a job," he said. "And what's happening to you anyway? What's with the accelerated craziness lately?"

Sheldon shrugged. "Life's short," he said.

Sam felt a pang of compassion for his friend. "Still waiting for her to come home?"

"She will, one day."

"And when she does, you'll be waiting for her in clown clothes."

"I don't want her to think I've been bored while she's been gone."

Sam raised his eyebrows and shook his head. "See you later, Shel," he said, turning to go. "Thanks for opening the door."

"Sure thing. Watch that your 'work' doesn't upend your

monk life," Sheldon said, offering one last jab as Sam walked away.

CHAPTER FOURTEEN

S am fumed all the way home. He was finally in place in his seat at the counter—his hard earned, fought-for cup of coffee before him—when the doorbell rang. It was the bell to the house, not the store. He let his head fall into his hands for a moment before trudging downstairs to see who was there. Was it Sheldon, out for revenge? Or Katie? He went a little faster.

It wasn't Sheldon or Katie. It was his mom, and—if he wasn't mistaken—his fourteen-year-old niece, Maddie.

"Hi," he said, surprised. "What's going on? Maddie! I didn't know you were coming!"

"No one did, that's the point," his mother said, pushing past him. Sam gave Maddie a quick hug, then stood aside to allow her in as well. She looked like a different person from the last time he had seen her. She was taller, for one thing, her hair dyed black, some of it braided into tiny braids around her face. She had heavy eyeliner, a lip ring, and she was wearing a large black trench coat. She paused in the doorway, looking around at the store in awe.

"I remember this place," she said, and Sam was surprised by how soft her voice was.

"You would have been around four when you left," Sam said. "You spent a lot of time here with your grandpa. It makes sense that you would remember it. Straight through this way, it looks like your grandma has already let herself up the stairs."

He found his mother pacing in the living room. Sam retrieved his cup of coffee and made a final effort to drink it, staring glumly into the mug. The coffee wasn't hot. He drank it anyway.

"Come on, you two," he said. "Have a seat." All three sat on a different chair or sofa, awkward, like strangers. Birds chirped outside the open window.

"Start at the beginning," he told his mom, who seemed to be suffering from some kind of fit, huffing and sighing and tugging at her shirt. Sam suddenly noticed that she was only wearing one earring. That was alarming.

"You know how Reesey has been acting lately," his mother started.

"Yes, I've been worried. Is your mom okay?" he asked Maddie, and she shrugged and stared at the carpet.

"Well, this morning I got a text—a text!—that I needed to go down to the Greyhound bus station because Maddie was waiting there, and get this, Maddie is going to live with me now, *indefinitely*."

Her voice had been rising as she spoke, and she drew the last word out until it was nearly a wail. Sam glanced at

Maddie, who sat hunched on the couch with her arms wrapped around her stomach. He tried to give his mother a look that told her to get a hold of herself, but she was beyond the point of paying attention.

"Do you know what's going on?" Sam asked, directing his question to Maddie.

She darted a glance at his face, then looked back at the ground in front of her. She shook her head. "Mom's been frustrated with me lately," she said, in that same soft voice. "She thought it would be a good idea to send me without asking because you wouldn't be able to say no."

Sam ignored the exaggerated sigh that came from his mother's direction. "Do you think your mom is okay?" he asked. "You know, like, okay?"

Maddie shrugged. "No worse than usual. She'll probably be okay now that I'm gone."

Her words hit Sam like a fist in the gut, and even his mother paused her spluttering to touch Maddie's hand. Maddie seemed frail, and thin, sitting as though like she was trying to hold herself together with her arms, enveloped in that black coat.

"Mom, can we talk for a minute?" Sam asked, standing. "Maddie, if you don't mind waiting, I've got some things I need to discuss with your grandma."

Maddie nodded and sank farther into the cushions of Sam's couch.

Sam led his mother to his room. She was momentarily distracted when they entered.

"Sam, dear, you don't have one thing on your walls. You should let me decorate."

Sam laughed. "That will never happen," he said. "Besides, I have a painting on the wall." He gestured at his whale painting.

His mother snorted. "Everyone in Aveline has one of those. It doesn't count."

"I like it. But let's stay on topic," Sam said, dropping his voice to a whisper. "You can't act like this around Maddie. It's not her fault what Reesey does. And, though permission is usually granted first—" he made a face, "it's not that strange for a grandmother to take care of her grandchild for a while. Frankie's parents do it all the time!"

"That's different, Sam. Francisco lives with Lupe and Juan! I can't do it. I can't take care of someone else right now. That's all I have to say." Tears were standing in her eyes. She looked lopsided, with only one earring in, and something was wrong with her eyes. Sam looked closer and saw that she wasn't wearing makeup. He didn't think he'd seen his mother without makeup since he moved out of the family house.

Sam looked at her for a long moment, then settled back on his heels and crossed his arms. He knew his mother well enough to know when she wouldn't change her mind.

"Then what do we do?" he asked.

"It's obvious, Sam. You need to take her." Dorothy nodded decisively as she spoke.

"Me?" Sam couldn't have been more stunned if she had flown out the front window. "Why me? How am I a better choice than you?" He was still whispering, but his whispers grew louder. He tried to calm down.

"You're young. You have an extra bedroom, and I don't. And you haven't raised two horrible children already."

"You've always said we were angels!"

She shook her head and put a hand up. "I'm doing something here, Sam. After a lifetime of caring for your father and you and your sister, I'm discovering what it means to do as I like. You can call me selfish or terrible, but I didn't sign up to take care of Maddie. I'm not going to do it." Sam did think she was being rather selfish. At the same time, he couldn't blame her. He ran his hands through his hair, feeling his throat constrict. *God, what are you doing? I thought we had an agreement! What about the monk life?* But he couldn't escape what God would want him to do. He couldn't turn a child away.

"Okay," he said, lifting his hands. "Okay, I'll do it. But I'm starting a contract at the Grace house, and school's out in two weeks. I can't enroll her. What am I supposed to do with her?"

"Leave her here—she's not a baby. Or take her with you. I don't care."

Sam leaned his head back against his door, thinking about how messy this would make his life. Theresa, argh. He silently berated her and hoped for her safety at the same time, then took a deep breath and walked back out to where Maddie sat, staring straight ahead, her face unreadable. He was going to have to be with her most of the time! He felt the blood rush from his face at the thought. He wasn't prepared for this. The only teenagers he knew were the ones who worked for him. That thought was encouraging, though—he was famous for being an excellent boss for students. Maybe he could handle a fourteen-year-old. She couldn't be that different than an eighteen-year-old, right?

"Good news, Maddie. You're going to be staying with me!" Even he could hear the fake cheer in his voice, but Maddie simply nodded. "Let me show you your room. Where's your stuff?"

"In Grandma's car," she said, her voice barely audible.

"I'll grab that. Mom, can you show Maddie the spare bedroom?"

As he went, he heard his mother, now overflowing with hospitality.

"You're going to love living here," she bubbled. "Everything you could want within walking distance, and Sam makes great coffee!"

Sam shook his head, feeling a bit panicked as he moved out of reach of their voices. He made great coffee, sure, but that was about it. He was going to have to feed her, wasn't he? *God, help me*, he silently prayed. He stood staring at the sidewalk, stunned, for at least five minutes, before he finally remembered to gather Maddie's bags out of the car.

CHAPTER FIFTEEN

Sam showed up late to the first day of work at the Grace house. He had texted Katie to let her know there was a family emergency. He had called his work crew of three men and asked them to wait until he arrived.

"Yes," he reassured them. "I'm paying you for the full day. Just don't start anything before I get there."

Sam hadn't told Katie the nature of the family emergency, and as he walked along the footpath with Maddie trailing behind him, he saw Katie standing on the porch watching them, her eyebrows so high they were almost in the roots of her hair. He glanced back. Maddie was a sight, wearing the crazy black coat, dragging her feet, eyeliner even thicker than when she arrived. He supposed she had used the moments when he was whisper-arguing with his mom to draw more on her eyes. Paint more on her eyes? Oh, man, he knew nothing about teenaged girls.

"Hi, Katie," he said. "I'm so sorry that I'm late."

"That's okay," she said.

"This is my niece, Maddie," he said. "She's staying with me for a while. Her mother is..." Words abandoned him.

"Taking a break," Maddie said, helping out.

"Wow, that's awesome for you," Katie said, still smiling. "I wish I had a niece."

Maddie's face softened, and Sam felt a rush of gratitude. Katie towered over the younger girl, her hair in a loose braid, dressed in a T-shirt and jean shorts. He shrank inwardly from the thought of working side by side for weeks with Katie running around looking like a summery frayed denim goddess. *Monk life,* he reminded himself. *Monk life with a kid.* He leaned against the porch railing, jumping up when it let out a creak.

"It's too late in the year to enroll Maddie in school," he explained, "and I don't want her to be at home alone all day, so I brought her along. Maybe after the demolition, she can help me with work around here, but for now, do you have any work for her?"

Katie blinked at him. Sam felt a twinge of guilt for putting her on the spot.

She collected herself. "Actually," she said, "I do have some work. I'm putting garden beds in, Maddie, to grow salad greens for the restaurant. And I'm going to test another recipe this afternoon. Can you handle a shovel for dirt and a knife for vegetables?"

Maddie's eyes widened. "I think so," she said. "I mean, I can chop vegetables, but I've never used a shovel before."

"First time for everything," Katie said. "Let's put your coat somewhere so we can start."

The day went smoothly after that, but there was a lump in Sam's throat that made its presence known every time he spotted Katie and Maddie digging the garden bed. They both wore gloves and big straw hats, Maddie elfin in hers, Katie tall and glorious, copper hair trying to escape its braid. By midday, Sam's crew had taken three walls down, and Katie and Maddie had dug one garden bed. As Sam looked over what they had accomplished, he felt some of the tension drain out of him. The week before, he and Katie had spent two days moving all the furniture into the cellar under the house—a frustrating job that involved a lot of muttering and whispered cussing from Katie—and with the space cleared it was easy to see the morning's progress.

The rooms on the lower floor had been small and separate, but Sam and the crew were working to transform the three little rooms into one large one. Sam craned his neck to admire the tall, scalloped ceilings and brightness of the house now that it was open.

Katie came in and shrieked. Sam spun around, startled.

"I'm sorry," she said, her hand on her mouth. "It's just so surprising. Sam... it's beautiful." He let out the breath he was holding. Maddie walked into the house behind Katie and looked around, her expression neutral.

"I think so too," Sam said. "We'll open that kitchen wall this afternoon." They had decided to double the size of the kitchen by opening the wall between the kitchen and what had been the dining room, making one large, bright space for Katie to work. She was still gazing from one side of the house to the other, smiling, one hand on her chest.

"This is going to be the most beautiful restaurant ever,"

she said. They stood in silence for a while until the doorbell rang.

"That'll be lunch," Katie said and went to retrieve the six giant burritos she had ordered from the taqueria down the street.

AFTER THEY ATE, while the crew took down the last wall, Katie and Maddie sat on the porch swing, talking. The two of them had begun chopping in the kitchen, only to stop in dismay as the dust from the demolition began to sweep over the room. Laughing, Katie ran around throwing sheets over everything, and then she and Maddie retreated to the swing with glasses of icy hibiscus tea. Sam wondered what they were talking about. Could Katie give him any tips about four-teen-year-old girls? She made it look easy. Every once in a while, he checked on them as they sat with their heads together on the swing. Katie winked at him on one of his trips, and he pretended to scowl at her, then went back to knocking down the wall, a broad smile spreading across his face.

MADDIE WAS ENJOYING HERSELF, and no one was more surprised than her.

She sipped at the hibiscus tea in the glass—it was sweeter than her mom's blend—and looked at the blisters forming on her hands. Just a little bit of digging had given her three blisters, despite her gloves. The digging felt good after a cramped night on the Greyhound bus, though. She didn't think her uncle realized that she hadn't really slept the night before. She felt sleepy, but the warm, contented kind of sleepy, wrapped in her coat—she had found it draped over a post on Katie's stairs and had put it on again. Wearing it made her hot, but it was comforting. It smelled like home.

This morning after her grandma had left, Sam told her not to call him Uncle Sam. "It sounds weird. Like the man in the stars and stripes hat."

"What should I call you? Uncle Max?"

"No," he said, grinning at her. "Sam will do if it's okay with you."

"It's fine with me."

Then Sam brought her to Katie's house, and Maddie liked Katie immediately because she didn't seem to pity Maddie or be put off by her. While they were digging and squishing dirt with their hands to make a garden bed, they had talked about books and poetry, which Maddie loved. Katie knew about a lot of poets. Now they sat in silence on the porch, all talked out.

"Tell me about your mom," Katie said, after a while, looking over at her. "What's going on there?"

"My mom?" Maddie asked, taken aback. She didn't like to talk about the trouble with her mom.

She stalled, taking a sip of tea, thinking about what she should share. "My mom's great. But she needs a lot of time on her own. She's a potter." Maddie looked up at Katie, who nodded. "She did something different here, but when she moved to Minnesota, she started work as a potter, making cups and pots and lots of weird sculptures. Now she's pretty well known. Her art is beautiful."

Katie smiled at her. "You seem very protective of her."

Tears sprang into Maddie's eyes, and she blinked rapidly. "Well, she's not bad, lots of people send their kids to stay with their families. And I've been getting into trouble lately. It was hard for her." Katie's eyes were very kind. Maddie's back stiffened. Was it pity? She hated being pitied.

"What kind of trouble?" Katie asked.

"Mostly school," Maddie said. "I hate stupid school." She sat up and used the backs of her hands to wipe her cheeks. "Is there a bathroom upstairs that I can use? I don't want to use the downstairs one after all those construction guys."

Katie laughed. "I don't blame you. There's one upstairs, beside my bedroom at the back of the hall."

Maddie walked up the stairs slowly, a wave of exhaustion crashing over her. She found the bathroom and used it, then stood in the hallway looking into a room that had to be Katie's. The door was wide open, so that Maddie could see all of it—a single bed with a quilt, a desk, and a dresser covered in beautiful things. She quietly walked over to the dresser and picked them up one by one. There were several rocks, some tiny clay pots, and a cactus. A brooch, three necklaces, a photograph of an old woman and a little girl. She put each one down, then found the thing that was calling to her. A small clay bird. The bird reminded Maddie of her mom, and fit perfectly in her hand. She held it for a moment, then dropped it into her pocket. She left the room and walked back down to the porch, feeling the cold, controlled feeling that came to her whenever she took something. The bird was a comforting lump in her pocket.

CHAPTER SIXTEEN

The renovation progressed step by step. Sam had hired Lucy for the duration of the project, and when Sam and Katie went to Grant Hardware to pick up paint for the kitchen, Katie got a good look at how Lucy and Larry worked together.

"Get the log book, Larry," Lucy said. "And straighten your shirt. The boss is here. Did you shower today?"

Larry looked at Sam, his eyes frantic.

"You've ruined my life," he muttered, passing by to retrieve the log book.

"It won't be forever," Sam whispered. "Don't worry. I'll turn her out on her ear when this is over."

Katie laughed. She knew Sam loved Lucy, and Larry loved his mother. But there was no denying that Lucy spoke at a volume nearly twice the level of anyone else in the world, thought at a million miles a second, and bossed everyone, including Sam.

"I'm sure I told you to order new Dewalt stock!" she

shouted across the store. Katie winced on Larry's behalf, but it was Sam who replied.

"Done, Luce!" Sam called back. "Truck's coming Thursday!" He popped his eyes at Katie, and she dissolved into giggles.

Sam mixed two buckets of paint while Katie collected brushes and rollers. After they wrote the supplies on Katie's ledger, they hauled the supplies back to the truck. Katie got in first, and then Sam climbed in, putting one arm behind Katie's seat to back the vehicle out of the parking spot behind the store. His hand brushed her neck as he pulled it back to the steering wheel, and it was only the lightest touch, but she was very aware of him, and his minty soap smell. He glanced at her once on the way back, and she smiled at him. That familiar blush crept over his cheeks. He left the truck quickly when they got back to the house.

Katie went back to the kitchen and was working with Maddie, testing recipes, when a loud crash came from the other room, followed by a stream of curses. Katie flinched and sighed.

"I'm going to have a permanent twitch before this is done," she told Maddie. Crashes and booms came at all times of day, as Sam and his crew dropped things or hammered or sawed, or whatever it was they did.

She left the kitchen to make sure everything was okay, thinking about how she and Sam hadn't been alone at all, besides that one charged moment in the truck. Maddie was always with them now. It was probably for the best, Katie thought, rounding the corner and finding Sam on his hands and knees sweeping piles of nails into his hands. She didn't need the distraction. Sam dropped the nails into the bucket, brushing off the crew member's apologies.

"Never mind," he said. "Let's just get it cleaned up." He looked up and met Katie's eyes. "Sorry," he said. "I'm sure that was loud. Joe momentarily forgot how to use his eyes. He won't do it again." Joe nodded in agreement. "Are you sure you don't want to move out during the renovation?" Sam asked.

"I'm sure," she said. "Actually..." she looked around at the mess of sawdust and plastic sheeting. "I love this."

Sam smiled at her, his eyes crinkling around the edges. Katie turned and walked quickly back to the kitchen. Her heart was thudding strangely in her chest, and she needed to steer clear of Sam for a while.

Maddie stood at the sink, washing kale. Katie thought she might add a white bean and kale soup to her menu, but this was the third time she had tried the recipe. Something was still missing. It didn't taste the way she wanted.

She looked over at Maddie. The teenager was so helpful that it was hard to imagine she was trouble for anyone. Katie liked working with her. They had become surprisingly close over the last week, enough so that Katie figured she could say something about Maddie's skimpy wardrobe. The girl didn't seem to have enough clothes, and Katie wanted to do something about it.

"Hey Maddie," she said.

"Yeah?" Maddie said, looking up from her kale washing.

"I've noticed that you wear the same few outfits again and again," Katie said.

Maddie flinched, anger flashing in her eyes. Katie realized too late that she had miscalculated.

"I didn't know you were watching me so closely," Maddie said, her voice sarcastic. "I'll try to remember that."

"Hey, that's not fair," Katie said lightly, trying to think about how to go gently from here. She didn't say anything more as she rinsed the potatoes and got the peeler and chopping board out. Katie worked quickly, her hands flying. If she was going to run an actual restaurant, she would need to work fast, and she was working on her speed, turning it into a game. Maddie was into it, too, and she had improved a lot since her first laborious, twenty-minute carrot chopping. The two of them had watched Youtube videos about how to chop efficiently, then experimented on onions, tomatoes, potatoes, and garlic.

How could she fix this? She'd stuck her foot in her mouth. Maddie must be sensitive about how she looked. She looked over at the girl, whose shoulders were drawn up to her ears.

"You know I have a big mouth, Maddie," she said. "You don't need to worry about me watching you."

Maddie's shoulders relaxed, just a bit. Her voice when she spoke was so soft that Katie missed what she said the first time.

"What was that?" she asked, moving closer.

"It's just that I only brought three outfits with me," Maddie said. She put the kale out to dry, then pulled the bowl of onions toward her, attacking them with the chef knife.

Katie felt a pang of pity. "Well, we can fix that easily

enough," she said. Maddie looked up. "Eyes on the chopping board," Katie said, "you need to keep your fingers." She went on while Maddie chopped. "What do you think? We could coax some money out of your uncle's wallet and go shopping this afternoon. I want to get out of this madhouse anyway."

When Maddie looked up, Katie saw relief in her eyes. Maddie nodded. "Yeah, that would be okay," she said.

"Great," Katie said, keeping her voice light, as though she was approaching a fawn in the backyard." Let's finish the soup and eat, and I'll go talk to that clueless uncle of yours."

CHAPTER SEVENTEEN

K atie got the soup exactly right, that time. The trick was more lemon and a different brand of parmesan that added just the right smoky creaminess to the soft white beans. Sam and the workers smacked their lips and made a fuss over the flavors. Meanwhile, Katie wrote down every last thing she had done in her notebook. Was anything as satisfying as getting a recipe right? Katie didn't think so.

When she was sure she could replicate the recipe, she turned to the next task, pulling Sam aside to talk quietly with him.

"I'm going to take Maddie shopping," she told him. "We need money." She laughed. "Cough it up."

A look of relief crossed his face.

"You are such an angel," he said. She blushed and looked down. "I've been thinking that Maddie needs clothes, but I have no idea how to buy a girl clothes, and I'm not sure my mom would get Maddie what she wants."

"I'm happy to do it," Katie said. "We'll go to Billers. It'll be good to get out of here for a while."

In her bedroom, Katie put on a purple shirt dress and fixed her hair in two braids. She smiled at her reflection in the mirror over her dresser, then plucked some bracelets out of her jewelry box. Wait. Where was her clay bird? Nana had given the bird to Katie for her twentieth birthday, and she had treasured it ever since. Had it fallen behind the dresser? Or maybe she had knocked it into the top drawer? She rummaged through the drawer for a minute, then left it. She didn't want to make Maddie wait. She would have to pull the dresser out some other time. She slipped into sandals and flew downstairs, nearly crashing into Sam at the bottom.

"I put some money on the table on the porch," he said, then went back to the piece of trim in his hands. When the crew had knocked the walls down, they left the top corners there to frame each room, and Sam was hand-making trim for them.

"Thanks," Katie said, waiting for him to look up. He stayed bent over his work, though, and she shrugged and left, calling a light "Bye!" over her shoulder. She plucked the envelope from the table as she passed it. Maddie waited by the car, hunched inside her black coat. Katie frowned. The weather was scorching, the middle of a sweltering June.

"You have to be hot," Katie said to Maddie. "Do you want to leave the coat here?" Maddie shook her head with a look of panic. Katie shrugged, seeing that it was a big deal to Maddie, though she didn't understand it. "Okay! Suit yourself."

They drove out of Aveline in silence. Katie was deep in thought. Things had changed over the last weeks. She spent almost no time obsessing about the past or reliving the shame of the courtroom or the online anger and insults. The panic had been quiet. When Katie did feel panicky, she could calm herself by lying down in a dark room for a while. She hadn't cried on any curbs lately. She was preoccupied with the very full present; renovations, menu planning, and the fourteen-year-old girl who sat in the seat beside her. And she barely thought about Ed.

She thought about him now, though—his straight black hair and striking face. She had been smitten by him and all the attention he paid to her. He wore such excellent suits and smelled so good. His smile was devastating. But she also thought of him turning away from her when she tried to meet his eyes in the courtroom, desperate for support. He told her she humiliated him. He was embarrassed by her.

Katie had taken the fall for them. She was their scape-goat. They tried to drive her into the ground in their bid for innocence. Katie was shaky on the witness stand, having gone through so much accusation by then that she wasn't even sure what was true anymore. She had still testified against them, but Philip and the company had come away with light penalties. The penalty hadn't been light for Katie. She had paid nearly everything that mattered to her. Her boss, Philip, could have stood up for her character since she had been practically family all those years, but he was the accused. Ed could have stood up for her too, but he stepped aside and avoided the fall.

Katie's hands tightened on the steering wheel. This was why it was good to stay busy. Her thoughts always led in circles as she defended her actions in her head, facing a phantom courtroom. For months, she had relived it in her dreams, seeing the women and their eyes, or Philip's wife Rhonda, shrieking at her in the hallway. The flash of the knife.

"What's wrong?"

Maddie's voice startled Katie out of her memories. She blinked. She was in the car with Maddie, far from the trouble of the past. She had been there again—it felt so real—the room with its dingy hallways, the corporate heads who stared at her with such hatred as she walked by.

"What?" she asked, clearing her throat to get the word out.

"You were making sad sounds," Maddie said. "Are you okay?"

Katie looked at the girl, curled into her coat as though she wanted to disappear. Her face was lovely. She had big eyes and a delicate jaw. She had pulled her hair back today, and it showed off her graceful neck.

"I went through something horrible a while ago, before I moved here," Katie answered, choosing her words carefully. "Sometimes I get caught up remembering, though it's been better now that I have such good company." She smiled at Maddie.

"Something horrible with a man?" Maddie asked bluntly.

"Kind of. But it was more than that."

"I know what that's like. Do you—" The girl took a breath. "Do you ever feel like the horrible stuff is following you?"

"No, I left it behind," Katie said softly, feeling curious.

"But it follows me in my thoughts. Sometimes I get scared for no reason at all. Does yours follow you?"

"I feel like I can't get rid of it," Maddie said. "What do you do when you get scared?"

"I lie down in my room with the lights off and listen to music. Or I cook something."

"And that works?" Maddie's voice was skeptical.

"It does. You should try it sometime." She smiled. "Or whatever works for you. Some people listen to loud music when they get scared, my therapist told me. But that never worked for me. It just made my heart race."

"You see a therapist?" Maddie asked. She tapped her fingers on the car door, then let her coat fall back over her wrist, drawing her hands up into her sleeves.

"I did, for some time, right after the horrible thing happened." She cleared her throat. "Have you ever seen a therapist, for your hard thing?"

Maddie looked at her as though she was crazy. "I would never," she said.

Katie shrugged. "Just wondering," she said. She felt the fragile, bird-like nature of their conversation, and dropped it as she pulled the Subaru into the parking lot. Talking to Maddie had pulled her out of her own trouble. She stepped out of the car and stretched, letting the past go again, as she had tried many times before.

"Where are we?" Maddie asked.

Katie grinned. "I Googled the best thrift store in Billers. You're going to be amazed, if the reviews are right." She had the pleasure of seeing a look of delight flash across Maddie's face as they walked across the hot asphalt toward the store.

CHAPTER EIGHTEEN

Katie felt the afternoon was exactly what they needed. Maddie tried on about thirteen outfits in black and gray, but she allowed Katie to put some purple and blue in the pile of clothes. Maddie scorned a pink shirt, though, picking it up with her thumb and index finger as though it were a dead rat. Katie laughed at the look on her face. Katie did a little shopping for herself, scoring some clunky glass bead necklaces, a new pair of jeans, and in the vintage section, the red dress of her dreams; an A-line with a knee-length skirt and tight sleeves. It fit Katie perfectly. She bought it to wear at the restaurant opening, ignoring the butterflies that erupted in her stomach at the thought of the opening party.

She applauded as Maddie modeled outfits for her, praising the ones she liked. She watched carefully as Maddie stepped out of the dressing room in a tank top and short skirt, sighing with relief when she saw Maddie's thin, white, unscarred arms and legs. She still wasn't sure what the trouble following Maddie was, but she was thankful to see that the girl wasn't cutting herself.

Katie pulled out her phone and took a selfie of the two of them wearing vintage hats, and then decided to buy hers when she saw the result.

"It looks gorgeous on me," she said, preening. Then she smiled at Maddie's look. "What? The whole world criticizes women for every flaw, so we need to be our own best cheerleaders."

She winked at Maddie but turned away as her heart fell. She remembered the Katie who had existed before the incident, back when she had believed that she could do anything, had thought that if she only believed in herself enough, she couldn't fail. That had turned out to be a load of crap. Believing in yourself couldn't make you a good judge of character. She hated what had happened, what she had done and not done, and how it had marked her forever.

She had to take deep breaths for a few minutes as the panic and feelings of self-loathing nearly overwhelmed her. How could she ever get away from the cloud of shame? Or the futility of life? Katie could try and try, and still, everything would fall apart. She stood there with her head down, trying to pull herself together for her young friend, until a gentle touch at her elbow brought her back, and she blinked tears away and smiled at Maddie.

"Ready to buy this stuff?" she asked. "I'm starving."

They stopped for quesadillas at Katie's favorite taqueria, then dropped into Target for new underwear and bras for Maddie. Katie was tired as they drove back through Billers on their way home, the sun beginning its golden descent in the sky. *Home*, thought Katie, and exhausted as she was, the thought warmed her.

"I don't want you to think that I don't have stuff," Maddie said suddenly. "I have lots of nice things at my house with my mom. I just didn't think I would be here for long. So I didn't bring much. My mom takes good care of me." Katie could feel how badly Maddie wanted her to think well of her mother.

"Tell me about her," she said.

Maddie went on to describe a fun, quirky, fragile artist, who lived in her clay studio and sometimes couldn't be bothered to eat. She sounded like someone Katie would be friends with.

"She works hard to deal with life, even though it's tough for her sometimes," Maddie said. "I think my... horrible thing... sent her over the edge. She needed space to get her balance back." Katie felt sadness and admiration for the love she heard in Maddie's voice. The teen cared so much for her mother's well-being, even after she had been sent off to live with relatives.

"The problem that followed you..." she said. Maddie nodded. "Is that the problem with school?" Maddie hesitated, then nodded swiftly. "And your dad? What about him?"

"I don't know who he is," Maddie said, her voice so soft that Katie barely heard her. "My mom won't tell me. Maybe he's around here. We lived here until I was four years old."

"What made your mom leave?" Katie asked.

"I don't know." She glanced over at Katie. "Maybe something like what made you leave L.A."

THEY DROVE to the gas station at the edge of town, filling up for the long drive over the hill to Aveline. Katie saw Maddie looking at the animal shelter across the street and suggested, on a whim, that they check it out.

"We could use some puppy therapy after all that shopping," she said.

"And talking," Maddie added.

"And talking."

At the shelter, a volunteer guided them back to large, grassy fenced areas that contained puppies and older dogs. Katie was relieved that there were no cages. She wandered around, looking at the larger dogs while Maddie played with a group of puppies that had been found on the side of the road that morning. She passed a rottweiler, a dalmatian, and several mixes before she found herself standing in front of a dog—a very specific dog—who caught at her heart. He had short, golden fur, floppy ears, and soulful eyes. She reached over the fence and scratched his head. He nudged at her hand with his nose, whimpering, his tail wagging furiously.

"Oh my," she murmured, petting his short, soft fur, "you are the sweetest thing." She rubbed his head for a long time, whispering to him while he stared into her eyes. Then she stood reluctantly, avoiding the eyes of the employee hovering nearby. The dog whined as she left. He scratched at the fence and gave one short bark. Katie walked faster.

"We'd better go," she said to Maddie, "Your uncle is going to worry." They crossed the street to get back to the car, but the farther away they got from the shelter, the more Katie's stomach hurt. She went as far as turning the car on and sitting there for several spaced-out minutes before she shut it off and said, "Well, that's it then." She was smiling as she walked back into the shelter to retrieve the dog that was so clearly hers.

MADDIE WAS WORRIED. "But have you ever owned a dog before?" she asked on the way home, after the long process of adoption the shelter workers had led them through. The sun was setting, and Maddie was hungry again, but she didn't say anything. She didn't want Katie to spend any more money on her. Even the gas to get here must have cost a lot. She sat in the back seat, holding tight to the dog's new collar to keep him from jumping into the front seat. He wanted to be right on Katie's lap. Katie had bought the collar when they stopped at the pet store to get food and supplies. A massive pile of stuff, actually. Maddie had watched as Katie kept throwing things on the pile, the same way she had back at the thrift store.

"No, but what does that have to do with anything?" Katie said. She was glowing. Maddie was almost jealous of how happy Katie was. But she didn't have much room for jealousy. All her brain space was taken up by worry. Worry about whether the restaurant would work out, whether she would get to see it open before her mother called her back, whether or not she wanted to go back to Minnesota, whether Katie could handle a dog, and most of all, what to do about the necklaces from the thrift store that were burning a hole in her pocket. Stealing didn't help as much anymore. It was starting to make her feel worse. She didn't know how other people handled all the things they felt, how they got through days and days without doing things they were compelled to even though they didn't want to.

How they got through days without being bad. Maddie stared at the trees, dark against the luminous sky, as they started on the mountain pass to get to Aveline, wishing she was anyone else, anyone but Maddie.

CHAPTER NINETEEN

A wind whipped up, blowing leaves along the sidewalk as Sam walked to Frankie's house for backyard night. He welcomed the breeze after another hot day of renovations without an air conditioner. Sam had been looking forward to the evening at Frankie's all week, thankful for one familiar thing when so much in his life was changing so rapidly.

Back when Frankie arrived in Aveline to take over the old church, Sam had been in a bad way. Morose and isolated, he was nursing a grudge against his ex-girlfriend, finding no joy in the business he inherited with his father's sudden death.

Sam had always imagined leaving Aveline someday, moving to New York City or London, maybe becoming a writer or an antique dealer. Something away from his small town and its small ideas. But his mother needed him, and he couldn't see the business wither and die. He stayed, but he grieved his father, his ex, and his plans. He didn't see the point in anything. He worked and slept. Life felt meaningless.

But then the young, widowed Reverend Francisco moved into the old parish house with his family. With him came something Sam had never before considered: a life of purpose fueled by unshakable love from God. Frankie had joy that had nothing to do with where he was or how small his environment was. Frankie's parents had come to America when Frankie was a toddler, as refugees from the violence of the Civil War in El Salvador in the eighties. Frankie had grown up in a family that was devoted to God and human rights. He seemed to live and breathe possibility, his whole life radiant with all the little moments where love made itself known, every day. The town had not wanted to embrace him, but he was irresistible.

Sam was still on a slow journey toward the reality of love in everything, but he was committed to the journey. So were the other men who met for backyard night.

Frankie's house, which he shared with his parents and daughter, was a modest craftsman-style house next to the old stone church. Two tall redwood trees presided over one corner of the yard, while a giant oak spread its branches over another. The summer light lingered, and Sam could hear Sheldon and George in the backyard. George's deep laughter mixed with Sheldon's manic style of storytelling. Sam smiled and pushed the gate open.

"Sam!" Frankie exclaimed, giving him a hug and offering him a cold beer.

"What's this?" Sam asked, looking at the unfamiliar label.

"New brew from up north. Figured we would give it a try."

Sheldon sat poking at the makeshift grill over the fire, Carlo in the chair beside him.

"Last fire of the season," Sheldon said. "We might as well make use of it."

"Next week we're on charcoal," George said. "Wildfire season and the ban."

"Where's your mom?" Sam asked. Usually, Francisco's mom, Lupe, would be out here by now, unable to stop herself from offering food or drinks, no matter how many times Frankie told her she didn't have to work on backyard night.

"She took Flora out for dinner."

Sam nodded. "Nice for them both, I bet. George," he said, clapping his friend on the back.

"Whippersnapper."

"George, come on. I'm a dozen years younger than you!"

"Enough that I have a grown daughter and you don't, Son."

"I don't have any daughter. How is Faith?"

"She's well. Sometimes I worry about her, but I guess that's normal. But, Sam, I hear you have a new young woman in your life."

Sam felt his face grow hot and knew he was blushing furiously.

Sheldon snorted. "Calm down, Sammy. He's talking about Maddie," he said.

"I knew that," Sam muttered, sinking into a chair. Carlo burst into laughter, and George looked at him in surprise.

"What's going on?" George asked.

"You tell me," Sheldon said. "He forgot to buy coffee the

other day. Sam. Forgot one of his precious life habits. Pulled me out of bed at seven o'clock in the morning, grumpy as a bear."

"I called it," Carlo murmured.

George stared at them for a moment, then turned to look at Sam again, realization dawning on his face.

"The new woman. The one you're working for." He sat forward in his chair. His short hair was grizzled with silver, but his face was barely lined. "You like her."

Carlo laughed a long, deep laugh. Sam glared at Sheldon. "I thought we were in this together. Frankie, help me with these two. I'm here to pray, not gossip about new citizens of our town."

"You know I don't think you need to be a monk, Sam," Frankie said, his voice mild. "We've had this talk."

Sheldon smirked.

"You're a lot of help, Frankie. Thank you," Sam muttered.

Frankie walked over with a plate of burgers.

"I'd like to meet the woman who can have you red in the face for five full minutes," he remarked, as they all piled condiments on their burgers and started to eat.

"Careful," Sheldon remarked. "Don't all women fall in love with you?"

Sam felt a spike of jealousy at the thought but pushed it down quickly. Frankie was a widower, and though it was true that women fell for the tall Salvadorian in the clerical collar, Sam knew that Frankie never encouraged them, and the attention made him uncomfortable.

"You know I'm not interested in marrying again," Frankie said.

There was a long silence as the men ate. All of them had suffered a loss of some kind. It wasn't hard to see why they were drawn to each other and clung to faith. Sam remembered that his own losses had been so much less than Frankie's or George's. Or even Sheldon's, though they had suffered the same loss in a strange way.

"So how is Maddie?" Carlo asked suddenly. "How can we pray for her?"

Sam felt a rush of gratitude for his old friend and the change of subject. He told them about his niece and his new role in her life, and thankfully, he didn't turn red for the rest of the evening.

BACK AT HOME, Sam waited for Katie and Maddie on Katie's front porch. It had grown late, and the moon was bright in the dark sky, shimmering on the piece of lake Sam could see from where he sat. He could be getting work done as he waited, but he was tense with worry and couldn't focus. They were much later than he had imagined they would be. Katie's phone was going to voicemail on the first ring, and Maddie didn't have one, an oversight Sam needed to fix. He hoped Katie was okay driving the curves over the mountain in the dark.

When he finally saw headlights swinging around the corner and the car nosed into the parking space, he let his breath out in a long sigh. He shook his head at himself. This was not the simple life he had been working toward all these years. Worrying about cars going off mountain cliffs was the definition of complicated.

Sam slowly stood as the car doors opened, but took a step back when a dog leaped out and tore across the grass toward him, wriggling all over, clambering up the porch steps, throwing itself at his legs.

"Whoa!" he exclaimed. "Who are you?" He bent down to stroke the dog's head. The animal was extremely cute and very wriggly. Katie arrived with her arms loaded down, dropping a pile of stuff on the porch. Sam saw a dog bed, a leash, and some rubber dog toys among the stash.

"Sam! You've met our new friend!" she said. "We need help with naming him."

"Katie," he said. She looked at him, and he felt a familiar swooping in his stomach when she held his eyes with hers.

"Yeah?"

"I was a little worried. Your phone is off."

"Oh, no!" She dropped the stuff on the porch and pulled her phone out. "Dead. This battery is getting so bad." She walked into the house, calling the dog after her, "Here, boy! I'm so sorry, Sam. We were going to be back in good time, but then I met my soulmate, and we went to the pet shop, and that place sucked us in."

Sam followed her into the big front room, and she turned to face him.

"What do you think his name should be?"

"Your soulmate, huh?" Sam turned as he heard Maddie

coming in. "You okay, Maddie?" he asked, and she nodded, giving him a fleeting smile. Sam felt shaky from the worry that had been coursing through him just a moment before. He was not in the mood to linger and play around. "I don't know what you should name him, Katie. I think Maddie and I need to get home now."

"You should eat first. I have so much of this soup left."

"I ate dinner."

"Well, Maddie didn't," Katie said.

Can we take it home with us?" he asked.

She stared at him. "Are you mad about us being late?"

"No, it's not that." He smiled, reluctantly, at her expression. "Don't worry. Just pack up some of your soup, and we'll see you in the morning."

MADDIE HELD the pot of soup on her lap while he drove the few blocks home. He looked at her. He thought she looked sad, but he wasn't good at reading her emotions.

"How was your day with Katie?" he asked.

"All right," she said, looking out the dark window rather than at him. "Fine."

He considered trying to get clearer answers from her, but decided to drop it, and hauled his tools out of the truck bed while Maddie disappeared up the back stairs, two large bags in tow.

Sam sighed. He wasn't exactly failing with Maddie, but he wasn't succeeding either. He thought of the backyard prayers for wisdom and much-needed peace for him and Maddie. They needed those prayers so badly. He locked his tools in his tool closet, then headed upstairs, feeling like an old, old man. When he reached the top floor, he looked briefly at Maddie's closed door, wondering if she needed to talk, then turned the other way and took a shower, thinking about life and complication and relationships. He was asleep almost before he fell into his bed.

CHAPTER TWENTY

The next morning, when they pulled up at the house, Katie was sitting on the porch steps, watching the dog run circles on the grass. When she looked up, Sam saw shadows under her eyes. She wore a skirt and tank top, and despite her tired face she was so beautiful he could barely look at her. He pulled his tools out of the truck and went to sit beside her on the porch.

Together they watched as the dog careened around chasing invisible things—a crazy, happy bundle of fur. Maddie pet the wriggling dog on the head, then went off to the garden bed to water the lettuce seeds she had planted the day before. She had been talking about the seeds since she woke up, and Sam had had a brief moment of thinking they might all be okay, thanks to Katie and her seeds, shopping, and care for Maddie.

"I'm sorry," Katie said in a low voice. "I could barely sleep last night. I felt terrible about making you worry."

He sighed. How could he possibly explain the truth to

Katie—that he wasn't mad at her, but at himself for caring, for thinking about her when he woke up and before he went to sleep, for trusting her so much, for becoming so wholly, thoroughly involved with her in such a short time? She was swiftly knocking through every wall of protection he had put up in his life.

"It wasn't a big deal," he said. "I was just tired."

She turned to him, then. Her dark eyebrows framed her face perfectly. He stared at the corners of her mouth, dragging his eyes up to hers.

"I feel like I know you pretty well by now," she said, "and I know that you were upset about something. I wish I knew what it was."

He swallowed. It was true that friendships were based on honesty, but he couldn't be completely honest with Katie. Sam couldn't tell her that he was tormented because she was becoming everything he wanted and everything he didn't want.

"You might have to be okay with a little mystery," he said, then smiled as she frowned, seemingly unimpressed with his answer. "What did you name him?" he asked, changing the subject.

She sighed, then shrugged. "I named him Sirius Black," she said.

He laughed. "A Potter fan. And a dog with a first and last name."

"Isn't everyone a Potter fan?"

He grinned and stood up, offering her a hand. "I wanted to talk to you about our deadline," he said. "The work's going well, and I think we might be able to be finished by the end of

September. Would you want to open in the middle of October or so?"

She nodded slowly. "Back on track! Feelings put neatly away," she quipped, her eyes wistful. He dropped her hand and looked down at his phone, flicking through his calendar, waiting until his heart was under control before looking back at her.

"What do you think?" he asked.

"That sounds fine," she said, then turned and whistled.

"Sirius! Come here!" And whether the dog knew his name already, or whether he just liked the sound of Katie's voice as much as Sam did, he came.

Now THAT HE had a firm deadline, Sam put every bit of his energy into the work. The front rooms were nearly done. Sam had finished the corner arches in the front rooms, shaping them to reflect the same curves as the lace on the eaves of the house. The crew had painted the entire lower floor a rich, golden yellow, and Sam had finished repairing the old molding, painting it the blue that Katie had chosen. These rooms and the porch would be the restaurant's seating area. When Sam installed the new lights, the rooms glowed with warmth.

Sam set his crew on finishing the front hallway while he focused on the kitchen, working well past the time when the team was gone for the day, designing cabinets for the new half of the kitchen. Sam had ordered the two large professional stoves that would line one wall and now needed to build the two long islands with butcher block tops. The remaining walls would hold his custom cabinets and shelves. Cabinet making was Sam's dream job—he loved the precise nature of fitting cabinets and building drawers—but he was endlessly distracted by Katie as she worked at her stove, trying new recipes, humming to herself. He worked farther and farther into the night, allowing Maddie to stay by herself at the apartment. She had a phone now that she could use for emergencies.

"You don't mind, do you?" he asked Katie one night when he couldn't tear himself away from his work.

"I don't mind. I stay up pretty late anyway, and if it gets too late, I'll just head for bed and let you lock up. I can trust you not to take off with my new knives, can't I?"

Sam smiled at her. "Maybe. They're nice knives. If I'm too loud, let me know, okay?" He pushed his safety glasses onto his face and went back to work with the circular saw. When he noticed Katie yawning, he packed up and headed home, waving to her at the doorway before she closed it and locked up behind him. He drove home trying to avoid images of Katie padding up the stairs by herself, sleepy and warm, and ready to curl up in bed.

SAM WAS BACK at Katie's house with Maddie early the next morning, working on cabinets, measuring, sawing, and sanding. The kitchen was fragrant with the scent of pine, and the sun illuminated tiny shavings of wood that danced in the air. Katie yawned at the other end of the kitchen, and Sam tried to ignore her. He had things in his heart well under control now. He would be fine as long as he didn't allow too many opportunities for the two of them to be close to each other. It was all about maintaining distance—not the easiest thing when they were spending hours on end in the same kitchen.

After he finished with the cabinets, he would add height to the countertops for Katie. She was so tall she had to stoop over the current counters. She leaned her elbows on one now, muttering to herself as she wrote in her notebook. Her hair was loose, falling nearly to her waist, but as he watched, she twisted it up in one fluid motion, coiling it on her head in a messy knot. She reached for one of the many clips that were stashed everywhere in the house, and pinned it in place, then turned to him.

Caught! He didn't turn away, knowing it would make him look guilty, but he hated that she had caught him staring.

She, however, gave him a brilliant smile and walked over to his work table. She was barefoot, her toenails painted light pink. He swallowed a feeling of panic.

"It's Saturday," she said.

"True," he replied.

"Will you go to the Farmer's Market with me?"

He waved his hand at the half-cut wood in front of him. "I have a lot to do."

"It's Saturday," she repeated, shaking a piece of paper at him. "You need a break."

"What's that?" he said, pointing at the paper.

"It's a list of people I need to talk to at the Farmer's Market. I have questions to ask."

"What about Maddie?" His niece was reading in the other room, Sirius curled up beside her.

"We'll bring her."

"I meant that she could accompany you instead of me."

She frowned at him. "Sam! I want you to come! You can introduce me to people I don't know. Get out in the sunshine for a while."

He sighed. "Okay, I guess."

She clapped her hands. "Yes! Great! I'll go change my clothes!"

"You get to change, but I don't?" he griped.

She was already leaving, but she turned and laughed at him. "Everyone already knows you're messy. I have to make a good first impression."

She was back soon, wearing her green sundress, carrying a large tote bag, smelling of roses. They collected Maddie, who put her book down and heaved a sigh.

The weekly farmer's market was held in the parking lot near the lake, only a couple of blocks away from Katie's house.

"You haven't been here yet?" Sam asked as they reached the outer stalls of the market.

"Of course I have. I haven't talked to vendors about supplies yet."

He glanced at her. She walked beside him with her loose, energetic stride, arm linked with Maddie, who only came up to her shoulder. She met his eyes and smiled.

"That's where you come in," she said. "You're the ice breaker."

"You are using me without any guilt whatsoever."

"That's not true. I have a little guilt." She laughed. "No, the truth is that I'm really shy and this part is scary. I need your help." She looked at her list, then from stall to stall as though she couldn't decide where to go first. He could see her preparing to be brave.

His face softened, and he sighed, plucking the list from her hand.

"Let's see. No, we don't want to talk to the tomato guy yet, he's really not a morning person—I don't know how he decided to be a farmer. Best to save him for last. The honey stall...yes, they're nice—let's start with them." He looked up to see her worried look smooth over as she smiled at him.

"You're an angel, do you know that?" she asked.

Maddie rolled her eyes. "Gross. Can we get this over with?" she said.

"Oh, this will take a while," Sam said. "Buckle up."

They spent the rest of the morning talking to vendors and farmers about wholesale prices and delivery. Katie had her account at Greens, but one of the words in her vision list was local; she wanted to get as much as possible from farm to table, at least when things were in season. She could use Greens for everything she couldn't get locally. Sam watched in admiration as Katie bartered, her shyness falling away. He stood back as she won over farmers entirely on her own, and he had a good morning despite himself. They sampled grapes and bought honey sticks.

Katie decided she had to have the lavender honey despite the expense, and talked her way to a better price after leaving and coming back several times.

Sam introduced Katie to Lewis when she said she needed a produce connection. "I'll have to supplement my garden greens," Katie whispered to Sam. "At least I will if I get enough customers."

"You'll get enough," he told her. He couldn't imagine people not lining up around the corner, even for a glimpse of Katie.

Sam liked Lewis and remembered that Frankie had mentioned he might invite the younger man to backyard night. Lewis's farm was only about five years old, in the outer edges of Aveline, but it was flourishing. Lewis was a young black man with short starter dreadlocks and gold-framed glasses. He was originally from Oakland and had graduated from Berkeley with a degree in literature and a dream of sustainable living. He taught workshops at his farm and hosted workers from a network of travelers who volunteered at farms in exchange for a place to stay.

"Nice to meet you," Lewis said now, shaking hands with Katie. "What kind of produce will you need?"

Sam left the two of them talking and wandered. He rubbed at his forehead, tired from trying to resist her, especially as she insisted on grabbing his wrist or hand whenever she got excited. He saw raised eyebrows on more than one familiar face. He put more distance between them once she was done talking with Lewis, letting Katie and Maddie walk ahead as he lingered at various stalls, looking over things without seeing them.

Now Katie and Maddie huddled over the goods at an Indian stall. Maddie was holding a small, beaded mirror. Katie looked around to find him, didn't see him, and turned back to pick up a shawl, holding it up to the light. He needed to get out of here.

"Katie," he said, walking to the stall. "Hi Patel, Sharma," he said to the couple at the stand. Katie looked up.

"There you are..." she said, but he interrupted.

"I need to go talk to Sheldon—I'll meet you back at your— the workspace." He changed his wording when he realized that everyone within earshot was listening. She looked at him.

"Is something wrong?" she asked.

He shook his head. *Yes, you're too beautiful.* "No, everything's fine."

He left as she turned back to the stall to barter with Sharma.

CHAPTER TWENTY-ONE

S am walked to Green's, shoving his hands in his jean pockets and kicking at a stone along the way. He felt irritated, riled up, despite the perfection of the weather, the heat of summer slowly giving way to the crisp air of fall. He pushed through the doors of the store, looking for Sheldon. His friend was nowhere to be seen.

"Where's the boss?" he asked the girl at the cash register.

"Back in the office," she said, pointing her chin toward the back of the store.

Sam frowned. Sheldon holing up in the office was never a good thing. When Sam reached Sheldon's office, he found his friend wearing a striped shirt with suspenders and torn jeans with the yellow scarf around the knee—all fine and good—but he was sitting in a beach chair sipping a glass of whiskey, reading a book.

"Are you not at work today?" Sam asked, walking into the room to sit in the desk chair.

"Of course I'm at work. Where are we, Sam? This is work."

"Shel, I need to confide in you, but I come to your store to find you falling apart."

"Does reading a book constitute as falling apart these days?"

"I know what the whiskey means in the middle of the day. You're not coping."

"Fine." Sheldon set the cup on the floor beside him, folding his hands and sitting straighter. "Fire away. I'm ready to listen, even though you have come to my office and insulted me."

Sam leaned back in the desk chair. He let out a long sigh and shook his head. "I don't even know what to say, but I'm in trouble. When we made the vow for a single life, I don't think I knew that there were women like Katie."

"Tall women?"

"No, women who were funny and brave and beautiful."

Sheldon shook his head, gravely. "Oh dear, you're well past 'in trouble.' You've gone to where there's no coming back. I've been there."

"You can hardly compare the two of us."

"Why not?"

"Because she left you, Shel, but Katie is here and possibly open to being together."

"She left me." Sheldon picked up his glass again and took a large gulp.

"Yes, she did. A long, long time ago. And maybe I'm not supposed to say this, but it's probably for the best. You don't need her here."

Sheldon shook his head at Sam, a pitying look on his face. "If you really think that, then you're not as far gone as I thought. You can most likely get out of your own trouble with no side effects." The pitying look turned into a glare. "'It's probably for the best.'" He imitated Sam's voice with a harsh nasal tone. Sam's eyebrows shot up. "It's not for the best, and I would gladly deal with any kind of complication if she would come back."

"You say that now," Sam said, "but only because you don't think she will."

"She will, that's what the bandanna is for. Plus, there's more for her to come back for these days, isn't there?"

Sam smiled at his friend, feeling sad for him. He didn't think she would be coming back any time soon. "So what should I do?" he asked.

"What do you want, Sam? That's the first thing. You need to figure out what it is you want," Sheldon said, looking very wise, but then he ruined the effect by carefully untying and retying the bandanna that was around his knee, giving it a pat, and settling back into his chair.

SAM WENT BACK to work and mulled over Sheldon's question all afternoon. What did he want? He thought about it while his hands were busy at the saw and the lathe, shaping corners that fit together perfectly, drilling into wood, surrounded by the smells of work—glue and fresh pine sawdust. Sometimes when Katie called to him from the other side of the kitchen, it took her three or four tries before he heard her. After a while of this, she laughed as he looked up, foggily, from far away.

"Where are you?" she asked. "You're so far away today."

He was not far away. He was right here trying to figure out which he wanted: her, or the monk life he decided on long ago. Part of him was adamant, insisting that manifestos were made for moments like this—when a man was tempted away from his ideals. And part of him said, "Yes, but her laugh, her hands, her perfect jawline, her sense of humor, her smile." And that part was very persistent.

He took a break, wandering through the house to find Maddie. She was sitting in the front room on the floor, scratching Sirius under the ears, and the look on her face was so sad that Sam took a step back. He cursed himself for being too involved in his own worries to notice that his niece had very real problems as well. He sat down beside her.

"Hey, what's going on?" he asked, slinging an arm around her thin shoulders. She looked up with tears pooling in her eyes. They fell as she blinked and shook her head without saying anything. They sat there for a long time, silent, playing with the dog as Maddie tried to pretend she wasn't crying. Sam felt frustration growing toward his sister. What was Theresa thinking? Her daughter needed her.

THAT NIGHT HE CALLED HER. "Reesey, it's Sam."

"Oh," she said, her soft voice at once so completely familiar and lovable that a little of his anger dissolved. "Are you still mad at me?" she asked, her voice wistful.

"A little."

"What about Mom?" her voice quavered.

"Not so much anymore, now that she doesn't have to worry about Maddie. She's with me, Reesey."

"I know. Maddie told me."

"She needs you, Theresa. She's going through a lot, and she won't talk to me."

"I can't do it on my own anymore. You don't know how lonely it's been. I need a little time."

"If you can't do it on your own, why don't you come back here? Then we could help you."

She heaved a huge sigh. Sam was sitting on the kitchen floor, nearly whispering into the phone so Maddie wouldn't hear over the TV in the other room. "I can't do that, Sammy. You know that. There's no way."

"He's still waiting for you, you know."

"That's exactly why I can't come back. He's the most persistent person that was ever born. I'll collect Maddie sometime, Sam, maybe in a few months. For now, can you please keep her? Put her in school? Please? I'm starting to come back to myself, to the ground I gained after the... thing. But I need the space."

He shook his head. "Of course." He knew his sister well, her wild battle for mental health that took over her life. He knew that she had left to protect them all, that she had sent Maddie away to protect her, rather than the selfish reasons others might assume. He hung up in the dark, staring at the phone for a long time after her voice had already faded out of his head.

. . .

ON THE COUCH in front of the TV, Maddie lay in her big coat, holding the jeweled mirror she had taken from the friendly people at the Farmer's Market, crying until she fell asleep.

CHAPTER TWENTY-TWO

When Sam woke the next day, sadness lingered in him, teasing at the edges of his brain. After the phone call with Theresa, he had dreamed of the horrible day when his sobbing sister had left Aveline, packing a heartbroken, four-year-old Maddie into her car and driving away.

He rubbed at his face, groaning, then slowly got up and pulled on a pair of jeans before walking out to the kitchen to make coffee. Walking around in his boxers was out of the question with a fourteen-year-old in the house. She was rarely up this early in the morning, but he wasn't taking any chances.

He filled the coffee machine and turned it on, gazing out the window at the street below. It was the last week of sleepy summer quiet before the students came back. Soon, everything would be noisy and active again, with students traipsing around town, falling over themselves, giggling, making a big deal about their course schedules.

He needed to register Maddie in school. He had barely

spent any time thinking about it, still holding out hope that
Theresa would have called Maddie back by the time school
started. He heard the click of the coffee maker, and poured
himself a cup, flicking through his news articles. He read over
breakfast. A second cup of coffee, then a bowl of cornflakes
and milk. His phone rang, startling him as he stared at the
screen. Katie. He answered it.

"Hello?"

"Sam? Oh good, you're up! Oh, guess what—you'll never
guess—the stoves are here! A whole week early!" He pulled
the phone away from his ear and looked at it.

"They're there now? It's seven o'clock in the morning!"

"Sorry it's early, but we need you down here. It's happening, Sam!"

He smiled. "Okay, okay, I'm coming," he said in his
grumpiest voice.

"Thank you!" she squealed, and Sam went to wake a very
reluctant Maddie.

When they pulled up twenty minutes later, Maddie
dozing beside him, Katie was turning cartwheels in the yard.
A pair of very interested delivery guys were leaning against
their truck, enjoying the sight. Sam stepped out of his vehicle
and scowled at them.

They quickly looked away, and Katie bounded over to
Sam and caught him in a hug. All the breath left his lungs.
He tightened his arms involuntarily before forcing himself to
let go and step back.

"Sorry," she said, her eyes dancing. "It's just such a
perfect day, and you're nearly done with the kitchen, and
now stoves! And I haven't even thought of the incident back

in the city or my ex in days! I haven't felt this happy in a long time." He couldn't help smiling back at her. Right at this moment, she reminded him of the old Katie Grace, the one who whirled in and out of town like a red-headed elf. The one who turned perfect cartwheels and had big plans to learn how to fly a plane. He cleared his throat.

"Okay," he said, turning to the delivery men, "let's get these monsters in place."

It took a lot of effort to heave the two huge ranges into the kitchen. When they were done, the delivery men, who weren't so bad after all, stuck around to properly install them, hooking up the gas and calling the company to have them turn it on. While he was waiting for the men to get done with the installation, Sam worked on the kitchen cabinets. On his way back to the bathroom, he glimpsed Maddie and Katie through the window—Katie racing around in the grass, Sirius leaping after her, stopping every once in a while to jump on Maddie, who was laughing again, Sam noticed. He sighed. Without Katie, taking care of Maddie would be much harder, impossible even. Was it a point for complication? Why was he thinking in points? What was he trying to decide, anyway? Whether or not to be her boyfriend? Whether or not to marry her? He turned away from the window and back to his work, his head pounding.

LATER THAT WEEK, Sam, Maddie, and Katie stood gazing at the bright, gleaming kitchen. Even in the morning sunshine, the work was seamless. It was impossible to tell that Sam had made a kitchen out of two rooms. The ranges stood against one wall, a row of shining sauce and frying pans hanging from hooks on a dowel above them. Shelves to the side of one of the ranges held the rest of the pots and pans. Two large butcher block islands were in the center, and the tall granite counters, sink, and dishwasher were against the back wall. All along the remaining other walls, Sam had installed his pride and joy: Victorian style cabinets that matched the house but held drawers and swung easily on their hinges. The walls were the same buttery yellow as the rest of the house, with the blue trim that Katie had chosen. The kitchen was a vision, but Sam still held his breath as he waited for Katie's final verdict.

"You're a genius, Sam Grant," she said finally, turning and kissing him on the cheek, her soft lips brushing the space just above his beard. He nearly choked, frantically trying to keep his face blank.

He cleared his throat. "I love this kind of work. There are a thousand things I can't do, but I think I'm okay at renovations."

"More than okay," Katie said, elbowing him and turning back to look at her kitchen, her eyes shining.

"So... are we done?" Maddie asked.

"We are not done," Katie said decisively. Maddie sighed. "We have to do the porch and the grounds next, and then we'll be done. But all of life is a process, Maddie dear, and we are never really done."

"Thanks for the talk," Maddie said dryly, but she smiled, her dimple flashing briefly and then disappearing again.

. . .

SAM THREW himself into the renovation of the porch and exterior of the house. He hired another crew to paint while he replaced boards and spindles in the railing, and fixed the trim around the windows and the wooden lace that hung from the eaves, hand cutting pieces to replace what was broken or gone. Katie busied herself with the grounds.

"I want it to be a garden restaurant," Sam overheard her explain to a potential landscaper one morning, "with tables and chairs on the porch as well as inside. The garden should feel natural but magical, like the garden of their dreams."

The man nodded, standing with his legs apart, arms crossed, looking at Katie with appreciation.

Sam crouched down to replace a broken board, scowling. "Do you want to get dinner, later?" the man asked. Immediately Sam hammered his thumb. He stifled a yell as it instantly began throbbing painfully.

"Oh," Katie said. "Well, thank you. But not today—I have plans with a friend. But maybe another time. I'm new to town. I'd love to get to know more people."

Katie's problem was that she was too nice, Sam thought, standing and shaking his head, glaring through the lilac bush at the landscaper, pleased to note that he was half a head shorter than Katie. The man spotted him and the look on his face and took a step back.

"Maybe later then," Sam heard him say as he thrust a card toward Katie. "I'll be back on Saturday with a quote and a design. Here's my card. It's got my number on it."

Katie grinned. "Thanks," she said, then turned and caught Sam's eyes, holding them for a minute before she smiled and walked off to see how Maddie was doing in the vegetable beds.

Sam growled with frustration. He could happily have punched the short nursery boy. He waited for the flood of emotions to subside, holding his hurt hand. This was precisely what he had been trying to avoid all these years. He went back to hammering nails, letting the pain in his thumb be a warning to him.

His mother dropped by later in the day—her first time seeing the house since Sam started working on it. She claimed she was too busy at her shop, but Sam could read between the lines. His mother was avoiding him because she felt guilty about dumping Maddie on him. Today she was subdued, her eyes red.

"Hi, Dorothy," Katie said when she arrived. "Let me know if you need anything. But maybe..." Katie seemed to understand something was up. She met Sam's eyes briefly. "Maybe I'll give you two a moment. Come on Maddie, Sirius," she said.

"What's wrong, Mom?" Sam asked when the others had left the porch.

"I talked to Theresa last night," she said. "She said you called her a while ago and you were having a difficult time with Maddie. She said she was always able to count on me, growing up, and she was shocked that she couldn't rely on me now."

"Oh, Mom, she's not well," Sam said, looping an arm

around her shoulder and squeezing her to his side. "She doesn't know what she's saying."

"She's right, though. I haven't been very helpful, and it's all been on you at the same time as this house... You poor thing," she wiped at her eyes, "...taking over the business, always getting the brunt of everything..." Sam's eyes widened. His mother was in danger of a full Dorothy meltdown.

"Mom," he said. "Look at me. It's all right. You know I've grown to love the business. I've never been happier. And it's okay for me to be a good uncle and take care of Maddie. I'm just a bit worried about her. She's going through a rough time and she needs a lot of love. She could use more adults who love her."

His mother stared up at him, her mascara dampened into spikes around her eyes. She took off her glasses and wiped them with her shirt. Then she pulled a pack of tissues out of her purse and blew her nose.

"I want to help," she said, her eyes wide. "I'll be back this afternoon for Maddie. Tell her we're going to see a movie and go out for dinner."

"You can come tell her yourself," Sam said. He felt waves of relief as he led his mother into the house to find Maddie. Maybe this was an answer to their prayers.

CHAPTER TWENTY-THREE

True to her word, Dorothy picked Maddie up that afternoon. Sam saw the two of them off from the porch. Katie came to the screen door, freshly showered and smelling of roses. She and Maddie had waged a dirt war earlier in the afternoon, laughing like crazy people while they threw clods of soil at each other from either side of a garden bed. Every day, Katie seemed more like the girl Sam remembered from their childhood.

Her hair was wet, and she was wearing a pink shirt dress he hadn't seen before.

"This is perfect," she said. "I have you to myself. I've been hoping to put together a sample dinner with a full appetizer, entree, dessert. I need your opinion. Can you stick around for dinner?"

The two of them alone was a terrible idea. "Oh, well, no I, well, I..." He had nothing. There was no excuse she wouldn't see through. And his stomach growled at the thought of eating Katie's cooking. He swallowed. "Sure. I can stay."

He worked a while longer, stretching out his baseboard job to put off being alone with Katie. He could hear her singing in the kitchen with her deep beautiful voice. He finally packed up when the light was gone. Incredible smells wafted from the kitchen and Sirius lay at the bottom of the stairs, exhausted from racing around all day. Sam leaned down to scratch him under the chin.

"Do you mind if I take a quick shower?" he asked when he reached the kitchen. "I feel sweaty and smelly, and you're all freshened up."

She looked up at him from where she stood at the island, frowning in concentration as she flipped through the many pieces of paper scattered around the room.

"Of course," she said. "Towels are in the closet at the top of the stairs."

He climbed the stairs slowly, noting a few sagging steps that needed to be replaced. Would Katie hire him to renovate the second floor when they were done with the restaurant? It needed a lot of work but could be glorious if he got his hands on it.

Sam glanced into the front bedroom and saw that it still wasn't occupied. He peeked into the little back room. There was something sad and sweet about Katie's narrow single bed with her bright quilt spread across it. The room was tidy, except for scraps of paper that contained thoughts like, "Ask Sam about water heater," and "Talk to Sheldon about grape leaves."

He smiled and went to the bathroom to shower. The hot

water soothed the ache in his muscles. Working on the exterior meant holding his arms up for hours at a time, and he was feeling the extra strain. Shampoo and conditioner, sweet smelling soap, and a pink razor were lined along the shower wall. Sam used the soap and got out quickly, toweling off. He put his jeans on again, but stared at his sweaty T-shirt with revulsion. No way. He had an extra shirt in his truck cab.

Sam left the bathroom after hanging the towel on the rack and was halfway down to the lower floor before he realized that Katie was at the foot of the stairs, staring up at him. He glanced down at his bare chest and felt heat rising to his cheeks.

"I... just wondered if you needed anything," she said.

"No, I'm fine. Heading out to the truck to get a clean shirt." Sam walked out the door, and when he glanced over his shoulder, he saw that she was still looking at him. At the truck, he pulled the shirt over his head with a tiny smile on his face. It was nice to see her flustered, for once, when he spent every day trying not to notice how beautiful she was.

When he got back to the house she was in the kitchen again, leaning over the counter, standing on one leg, her other foot balanced on her knee. He went to stand next to her and saw she was putting the finishing touches on dessert.

She smiled up at him. "I see that you have clothes on now."

"I do."

"Good," she said. What did that mean?

He cleared his throat. "How's it coming?" he asked.

"Just have to put the panna cotta in the fridge." His stomach roared loud enough for both of them to hear it, and she grinned. "We need to feed you, Sam—quick!" she said, but she kept her eyes on his face.

"What?" he asked.

"Nothing. Well...I guess I thought contractors had beer guts rather than abs," she said, avoiding his eyes now, playing with her hair. "It feels a little more comfortable around the workspace, to be honest."

"I can work on getting a gut if you keep feeding me panna cotta," he said, smiling at her.

She glanced up and blushed, then shook herself.

"Okay, here we go," she said. "We're eating in here because this trial has nothing to do with the seating or the ambiance. I want you to tell me exactly what you think about the food." She pushed the two bowls of panna cotta onto a shelf in the fridge.

"Where do we sit?" he asked, looking around. He saw no chairs.

"On the floor," she said. "Here, sit against the cupboard."

He obeyed, sitting on the floor with his back against the island cupboard. His sore muscles didn't love it. "This is odd," he said.

"Well, I'm odd. Here's the appetizer—smoked salmon salad with arugula from the garden."

"Your greens are ready?" he asked.

"The baby stuff is, and it's the best," she said. They sat side by side, shoulders touching. "What do you think?"

He was overwhelmed. The warmth of the kitchen, her closeness, the wild, tangy taste of the salad. "It's perfect," he managed to say.

"Really? Wait—I forgot!" She leaped up and pulled a

bottle out of a cupboard. "Wine. I bought this from Sheldon yesterday. He was insistent that I buy this one when I told him we were doing a taste test today."

"Wait, you told Sheldon that we were doing a taste test before you told me?" he asked.

"Yes, because I needed to buy wine! I thought Maddie would be here, but it's better when it's just us." She uncorked the bottle and handed him a glass of wine, then sat and gently clinked his glass with hers. "Sheldon said this would go well with both salmon and beef." Sam took a sip. Wow, Sheldon was good with wines. It was intense and rich, spicy, yet smooth. He took another sip and felt his shoulders relax.

Katie was staring at him, her face slightly worried. "It's good," he said, and her face cleared. She got up again.

"Entrees!"

She handed him a plate with lightly curried beef on a bed of saffron rice, surrounded by roasted vegetables. He moaned, and she laughed and picked up her plate, settling herself beside him again.

They ate for a while, sipping at their wine. Sam didn't have anything to say. The food was heavenly, and her arm was touching his again. The kitchen was cozy. He felt happy, but also as though he could barely breathe.

She turned to him when her plate was empty. "What do you think?" Again the slightly worried look. He reached out and put his thumb on the little line between her eyebrows, pressing it gently.

"It's perfect. You're perfect," he said.

"Sam," she said, catching her breath. "You don't know what you are, do you?"

She stood and poured them more wine, then opened the fridge door and pulled out the panna cotta. She stood there with the bowls in her hands, looking at him. She seemed slightly feverish as she placed one of the bowls in his hands and sat down again.

"You're my best friend, Sam, sorry. You're stuck with me." He took another sip of wine, feeling warm all over, slightly sleepy from the food, woozy from Katie's rose fragrance. "Lavender panna cotta," she said, "made with the lavender that restarted our friendship. And lavender honey. Tell me if it's too much."

He took a spoonful and closed his eyes. The dessert was creamy and sweet, with just a hint of lavender and the wild honey she had bought from the honey stall. Pistachios dusted the top. The panna cotta was the best thing he had ever tasted. He turned his head to see her looking up at him, a tiny bit of cream stuck in the corner of her mouth.

"Katie..." he said, and then he bent his head and kissed her. If he had thought the dessert was sweet, it was nothing compared to her as she turned to reach him better. Softness, her breath, her mouth on his, her hand on his cheek. He reached out to pull her close, his hand on her neck. Her skin was so soft. She made a small sigh, and he blinked, pulling away from her. He stared at her. Her eyes were very wide, deep green with gold sparks in the depths. He frowned and touched her lips again, kissing her softly one more time before he slowly stood, leaving her sitting on the floor.

"The wine must have gone to my head," he said. "The food... was amazing. You are a wonder, Katie Grace."

"Where... where are you going?" she asked, her voice shaky.

"I think it's time for me to head home." He looked away from her face, which was falling, slowly, as she realized he was really going. In a minute, he would be tempted to kiss away the sadness, and that would be... He needed to get out of this room and clear his head. "Thank you for having me, Katie," he said. At the door, he turned. "You're my best friend, too," he said. "I'll see you tomorrow."

CHAPTER TWENTY-FOUR

Katie taped a note for Sam to her front door, then climbed into her car and drove away. The note explained where the keys were, and that she would be away for a while.

It was early, the sky purple and sleepy before dawn, the woods dark as Katie drove around the lake. She had the slightly hungry feeling she always got when she woke up in the dark. Her sleeping bag and extra clothes were in the back of the Subaru. Sirius sat beside her on the passenger seat, holding his head out of the window, his tongue swinging in the wind as they drove the winding road.

"You're going to like the cabin," Katie told him. "Lots of interesting things to smell there. Probably bear pee. Maybe even bears." She glanced at him. "Be careful, okay?" He pulled his head inside the window and panted at her, wiggling his back end in happiness. Katie smiled.

The road was clear of traffic and Katie drove quickly,

taking the corners expertly, windows down, cool air rushing through the car. The drive around the edge of Lake Aveline to her parents' cabin took about half an hour. Katie hoped the cabin was far enough to get a long-distance view of her life. Everything had changed since the incident in L.A. Every single thing.

She sighed, her brow furrowed, reliving last night for the hundredth time. Sam's mouth on hers, his hand on her face. She had been kissed plenty of times but never like that, never with her heart trying to escape her body. She hadn't been trying to seduce him. Anyone with half a brain could see the man didn't want a relationship. Katie knew she was pretty, at least to people who didn't consider her too much of a giant, and they had been spending a ton of time together. If Sam thought of her that way, he would have made a move, changed something, kissed her weeks ago. No, he didn't want a relationship. She knew that and had somehow relaxed into what they did have—a practical yet flirty friendship.

The sky grew lighter at the edges, violet and blue until suddenly the sun rose and the whole world was visible. She drove and drove, trying to push away panic at the thought of more change.

But he did kiss you last night, Katie Grace. And you liked it!

Nope, she told herself, *not going there.* She turned onto the gravel road that led to the group of cabins. The Subaru rumbled along for a few hundred feet before Katie parked and shut off the car. She sat in silence, looking at the cottage where she had spent endless summers as a girl.

Sirius licked her face and brought her back to herself, and she opened the car door, Sirius leaping out after her and running from tree to tree to investigate. The car door echoed when she shut it behind her. This side of the lake had a rich quiet, as though the forest was listening. Katie heard birdsong and the quiet shushing of lake water in the wind. The cabin was achingly familiar. Katie couldn't remember what her childhood homes in L.A. looked like, but she remembered this cabin. Every summer her family had come up to spend a week or two in the cabin, and then Katie went to spend the rest of the summer with her grandmother in Aveline town, while her parents went back to their jobs in the city.

Her parents rented the cabin out for vacation use these days, but Katie had checked with her mom, and it was empty for the time being. She unlocked the blue front door and threw it open, looking around, memories cascading over one another. Firs backed the cabin, but the large front windows faced the lake, and the room was bright with sunshine. Katie pulled back the curtains and gazed out at the water of Lake Aveline. It shone softly in the morning light, calling to her. She left the house and called Sirius, walking down to the rocky shore, Sirius at her heels.

The dog ran joyfully back and forth, in a dozen different directions, racing back every so often to make sure Katie was still with him. Katie sat on the stony beach and wrapped her arms around her legs, leaning her chin on her knees. Everything in her new life had come so quickly, and the kiss had pushed it all over the edge. Last night after Sam left, she felt panic stirring in her lungs.

Katie couldn't find herself in the midst of it all. Half a year ago she had been a manager in a large corporation, wearing high heels to work, walking quickly, frustrated if her coffee order took longer than five minutes at the coffee shop in the lobby. Everything in her life was different now, and not in a bad way. But would her new life collapse as the old one had, like a poorly constructed bridge?

Katie hadn't been making it up when she told Sam he was her best friend, but she was gaining other friends as well, and that was new for her. Mercy and the other women from the women's circle seemed like they could be good friends. She was always happy to see Sheldon. Even Maddie was becoming a friend. In her old life, she hadn't had that kind of companionship. Ed took up most of Katie's time. She had her parents and grandmother. Things here were so much more connected.

Would it all dissolve? It wouldn't, right? Katie wasn't under the same kind of pressure here. She picked up a handful of stones and tried to think of possible danger. Her mother wasn't happy about the restaurant, but she always thought Katie was too impulsive, and she hadn't approved of Katie's choice of a career back in the early days. She had been relieved when Katie left culinary school and went into human resources.

Maybe Katie *was* too impulsive. But she thought her grandmother would approve of the restaurant. There was the letter from her Nana. She knew Katie was missing something. She had known even before the incident, before the panic and the days of weeping. And Nana knew her, perhaps better than anyone else in her life.

Katie had made friends in Aveline. She even had a best friend here. His name was Sam, and he was the most beautifully put together human being she had ever seen in her life, as she had noted last night when she saw him without his shirt. Oh dear. No more thinking about Sam. *Focus, Katie.*

Katie knew there was a flaw in her restaurant plans, and it was like a stone in her shoe, a shadow in her vision, but she couldn't figure it out. What was wrong? She felt the wrongness of some kind of mistake, but it disappeared when she turned to look at it.

So, last night, when she couldn't sleep because of the kiss, the threat of change, and fretting over her vision, she decided to come to the lake. She needed a spacious place to figure it out.

The food she had made for Sam the night before was good, really good. It was delicious. But something was wrong —what was it? Katie dropped the handful of stones, standing to walk along the lakeshore, throwing a stick for Sirius, who retrieved it and tore back to her. They did this again, and again. She walked hard, fast, trying to jog her brain.

Was it that she didn't have enough confidence? She didn't, but she was trying to focus on one day at a time, the way Sam said. It seemed to be working. Katie's anxiety had subsided to a dull roar, with the occasional breath of panic. But she was eating, bathing, planning, and cooking. There was much less conflict in her new life, far from the complaints and noise of human resources. And she started every day sitting on her porch, gazing into the trees around her house, and the glimpse of the lake in the distance.

Katie had even begun to pray again, and that hadn't

happened for a long time. Nana had been a woman of faith, and the smell of the prayer-soaked house had possibly unlocked something in Katie's heart. She whispered the tiniest prayers in her morning spot. Just thanks and help—the tiniest of prayers—but her heart was changing. Cooking every day helped, too, as she immersed herself in picking greens from the garden, flavors, textures, and the fragrance of sautéed garlic. She loved her life here. It didn't seem to be a problem with her mindset. Was it a problem with her design? Or the menu?

The answer came after she had been hiking full speed up the hill for nearly twenty minutes. She stopped dead in her tracks and stared at the firs in front of her. After a moment, she laughed, the sound loud and ringing on the quiet hillside. It was so simple. When Katie had come to Aveline, the first thing she noticed was that the diner was gone. She'd been sad because of all the mornings she'd spent sitting at the diner with Nana, listening to the chatter of a close community. The Aveline Diner was the place to gather and discuss everything under the sun, all while eating mashed potatoes and fried chicken. Now there was no place to congregate in the same way. The coffee shop was great but lacked the meals. And a pizza shop was something completely different. There was just something about talking over food done with care. It brought people together.

That was the gap Katie had noticed, the loss she had felt in the town. But here she was, designing a fine dining experience with appetizers, entrees, and fancy desserts. She was making a restaurant most students wouldn't be able to afford, that even locals would only be able to visit once a month, if that. It meant Katie's restaurant would be full of tourists, and that wasn't what she wanted, that wasn't what she missed about Aveline, what she wanted to offer this lovely town.

This was the stone in her shoe. Katie needed to change course ever so slightly. She would open a café, with a simple menu and affordable food, fresh from the garden. She wanted her café to be a town establishment, not only a place for wealthy tourists. She felt goosebumps all up and down her arms as her brain went to work.

She would dream up a simple breakfast and lunch menu with specials every day, maybe a few baked goods. The Aveline Café. She jumped up and down a few times, delighted by the new idea. Sirius turned away from the rock he was investigating and wound around her legs, his tail wagging madly. She leaned down and hugged him.

"Oh, Sirius," she said. "We figured it out."

When she got back to the cabin, she fed Sirius, then sank into a chair while he scarfed his food down. Her phone dinged, telling her a text had arrived. She pulled it out of her purse and looked at the screen. It was from Sam.

"U Okay? Sorry about last night."

She smiled and texted back quickly. "No need to be sorry. Just sorting some thoughts out. About the restaurant, not u." She looked at what she'd written for a moment, then deleted the words, 'not u.' "Staying here tonight." she wrote. "See u tomorrow." She pressed send and felt clearer than she had in a long time.

For the rest of that day, Katie worked on her new menu,

crafting meals like the mushroom soup and quinoa salad she had first made for Sam. She sketched out ideas with her version of a garden diner, a café with healthy food, made with a lot of love. She sat back as the sky turned violet in the dusk, grinning to herself, happy that she had solved her elusive problem.

CHAPTER TWENTY-FIVE

The next day Katie drove back into town with the windows down, singing at the top of her lungs. She still didn't know what was going on with Sam, but she felt content to wait and see. Sam wasn't at her house when she arrived. She texted him.

"Where are you? Just got back."

The answer popped on her screen immediately.

"Enrolling Maddie in school, See u tomorrow."

She thought for a minute, then texted again.

"Are you keeping Lucy after we're done?"

"Why, want to hire her?"

She smiled, then texted, "YES."

"Go right ahead but she'll boss the life out of u. Don't say I didn't warn u."

She grinned. She realized she had been a bit worried that Sam would be mad at her for leaving without warning. But he was fine. They were still friends.

. . .

SHE WALKED to Grant's hardware, half expecting to see Sam, but he was still out. She did find Larry squatting in an aisle, stocking a shelf with cans of wood varnish.

"Is your mother here?" she asked.

"Yes," he muttered. "Unfortunately. She's in the back, watering the plants." He looked up, his eyes pleading with her. "Please, please take her away from here, Ms. Grace."

Katie laughed. "You can call me Katie," she said. "But I appreciate your manners. Probably a gift from your mother." He shook his head at the can of varnish in his hands, the picture of despair. Katie patted him on the shoulder.

She found Lucy wrestling with a garden hose.

"Oh, thank the sweet Lord," Lucy said. "This wretched thing is beyond me. It isn't even in my job description, but Sam didn't have time today with school registration, and the plants need to be watered, so here I am, fighting a serpent."

Katie grinned. "I can help." She took the hose and worked to untangle it while Lucy sank onto a stool with a huff, wiping her forehead with a handkerchief.

"I have a question for you," Katie said, hesitantly.

Lucy looked up. "Why is Sam so relationship shy?" she guessed. "It's because of the girl who broke his heart in college."

Katie's jaw dropped. "What? I wasn't going to ask that!" She felt her face growing red. "But now that you bring it up...what?"

"Oh, honey, she was clearly a parasite. Anyone could have seen that. But Sam is too sweet to think badly of anybody, and she was gorgeous. He got led right in, same old story. Sweet boy gets cheated on; the girl runs straight to a boy who will mistreat her. Anyway, she got pregnant by some rich jerk and came running to Sam. He wanted to help her, but her wealthy parents swept in and took her away. Told him she wasn't available, to leave her alone. She never came back. He loved her, and he was heartbroken. He would have taken her back, even after she cheated. He tried to contact her a few times, I think, but she never took any calls. Heard she married a senator out east."

Katie blinked as the blood drained from her face. Poor Sam. No wonder he was shy. She felt a rush of tenderness toward young Sam, who loved a girl ten years ago. Then she felt a sudden jab of jealousy. She didn't like the sound of that: he loved her, and he was heartbroken. It was Katie who had been Sam's first kiss, not some other girl.

"Why do those girls get the guys like Sam?" she asked.

"They know how to use their eyes," Lucy said. "They know their power. It's time for nice girls to figure out their power and use it."

Katie stared at her. "Really? Is that fair?"

"Heck, yes! If you're going to be nice and care for some-one, there's no harm in using your hips to reel him in." Katie giggled as Lucy stood up and demonstrated. "You're the one," Lucy went on. "I can just tell. I'm the village sage. I see all. Don't be shy, sweetheart." Her eyes became serious, and Katie stopped laughing. She looked at her hands.

"Well, Lucy, you've given me a lot to think about, but the real reason I'm here is to ask if I can hire you."

"What? Away from Sam?"

"No, after Sam is done with the renovation. How would you feel about being my café manager?"

Lucy stared at her. "Me? I don't have any management experience."

"I don't know about that. You're managing this place right now. Besides, you're the village sage, as you said, and I want this to be the town's café. You'll know how to make that happen."

Lucy stared at her for a few more moments, then her face shone with a huge grin, despite the tears that sprang to her eyes. She grabbed Katie and hugged her around the waist.

"Sam's right," Lucy said, hugging her. "You are an angel."

Katie blushed at the thought that Sam had said that about her. Then Lucy stepped back and looked at her with a determined face. "I assume there are benefits? Healthcare?"

Katie smiled at the sudden change. She nodded, and they sat down to talk about money and specifics.

As KATIE WAS WALKING through the store to leave, she passed a man, and it wasn't until she had taken a few steps past him that she realized. She froze. His scent had wafted in with him, and Katie knew that smell—mint and pine and soap. She turned, slowly, to stare into Sam's face. He no longer had a beard, just a face, a very nice face, with a very nice chin and jaw. She could barely breathe. He was smiling.

"I didn't even recognize you," she said, her heart hammering wildly.

"I noticed." He had dimples. Dimples. And the sweetest curved mouth.

"Your beard is gone," she said stupidly.

"I always say I don't have a beard; I just don't shave very often. That was a record for me, actually. I blame your house. But I wanted to look good to enroll Maddie in school."

"You...look...good," Katie said, nodding. She could barely think with his face all naked like that. What would it be like to kiss him without a beard? She shook her head, trying to clear it. "Maddie," she said. That was a safe topic. "How did she seem?"

His face fell. "Not happy. She's pretty bummed about a new school."

"Maybe she can come over after her first day? I'd love to talk to her about it."

"Mm, not today, we have some meetings and things, but later in the week, maybe."

"Will I see you tomorrow?" Katie's voice sounded wistful even to her. She could have kicked herself. She loved him, she realized, she was actually in love with him. Well, this was awkward.

"Yeah, I'll be there." He picked up a bottle of glue and stared at it as though it was the most important thing in the world. "Where did you go? Did you figure things out?"

And like that, it was as though she was released to be her usual self. Sam's face was less glaringly beautiful, and Katie could think again.

"I went to my parent's cabin—out on Douglas road, around the lake."

"Is your parent's cabin the A-Frame?" he asked.

"No, theirs is the one next to it. But it was so good, Sam. I figured so much out. I have to tell you everything tomorrow!"

He smiled at her. "That's great. I can't wait to hear about it."

SHE TOLD him her plan the next day while he finished fitting spindles into the porch railing. She sat on the steps, arms around her knees, waiting for his response.

"I get it," he said finally, squinting over at her and wiping wood shavings off his face with the back of one hand. "A place where everybody knows your name." She threw the pen she was holding at him, and he ducked, laughing. "Whoa, good arm," he said. "But really, I get it. I guess this means no panna cotta?" he asked, then quickly looked back at his work. Katie watched in fascination as he blushed.

"Maybe there could be some panna cotta," she said. "For special." He met her eyes and smiled.

She was chewing her lip and staring at her menu notes when she heard feet thudding down the pavement. She looked up to see Maddie running toward them, her eyeliner smeared down her cheeks.

"Maddie!" Katie said, jumping up to catch the girl. "What's the matter?"

Maddie only burrowed into Katie's arms and sobbed. Sam put a hand on Maddie's back, and together they led her into the house and away from the eyes of curious neighbors.

Finally, Maddie stopped crying long enough to tell them what had happened. A boy at school had called her a whore. He said he heard that Maddie's mother was a whore too, and when she stood up and overturned his desk, the teacher sent Maddie home for the day.

"Nothing happened to him," she said, still crying with little hiccups, "not even when I told the teacher what he said. This always happens to me. They always believe the boy."

"It's true, they do," Katie murmured. Sam shot her a glance, but Maddie was still talking.

"I'm not going back," she said to Sam. "I don't care what you do to me. I've had it with school, and I'm not going back."

Sam talked quietly with Maddie while Katie put a Tracy Chapman album on the house speakers and whipped up a pasta sauce. She poured cooked spaghetti into a large bowl and swirled olive oil into it, bringing it and the sauce into the front room so they could sit on the couch to eat. When she got there, though, she found that Maddie had already fallen asleep, her head cushioned on Sam's arm. He carefully got up, easing a throw pillow under Maddie's head, and took the sauce from Katie. "Front porch?" he asked, and she nodded.

"She really doesn't want to go back," he said. "She wants to be homeschooled."

Katie took a bite of pasta. She felt her shoulders relax at the taste of the tangy tomato sauce. It was perfect.

"So homeschool her," she said. She looked up at Sam, her eyes catching on a little divot at the corner of his mouth.

"What?" he said when he caught her staring. She put her finger on the spot, like a dimple right where his lips met each other.

"I never saw that spot until you shaved. You have a fascinating face, Sam Grant." She leaned toward him as she said it, but he shifted in his seat and moved away. His eyes glittered at her.

"Back on track," he said. "How do you even go about homeschooling?"

Katie looked at Sam and realized that he was actively resisting her. Lucy was right. She could make Sam realize that he liked her. She made a decision, there and then, still looking at him, that she would do it.

She tipped her head back and looked at the stars, clustered like jewels above the lake.

"I guess we're going to have to do some research," she said.

CHAPTER TWENTY-SIX

Katie did research, sitting on her new couch with her laptop, cross-legged, her bare feet tucked under her. She read through articles on homeschooling, and she searched "how to win a man's heart," checking first to make sure that neither Sam nor Maddie was going to catch her. One post suggested feeding a man to catch his attention. Katie smiled. That was easy enough. She learned about attention-catching ways of walking and flicking your hair. She read about perfume and wrinkled her nose. She liked to wear rose oil, but that was about it. And she wasn't going to start flicking her hair around like a girl in high school either. She tapped the keyboard with one finger. Hmm. Maybe she was better off figuring it out for herself.

The homeschool research was fascinating. As the day went on, she grew increasingly interested in what she was reading, calling out snippets to Sam and Maddie, who were working on stripping the old paint from the porch.

"Listen to this," she said. "'The only thing that stops kids from learning is to be forced to learn.' This is saying that if we left Maddie alone, she would pretty much do school by herself."

"Sounds good to me," Maddie said, a broad smile on her face. "No forced learning."

"Maybe a compromise?" Sam asked, eyebrows raised.

"There are so many resources on the Internet," Katie said absently as she scrolled. "There are even conventions for this, you guys! Let's hit a homeschool convention." She closed her laptop. "I'll bring the vodka."

"Did you find anything actually useful while you sat there browsing the Internet and watching us work for four hours?" Sam asked.

"I'm sorry, aren't you working for me?" Katie asked. And then she took the glass of water she was holding and turned it over his head, shocking herself as much as him.

Like a flash, she was running away, shrieking, as he tore after her. Katie was fast, but not fast enough, and as she tried to dodge him to get back to the front door, he tackled her, bringing her to the ground. She was laughing so hard she could hardly breathe, and they lay like that for a moment, looking at each other, before he jumped up and turned the hose on, spraying her until she was soaking. Katie grabbed the hose, kinking it, so the water stopped flowing. When he brought the end of it close to him, she let go, and the water hit him straight in the face. She doubled over laughing again at his expression until he turned to look at her again, and she suddenly got quiet. They stood there like that, both of them barely breathing until Maddie broke the silence.

"Am I the only one working today?" she called. "Has anyone heard about child labor laws?"

Sam went back to work beside Maddie. Katie ran upstairs to dry off and change. As she passed Maddie, she met her eyes and nearly flinched. The look on the girl's face bordered on dislike. Maddie turned away. She had never looked at Katie like that before. What was going on?

THE THREE OF them drove to the antique flea market in Billers later that day. They had pulled all the furniture out of storage under the house, but they needed more tables for the café, and they needed chairs. Katie thought they could find a bunch of mismatched tables at the flea market, then paint them in different colors and distress them.

"Let's distress them, sure," Sam said, as they were walking through the parking lot to get to the flea market. "But paint them the same color, or the café will look like a circus. If the tables aren't similar in shape, you need color to help them look like they belong together."

Katie considered this. "All right, I can compromise," she told him, eying him. "You're unexpectedly good at design."

"What's that supposed to mean?" he asked, smiling and elbowing her. Behind them, Maddie snorted. She had been barely civil to Katie all day, and Katie was starting to worry.

The weekend flea market was held in a large barn that was sweltering in the afternoon heat. Fans whirred overhead, stirring the warm air. There were hundreds of booths of antiques and used goods of every description. They passed collections of horrible rugs and booths brimming with exquisite Turkish carpets. Katie wandered over to a Turkish stall, entranced, but stepped back quickly after she looked at the price tag.

"Maybe if business is booming on my first anniversary," she said to Sam, wrinkling her nose. They pored over old books and magazines. Katie bought a stack of vintage books and magazines to scatter around the restaurant. She also purchased three granny-square afghans and twenty antique enameled salt and pepper shakers, all different in shape or design.

"I'm in heaven," she said to Sam as they flipped through a stack of old movie posters.

"I can see that," he replied, then held up a Citizen Kane poster to show Maddie, eyebrows raised in question. Her eyes lit up. She flashed him a brilliant smile and nodded. He made his way to the cash register and asked the price, reeling back in pretend horror at the answer. He appeared to recover himself and paid, handing the poster to his niece in its protective tube. She looked gleeful and gave him a quick side hug.

Katie didn't get any movie posters for the restaurant, but she did pick up a few old botanical posters of plant, vegetable, and fruit charts. They moved on to furniture. There were square tables, round tables, tables made of old doors, spindle legs or square legs, chunky round legs or legs with swoops like feet at the bottoms. Sam examined the furniture thoroughly, searching for cracks that had been covered with putty or simply painted. The air smelled of dust and wood polish. They picked over a dozen tables and bought stacks of chairs.

"I've never had this much fun shopping," Katie said. "It's

a shopping spree, courtesy of my grandmother, but in the flea market chaos of my dreams."

She glanced at Sam as she said it. Maybe it was time to call the fun to a close. He looked like he was wilting around the edges, and Maddie had already bailed on them to wait in the parking lot. It was time to finish up. And Katie should get home before panic came to call.

"We're almost done, I promise," she said.

"That's what you said an hour ago," Sam complained.

"Just a few...stalls...more." She pulled him by the elbow to a stall full of brightly colored Turkish lamps and bought six for the front dining rooms. She looked up from writing the total in her notebook to see Sam swinging a short door back and forth.

"What's that?" she asked.

"How are you going to block off your living space so people won't walk up there?" he asked.

Katie stared at him. "I didn't think about it. I assumed people would have the common sense not to go up there."

He snorted. "People need things spelled out for them. Who knows who might be looking for another bathroom and then find themselves in your toiletry kit?"

"Well, what do you think about that?" she asked, gesturing at the door in his hand.

"I don't think this will fit," he said. "But I can make something like this easily, and you should add another door at the top of the stairs. You need to be able to lock it, or your stuff will never be safe when you're at work.

"What's your door like?"

"It's a full door that locks, at the top of the stairs," he said, running a hand over the arch of the swinging door. He looked up with a startled expression. "Wait. Have you never been to my place?"

"No," she said, smiling. "We're always at my house."

"We'll have to change that. Maddie and I will have you over for dinner."

"I don't know if Maddie wants me to come over," she said, wandering over to the costume jewelry and looping a long necklace around her neck. She peered at herself in the little mirror on the shelf in front of her. "She seems mad at me today."

"She always seems that way to me," Sam said, wryly, but he nodded. "I have noticed that she's been a little cold to you. It's the opposite with me, actually. We've been getting along better than ever since I agreed to homeschool her." He picked up a fedora and stuck it on his head, then put a twenties style hat on Katie's head. They stood side by side, looking in the mirror. Katie held his eyes until he moved away.

"I think we need to buy these hats," she said lightly, hiding her disappointment at the distance he put between them. "We look like stars. My treat."

The day was a success. Not only did they walk away with eleven tables to add to the seven they had already, but they also had enough chairs for all the tables, various bits of pottery Katie could use for serving, and crates of decorative bits and bobs. Katie was exhausted by the time they were done, her feet and back aching, her stomach nauseous with the feeling that she had been out in the world for too long. She hadn't pushed herself this hard since her collapse, and she was feeling it. It was dark when they walked into the parking lot and found Maddie sitting on the hood of the truck, listening to music on her phone.

"Where's the stuff?" she asked, pulling her earbuds out and jumping down.

"They'll deliver it," Sam said. He crossed his arms and looked at his niece. "Are you going to tell us what's eating you? Why are you mad?"

Maddie glared at him, but her angry look melted into sadness after a moment. She shrugged.

"It's no fun to be a third wheel," she murmured.

Guilt washed over Katie. She recognized the deep loneliness behind the words, something that had been so familiar to Katie in the last months.

"I'm sorry," she said, slinging an arm around Maddie and squeezing her for a second. "We didn't mean to make you feel like that."

"Don't be silly," Sam said, frowning. "You're not a third wheel because Katie and I are not a bicycle. We're all just friends, the three of us."

Maddie raised an eyebrow and gave Sam a skeptical look. But she seemed comforted, and they played car games all the way home, twenty questions and the alphabet game, which Maddie won three times in a row.

Katie thought that they wouldn't be "just friends" for too much longer if she had anything to do with it, but she left it for the time being, listening to Maddie's laughter and thinking maybe things would be all right. She watched the sun dipping behind the trees, thinking about Maddie's education, when she had an idea. Perhaps Katie could put off the café opening, at least until they got Maddie's homeschooling figured out. Katie could put together a curriculum better than Sam could, now that she had done so much research. Opening the restaurant wasn't as important as helping Maddie get settled into a school routine. Katie didn't need the money right away anyway. She would run the idea by Sam later. She sat back in her seat and listened to Maddie and Sam joke around, feeling something that felt like the blooming of family.

CHAPTER TWENTY-SEVEN

Maddie left the apartment quietly, not wanting to alert Lucy, who was working in the back of the attached hardware store. Lucy always wanted to know where Maddie was going. Maddie was supposed to either help with the hardware store or Katie's house if she wasn't doing anything else, but her throat felt tight, and she needed air.

She was wearing jeans and a pair of clunky boots that Katie had found, as well as a purple tank top that Katie insisted looked great on her. When she looked in the mirror, though, all she could see was a small girl with big eyes and twiggy arms. She put on her big black coat over the tank top.

Not going to school was a massive improvement. Maddie had listened to Sam and her mom arguing about it the other night—or she had listened to Sam's side, though he tried to keep his voice down. She knew her mother well enough to be able to fill in the blanks.

"No, it's not letting her get her way," her uncle said. "She's sincerely anxious about school. It's making her sick. I can do this, Reesey, it's not that uncommon. Look into it. Especially look into college graduation rates for home-schooled kids. They're off the charts." There had been a long pause. "No, no, there haven't been any other problems. Problems like what, what are you expecting? She seems fine."

Maddie knew what her mother was digging at, and she crossed her arms over her chest, feeling a wave of longing for her mom, so intense that she gasped.

She closed her eyes and thought of her mom's pottery shed in their backyard in Minnesota. Maddie walked out there to kiss her mom goodbye every morning before school. She thought of the smell of incense, the kisses her mother planted on her head, the loud music she played when she was cooking, not jazz like Katie but rock that shook the house, even Maddie's room, and at the thought of her room, Maddie was fiercely homesick. She wanted to see her mom's face.

She kicked a rock, stomping along the sidewalk, trying to hold back tears. It was nice here, sunny and warm, with blue skies. She would miss Sam and Katie if she left. She had asked about snow, but Sam said it barely ever snowed enough to stick. Winter here would be way better than being stuck inside for months in Minnesota. She paused in front of Green's for a minute, considering, then walked in.

Her uncle's friend, Sheldon, nodded at her with a strange look on his face. Or maybe that was just his face. He was kind of weird. She liked to look into the store window every day to see what he was wearing. Today he wore a purple velour shirt with pin-striped pants and pink suspenders.

She picked up a basket and wandered to the back of the store to choose some snacks. Sam had put a jar of food money on the counter so Maddie could buy food if she wanted. She put honey-flavored yogurt and a bag of oranges into her basket. She picked out some granola bars and a bag of kettle chips, then wandered through the makeup aisle at the back of the store. Maddie quickly palmed and pocketed a sweet little tube of lip gloss, which fell into her coat pocket as though it belonged there. In the next aisle, she put some ramen noodle packets in her basket, then found some cheese in the dairy aisle. On her way to the cash register, she picked up a jar of soup stock, heavy and round and perfect in her hand, and dropped that into her pocket as well. A sense of relief cascaded down her spine.

She smiled at the cashier and paid for her groceries, full of energy and only slightly nauseous.

Sheldon spoke as she passed him, surprising her.

"Doing okay, Maddie?" he asked.

"Yeah," she said, her heart beating wildly. "Sure."

"That's good. Let me know if you need anything. I'm good friends with your uncle, and I told him I'd look out for you."

Maddie's heart was pounding so hard she could practically hear it. She told herself he couldn't have seen her, sitting at his desk the whole time. She left the store and walked home quickly, her stomach so heavy she was surprised it didn't drop out of her body.

SHELDON HAD INSTALLED the cameras a couple of years ago. His inventory was always off during tourist season. Still, he wouldn't have seen anything if he hadn't been watching Theresa's daughter on the screen behind his desk.

Sheldon was smiling at Maddie's food choices and trying to ignore the profound loss he always felt when he looked at her—the girl he had nearly adopted—when he saw her hand dart quickly toward her pocket, and her eyes dart around wildly. He leaned closer to the screen.

A few minutes later, he saw Maddie drop a jar of soup stock into her pocket. He was still trying to understand what he had seen when she came to the front and paid for everything else.

He was stunned. Reesey's daughter was stealing from him? He asked her how she was, not knowing what else to do, and saw her face turn white with guilt. She looked like a terrified rabbit, so he let her go. What should he do? He had no idea.

CHAPTER TWENTY-EIGHT

"Come on, old man!" Frankie called back to Sam, laughing.

Sam bent half over, trying to catch his breath. He had imagined that because he was strong and fit in many ways, running would be a cinch. That was not proving to be the case. Frankie was a natural runner, and Sam was having a hard time keeping up.

"How did you become a long-distance runner?" he gasped as he finally caught up to his friend.

"One word," Frankie said, slowing to a walk and swinging his arms to stretch. "Soccer. I grew up playing it. You run the entire time you're on the field."

"Aha!" Sam said. "An advantage."

"If you call growing up playing in a dusty field with a ball made of rolled up socks an "advantage," Frankie said. His voice was light, but Sam felt the weight behind the words.

He walked beside his friend, trying to figure out how to

ask. "We haven't talked that much about how you got here, or how it was at first," he said finally.

"We haven't, have we?" Frankie said, smiling over at Sam. "Don't worry, you'll hear more about it soon. I'm trying to get the town council on board with a refugee program for next year. We'll get a few families if they agree, and I'm sure I'll have to talk about my early life to help get people used to the idea."

Sam shook his head. The meetings and bureaucracy that Frankie sat through were beyond him.

"I don't envy you all that," he said.

"What?"

"All the talking and visiting, all the meetings."

"It's a different way to be devoted," Frankie said. He leaned down to pick up a stone and whipped it at the lake. Sam counted six skips.

"Not bad," he remarked, looking for his own flat stone. "What do you mean by that?"

Frankie looked over at him. "Just that I think we have narrow ideas of what it looks like to have a life that is devoted to God. For me, part of my devotion includes sitting in town meetings trying to convince worried citizens that we have enough to share with some of our less fortunate friends. It's annoying to listen to wrong ideas about refugees or the homeless, but I consider it all part of my work, just as much as prayer, study... Nice one!"

Sam had skipped a rock ten times.

"Can't beat me," he said. "I grew up skipping rocks on Lake Aveline."

"Ah," Frankie said, grinning and whipping another rock across the lake. "An advantage."

"Definitely," Sam said. He looked at his friend. "Whenever I talk to you, I'm reminded of my advantages."

Frankie laughed and squeezed his shoulder. "I'll take that as a good thing," he said.

"You know what I mean."

"Do you want to talk about your own narrow view of devotion?" Frankie asked.

Sam frowned, looking down at a smooth, flat rock. He smoothed it with his hand and then whipped it at the lake, turning to look at Frankie triumphantly after eleven skips. Frankie was still watching him with serious eyes.

"What do you mean?" Sam asked.

"The monk thing. You and Katie. And don't try to tell me there is nothing there. I've known you for ten years, and I've never seen you like this."

Sam sighed and slowly lowered himself down to sit on the pebbly beach. Frankie sat beside him, leaning back on his hands.

"I don't know. It doesn't seem right to decide on something, then give it up the first time a pretty woman comes into my life."

"You and I both know that's not what this is," Frankie said. "You're surrounded by beautiful teachers and fetching college students. You've never wavered until now. I think you've met your match, Sammy."

"What about a life of simplicity?"

"Like I was saying, there are different ways to be devoted.

Do you think there are ways you could love God by loving Katie?"

Sam looked out at the water and considered the question. He glanced at his friend again, who was holding a handful of pebbles, sorting through them. Frankie's black hair was getting wilder by the day. Sam was surprised that his mother hadn't wrestled him down and clipped it yet. Frankie looked up at him, eyebrows raised.

"Well?"

Sam sighed. "Yes. I think so. Katie has been badly hurt. And her faith in God seems like a little scared creature. It's there, but needs to be cared for. So yes, there are ways that I can love God by loving Katie. But isn't that how you love God, in one way? By loving people?"

"That's what I'm saying," Frankie said. "Love that is constant and self-giving, not fickle or transactional, is a high form of devotion. He dropped the pebbles and clapped a hand on Sam's shoulder. "I think what I'm saying is that the monk thing can stand. You can be a monk with a wife. You'll need devotion, in any case."

Sam dropped his head into his hands. "Now I just need to know whether I'm brave enough," he said.

"Well yes, there is that," Frankie said, laughing. "You're a bit of a chicken."

SAM PARKED the truck outside his mother's house and walked Maddie to the door. She shuffled her feet all the way there. She had looked miserable all day, and he didn't know what was wrong.

"You're happy about this, right?" he asked.

Maddie looked at him, her face open and surprised. She seemed to shake off her gloom purposefully, smiling.

"Of course. I love hanging out with Grandma. We eat ice cream and watch romantic comedies from the nineties. French Kiss is my favorite."

Sam didn't know what to say to this, but his mother saved him from having to answer when she opened the front door.

"Maddie!" she said. "You look beautiful."

Maddie looked the same to Sam—little, thin, a girl wearing someone else's extra large coat. But she did look radiant as she smiled at her grandmother and slipped past her into the house.

"Should I pick her up later or do you want her to sleep over?" Sam asked.

"She can sleep over. What are you up to tonight?"

"Katie's testing her menu on me again," he said, patting his stomach. "I've started running with Frankie, just to burn off all this food."

"What are you patting?" his mother asked. "You don't even have a stomach. Is that what you're wearing?"

He looked down at himself. Jeans, T-shirt. "This is what I always wear. It's not a date, Mom."

She raised an eyebrow but didn't say anything. Sam gave her a quick kiss on the cheek and turned around to walk back to his truck.

"She's good for you," his mother called after him.

He lifted one hand to wave as he drove away.

CHAPTER TWENTY-NINE

Sam parked on the street outside the old Grace house and sat for a moment, admiring the renovation so far. The old Victorian was stunning. He had fixed the window frames and wooden lace, and now that everything was freshly painted, the house's lovely details were visible. Katie had planted a few new bushes and trees: lilacs, rhododendrons, and wisteria, as well as a handful of Japanese maples. The landscaper had trimmed the old trees and hedges on the property. Just two weeks remained before the opening party, and Katie had ordered flyers to hand out around town, describing an evening of food and music. Katie had hired the Aveline Swing Band after all. Sam could see that she was nervous about the party, but he admired how she kept moving forward, despite her nerves.

On the porch, he ran a hand over one of the tables he and Katie had finished painting and distressing. Several sets of tables and chairs were grouped on the wraparound porch. They had chosen to paint them a deep ultramarine blue, and it set off the sea blue of the house outside, and the golden light of the inside walls.

Sam let himself into the house. The front rooms were beautiful too. A couch and a low table sat on one side of the room, with a wingback chair in the corner. Katie had hung a varied collection of art on the walls—paintings from her grandmother's storage and modern prints she had ordered online. The effect was cheerful and welcoming, and as he looked around, Sam knew it would be the most beautiful café Aveline had ever had.

One table in the front room was set with candles and the thick glazed plates Katie had chosen as the café's dishware. He eyed the table. Candlelight was too romantic. Dangerous.

"Katie?" he called, walking back to the kitchen and blinking when he caught sight of her. She was putting the finishing touches on a salad that looked delicious, but it was Katie herself that stunned him briefly. She wore a dress that just brushed her knees, with her hair swept off her face, tied up at the crown of her head. It showed off the long sweep of her neck, the lovely line of her jaw. She was wearing makeup, he realized, when she looked up at him. Just a little. Something dark around her eyes that made them even larger and more luminous than usual.

"Um," he said. "I came casual. I hope that's okay."

"You look great," she said, coming near to hug him. She smelled like roses, and he had trouble letting her go.

He cleared his throat. "Do you need any help?"

"You can carry the salad. I'll bring the soup and bread."

"What are we eating?" he called back to her.

"Clam chowder." Her voice echoed in the empty house.

Sam set the salads on the table, frowning when he noticed the chairs were pulled together rather than sitting across from one another. He fixed it, pushing one of the chairs to the other side of the table, but then he had to rearrange the place settings as well. He was working on that when Katie entered the room with a bowl of soup in each hand. She cocked an eyebrow at him.

"It just...seemed...nice this way," he said, wiping his hands on his jeans.

"You're right," she said, coming very close. She stood a few inches from Sam, looking into his eyes. "This way, I can see your face." She smiled and walked back down the hallway. "I'm going to get the bread and butter."

"You doing okay?" he called after her. She was acting a bit weird.

She came back into the room, grinning, holding a giant loaf of crusty bread. "I feel great," she said.

He watched her for a minute, but then shrugged and sat down as she did and took a forkful of salad.

"You have to tell me what you think," Katie said. "This is for the new menu."

"So far, it's delicious," Sam said. The salad was a mixture of fresh lettuce and caramelized nuts, bitter arugula, and tart strawberries. Sam kept his eyes on his food because Katie seemed to be staring at him a lot. He looked up at her. She was still looking at him, and he caught his breath at the look in her eyes. "Are you sure you're all right?"

She smiled. The candlelight turned her skin to gold. "I'm sure."

He took a large gulp of soup and closed his eyes. "Katie, this soup is divine."

She smiled again. "I'm glad you like it."

He focused on putting every bite into his mouth. The chowder was creamy, dusky with pepper, rich with clams and crumbly bits of bacon.

"I wanted to talk to you about something," she said, as he was wiping the bottom of his bowl with a piece of bread, a little sad to see that he had eaten it all. He looked up.

"What's that?" he asked.

"I'm thinking of postponing the restaurant opening," she said.

He stared at her. "Why? We're ahead of schedule."

"That's true, but I've been thinking that I could help with Maddie's homeschooling if I took a little time away from café prep. I have all these ideas, and I've been doing a ton of research." She stopped talking as he stared at her. He realized his mouth was hanging open slightly, and closed it, swallowing, not sure if he had heard her right.

"You want to postpone the opening...for Maddie's home-schooling?" he repeated. "Are you serious?"

"Yes, totally serious," she said, but her words turned up in a question as she reacted to the look on his face.

"That's crazy, Katie," he said, taking another bite of bread. When he looked up, she was biting her lip. She looked hurt. "I mean, no offense, but homeschooling Maddie is my job. It has nothing to do with you."

"I thought you wanted my help!" she said, her voice rising. She sat back in her chair and stared at Sam. "I did all this research because I thought it was something we were doing together."

Oh. She was definitely hurt. Sam caught her hand and squeezed it.

"Katie. I have a plan. She's going to do an online chartering school. They'll keep tabs on her and even give us money for her schooling. I know you had a lot of ideas, but don't you think this is about something else?"

"About what?" she asked, her voice injured.

"Are you maybe just distracting yourself from the café?"

Tears welled in her eyes. She looked so sad and so beautiful.

"Distracting myself?" She shook her head firmly, not meeting his eyes. "I just thought I had plenty of time to open the café and Maddie needed to start school soon. I thought you would be happy."

"She will start school. You can postpone if you want, but I don't want it to be because you're taking on responsibilities that aren't yours. What would really make me happy is to see you move forward with your dream. I mean, really, Katie, we're talking about someone whose mother sent her to her grandmother, who sent her to her uncle, who happens to be your friend. She's not your responsibility."

Katie laughed, but a few tears escaped and rolled down her cheeks. She pulled her hand away and wiped them quickly. He missed her hand in his.

"Do you really think I'm distracting myself?" she asked.

He nodded. "It makes sense," he said. "The opening party is a big thing. It's enough to make anyone want to run away."

She nodded, tracing circles on the table with the tip of one finger. Sam saw her gathering herself together and felt a wave of tenderness toward her. She stood suddenly, pushing back her chair.

"I'll get dessert," she said.

HE WANDERED AROUND THE ROOM, waiting for Katie to come back, looking at the pictures and brushing a hand over the wainscoting he had installed. After a moment, he heard Billie Holiday playing over the speaker system his crew had put in. The sound was perfect. He was admiring his work when Katie came back. She had a strange, determined look in her eye as she set the dessert on the table.

"I want you to try my pie," she said. She pulled a piece of it off with her fingers, then walked close to Sam and held it up to him. His stomach tightened, and he obediently opened his mouth, his eyes locked on hers. Her eyes moved to his mouth as she fed him, then back to his eyes as she licked the mulberry filling off her fingers. He could barely breathe.

"What do you think?" she asked.

His voice wouldn't seem to work properly. "It's amazing. What are you doing, Katie?" he asked, as she came closer to him.

"Using my eyes," she said, putting a hand on the side of his face. And then he couldn't think anymore, he pulled her close to him and kissed her, softly, tasting the mulberry on her. She lifted her arms and put them around his neck. She was perfect; she fit in his arms perfectly. They stood for a long while like that, kissing each other. He touched his lips to her chin, and she kissed his eyebrows. He felt like he would fly into a million pieces, but then she drew back. She looked at him very, very seriously, and he drew close to kiss her again, but she put a hand on his lips.

"Come," she whispered. "Let's sit." She drew him over to the couch and settled herself close to him, still staring into his eyes. He wanted to kiss her again. "You can't deny this, Sam Grant," she said. Her eyes were intent on his face. "This is real. This is serious. I don't know why you want to avoid what's happening, but I'm not going to pretend that I don't really, really like you. I like you enough to want to know everything about you. I like you so much that the first thing I think every day is that I can't wait until you show up for work and I can see which ridiculously plain, sexy T-shirt you're going to be wearing."

He blushed and looked down at his shirt, then back up at her. "I like you too," he said. He touched her shoulder and then her face with the back of his hand. "I...I've been a bit confused, Katie."

"I can tell," she said, her eyes crinkling in a smile.

"I don't know how to do this," he said.

"Just the next thing, right?" she said. "Someone told me that."

He leaned forward and kissed her again. She drew back again, her eyes soft.

"Is this real, Sam?" she asked.

"I think this is the realest thing," he said, and a brilliant smile broke over her face. He stood up. "How am I going to get anything done at all now?"

"We'll keep Maddie around," she said, laughing. "Our chaperone."

They sat at the table, next to each other this time, and fed each other the rest of the pie. Sam stole kisses between bites and felt every bit of reservation flee. This wasn't complicated. It just fit. They fit. She was his match.

"Now I really need to go," he said. "I'll be back in the morning. Katie?"

"Yeah?" she said.

"I meant what I said. I want you in my life, you beautiful thing. But this will all be so public, and there's the opening, and Maddie, and..."

Her face fell a bit. "You don't want a relationship."

"No, I do, I do," he exclaimed. "I just don't want to put it out there yet, with all the changes. Can... can it be between us until all this has blown over?"

She looked at him for a long moment, her face serious and still, and then slowly, she nodded. "Sure it can," she said.

Sam walked halfway home before he realized that he had left his truck in front of Katie's house. He dropped his head into his palm, then turned around to retrieve it. She had eclipsed everything, every single breath, every thought Sam had. He had been in denial to think he could avoid it, and as he started his truck and drove away, he felt happiness beginning to course through him. The truth was that Sam didn't want to be alone anymore. He wanted to be with Katie. He wanted to see her all the time, to sit beside her on the porch forever, not just when he was working for her. He wanted to kiss her until they fell asleep. As Sam allowed himself to feel things that he had been shoving away, he was shocked at the depth of his feelings. He was overwhelmed by her. She was everything bright and good that he had foolishly imagined he didn't want.

CHAPTER THIRTY

On the night of the opening, Katie stepped back and looked at herself in the mirror. She had knots in her stomach, and her heart was racing, but she had to admit that she looked good. The red dress was perfect. Tonight, she had left her hair down, pulling some front pieces back loosely at the crown of her head with the rest cascading down her back. She wasn't handling food tonight and could leave it loose. The party was for introducing her café to the town. She would mingle with guests and make sure everyone felt welcome. She had hired servers for the food.

She fastened an amber necklace around her throat and closed her eyes, breathing deeply. She felt as though she were stepping off a cliff. The days to come were unknown, as thin in her imagination as air. She and Sam had done what they could with the house, and she had made the best food she could create. She had trained her cooks to copy her recipes. The rest was out of her control. Would people come? Would they like it? Would it make a profit? These were all questions she couldn't answer, though she had worked hard on a business plan.

Despite the uncertainty, Katie felt a sense of peace. The house was filled with the fragrance of sizzling garlic, baking bread, and roasted vegetables. She spent her days slicing carrots and harvesting lettuce rather than going over charts. She had set her heart on something she loved. It would have to be enough.

When she opened the door to leave her room, she yelped and jumped half a foot. Someone was standing right outside, hidden behind an enormous bouquet of sunflowers. Katie took the flowers so she could see who it was, even though she half-guessed it was Sam. She placed the flowers carefully onto the dresser and then not-so-carefully threw herself at him. He caught her, laughing, and kissed her, then set her down.

"You're trembling," he said.

"I'm so scared," she whispered. Sam put a hand on either side of her face and kissed her again, then looked at her seriously.

"You have nothing to be afraid of, Katie Grace. If anyone should be scared, it's me, because now the whole world is going to see what a wonder you are. Someone will steal you away from me."

She rested her head on his shoulder as he settled his arms around her. "No one could steal me from you, Sam. Unless they had a nicer truck." She could hear him laughing through his chest.

A shriek came from downstairs. Katie sighed, pulling away. "I'm going to have to talk to Lucy about her volume," she said, collecting her flowers and plucking her handbag from the bed.

"Good luck with that," he said. "What can I do? I'm here to help."

Tears sprang to her eyes, and she blinked them back quickly so they wouldn't spoil her makeup.

"You've transformed this house," she said.

"And you've paid me handsomely for it," he said, taking her arm as they walked down the stairs. "I mean, what can I do to help as a—uh—best friend?" She laughed at him.

"Oh, well, then as a—uh—best friend, you can finish putting candles on all the tables while I turn the fairy lights on. The tea lights are in that cupboard," she said, pointing. "They go in the pottery holders we bought at the flea market. I'm sure you can figure it out."

"Glad to see your confidence in me," he said. "Anything else I can do while I'm at it?"

She laughed. "No, thankfully," she said. "I think we're ready." She went out to the porch and switched on the fairy lights, then found a vase in the kitchen. Lucy stood behind the island countertop, her round figure swathed in a chef's apron and hat.

"What's with all the shrieking?" Katie asked mildly.

"Larry put ice down my back," Lucy said. "I told you it was a bad idea to hire him."

Larry looked up from where he was stirring a large pot of soup, his face guilty.

"No more of that, Larry," Katie said, looking at him sternly. "This is a gala. Totally civilized. Keep it down until I need you to serve."

"Do you think there will be room for everyone?" Maddie asked. She and Larry were serving the free sample dishes Katie had made for the evening.

"I don't know," Katie said, feeling her stomach churn again. "Some people will be sitting at tables, but some people will be standing around. It depends—with the seats in the garden and the porch, we have a lot of room...but I don't know how many people will come. The drinks are out there already, right?" She had made three different kinds of cold tea so that each person received an icy drink as they arrived.

"Yes," Maddie said. "Who's serving them?"

At that moment, Katie heard a familiar voice. "Him," she said, her jaw dropping as Sheldon sauntered into the kitchen wearing a lime green suit with purple pinstripes. "Sheldon," she said. "You've outdone yourself."

"Thanks," he said. "Where do you need me?"

They walked out to the dining room, and Katie showed Sheldon the tea table.

"Just keep pouring so people can take a glass when they get here," she said.

"Got it."

Sam walked into the room with the empty candle bag.

"Done! There were candles left over, so I put them between the porch railings."

"Great," she said. "Will you light them now?"

"Sure. And Katie," he said, as he went back out to the porch. "Is there any panna cotta for dessert?"

Her eyes flashed at him. "Not this time," she said. "It's not great for big crowds. Or so I hear, anyway."

His eyes glimmered back at her. "Touché," he said, nodding before he disappeared into the other room.

"What was that all about?" Sheldon muttered, busy filling glasses with tea.

"Nothing," Katie said breezily. She wafted out to the kitchen as though she were floating.

CHAPTER THIRTY-ONE

Back in the kitchen, Katie paced, checking the soups and the hundreds of sandwiches she had made with Lucy and Maddie earlier in the day.

Katie had decided that the café would be open for breakfast and lunch, serving dinner only on special occasions, so she was showcasing sandwiches of every kind, three choices of soup, burrito bowls and platters of green salad. Everything looked like it was in order.

"Larry," she said. "You and the others need to load the dishwashers as fast as the dishes come back, okay? We're going to have a mountain of plates to wash, otherwise."

"Got it," Larry said, nodding.

Katie wandered around, trying to see the café as if for the first time. The band had set up in one corner of the room, and Katie could hear Carlo softly tuning his guitar. The large open dining room spread across the first floor; a large, meandering space with corners and nooks for privacy behind plants or screens. The ceilings soared, and the lighting showed off the golden warmth of the walls. Stained glass Turkish lamps glowed in each room, and a combination of tables with chairs, or couches and armchairs were spaced around the rooms, with afghan throws and potted plants adding texture. Katie's carefully chosen art covered the walls, the tables flickered with candlelight, and the whole place was bright with invitation.

Katie couldn't tell if it would be a success, but she knew she would want to eat here if she happened to walk past. She had created the kind of café she had always wanted. She walked out of the house and down the steps onto the grass, turning to gaze at the house, its porch lit up with lamps and candles. It looked like home.

"Where everybody knows your name," Sam said behind her, and she turned and knocked into him with her shoulder, laughing. He caught her hand, and she grabbed his chin, pulling away quickly when she heard Maddie call her name from the house.

"It's almost time," she whispered. "Stay close to me." He gave her the briefest, softest of kisses before they ran back up to the porch so Katie could welcome her guests.

Everyone was there. Of course George and Mercy with their daughter, Faith; Francisco and his parents, who exclaimed over the colorful house and told her it reminded them of El Salvador; Carlo and Juanita. Sheldon's friend Daniel, who worked at the post office and played bass in the band; Lewis, Ingrid, and Zoe with a group of professors from the university; and Dorothy, who stood on tiptoe to kiss Katie on the cheek. Katie stood there, smiling and shaking hands, greeting many people she didn't know, as well as the ones who had become so familiar. Sam didn't quite stand beside her, but he was never far away. Inside, Sheldon handed out icy glasses of tea and Larry offered bowls of soup while Maddie wandered around with a tray of sandwiches.

The band started up with soft music, prepared to play dancing tunes later on. Katie smiled in their direction. The four of them—lawyer, reverend, postal worker, and real estate agent—looked so different with instruments in their hands.

Then Katie saw her parents on the grass, outlined in the light that streamed from the porch. They walked up the steps slowly, and Katie's mother hugged her and kissed her on the cheek, gazing up at the house in awe.

"I've never seen it look so beautiful," she said. "You've done a great job, Katie."

"It was Sam," Katie said, catching Sam's elbow as he went by.

"Mom, Dad, this is Sam Grant. Maybe you remember him? We were friends when we were kids. He owns Grant's hardware, and he did all the renovation." Her mother just nodded at Sam. Katie frowned at the standoffish behavior. Her mother was usually very friendly. Sam must have noticed, but he only offered his hand to shake hands.

"It's nice to meet you two," he said. "Your daughter is one in a million."

"Katie," her mom said, after a quick handshake with Sam. "We have a surprise. We've brought someone very special with us. When we told him about your new restaurant, we couldn't keep him away." Her voice was tense with excitement.

"Who?" Katie asked, but her stomach plunged, as though

she knew. "What are you talking about?" She took a step closer to Sam. Then she saw him, emerging from the darkness of the garden. Ed. He was as tall and devastating as he had always been, with his black, immaculately cut hair, entirely out of place here, away from the city and the corporate world. His eyes appraised the house, and Katie couldn't help feeling the way she always had with him. Almost good enough, but not quite. Katie looked at Sam, her eyes wide with panic, but Ed arrived and bent to kiss her, aiming for her lips. She quickly dodged the kiss, and it landed on her cheek.

He held onto her hands, and she couldn't pull away.

"Katie," he said, his melodious voice causing waves of nostalgia to wash over her, years of memories. She was surprised to find that she didn't remember very many good things. She had thought she was devastated when he left. "You look good. What a very red dress."

Katie blushed, remembering that Ed had always told her that she shouldn't wear red because she looked like she was a walking tomato. The blush would complete the tomato effect, she thought, glancing at Sam, who was glaring daggers at Ed. From the look on his face, Sam seemed to want to fling Ed into the garden. The outright honesty in Sam's face gave Katie the courage to stick out her chin and answer her ex-boyfriend.

"I've always loved red," she said. "You know that."

"You didn't tell me that you had received an inheritance," he said, side-stepping her response. "I could have helped you with your investments."

"Why?" she said, eyes cold now. "Do you have experience, as a life insurance salesman, with investments?"

Her mother shot her a warning look, and her dad coughed and looked away. Katie could swear he was hiding a laugh. Beside her, Sam took a step closer to her.

Ed frowned. "I haven't met your friend," he said.

"This is Katie's contractor," her mother broke in. "Katie, don't you want to give Ed a tour?"

"This is my—uh—best friend," she told Ed, ignoring her mom. "His name is Sam. He's a business owner himself."

"Just a glorified carpenter," Sam said cheerfully, holding his hand out for Ed to take.

"Why don't you take Ed and get some food?" Katie asked her parents. "I'll finish greeting my guests and join you in a little while."

Her mother looked like she wanted to protest, but her father broke in.

"Excellent idea, Katie," he said. "The place looks fantastic, by the way. Nana would be so proud." Katie felt tears prickling behind her eyes, and she touched her father lightly on the elbow as he walked past her. Her whole body slumped in a sigh as the three of them walked inside.

She rearranged her face and greeted her next guests with a smile. Sam gave her some distance until it seemed that people were coming at a slow trickle, then he appeared and pulled her by the hand into a shadowy part of the garden. He kissed her on the forehead.

"Ed, huh? Tempted to go back?"

"I didn't know he was coming," she hissed. "Heaven help me. How did I date a jerk like that for two years? I don't even know why he's here. Clearly, he doesn't like the café." She looked into his eyes. They crinkled around the edges as he smiled at her. "Do you think I look like a tomato when I wear red?" she asked, hating the small wobble in her voice.

"I think you look glorious in red," he said. "I can barely stand to look at you tonight, all I want to do is bring you into some shadowy corner, um, like I did just now, actually." He kissed her, then pulled away. "I was thinking that we should get you a suit like Sheldon's," he said. "It would look fabulous on you."

She smiled. "I have to go in there," she said. "This is my party."

"Go. Are you going to make a speech?"

"I certainly am. Are you going to watch?"

"Absolutely. And I'm going to stick to Ed like glue, so he can't steal anything. Not a single spoon."

CHAPTER THIRTY-TWO

Every table on the porch was surrounded by talking, laughing people. Katie smoothed her hair and hoped her makeup was okay. She walked from table to table, asking her guests how they were enjoying the evening and the food. She got rave reviews on the food and exuberant praise for how the old house looked. Mercy stood and gave her a quick hug and kiss on the cheek when Katie reached the table she and George shared with Faith, Carlo, and Juanita.

"Thanks for playing, guys," Katie told George and Carlo.

"They'll use any excuse," Faith said, winking at Katie.

"We're not done," Carlo added. "But we got hungry."

"I thank the Lord you came to this town," George said. "Mercy, I think we can finally rest easy that we'll be able to spend our retirement in Aveline, right here at this café. You won't be able to budge us from the chairs on the porch."

"It's true," Faith said. "They'll sit and judge the neighbors. It'll be great!"

Katie laughed, feeling shy but happy with their praise.

Inside, she found Sheldon looking weary at the tea table, his jacket off and his shirt rumpled under his suspenders.

"Take a break," Katie told him. "I think everyone has drinks now. Have you eaten?"

"No, and I'm starving. Thank you." He bowed and disappeared into the kitchen, leaving Katie laughing. She almost didn't know what she had done without Sheldon in her life.

She kept walking through the house. People filled the couches and sat in the armchairs. Men and women stood around, talking in the middle of the room. The tables were full, and the room was loud with conversation. It dawned on Katie that the opening party was a success. Her knees were weak with relief. She joined her parents at a table when it seemed safe. Ed was off flirting with one of the cashiers from Green's. As she passed, she leaned in and whispered, "She's eighteen," avoiding his startled glance as she slipped away.

She chatted with her parents until Lucy, Maddie, and Larry brought out trays of pecan and mulberry tarts. Once everyone had their dessert, she stood to give her speech. She looked over at Sam, and he called everyone's attention. "Katie's going to make a speech!" Eventually, the room was silent and expectant, the quiet broken only by a toddler shouting, "I don't want the brown pie! I want the purple pie!"

Katie waited for the laughter to die down, then took a deep breath. "I came to this town broken down and scared," she said. "And you have brought me back to life. Thank you for being here for me, for inspiring me and encouraging me to make this café happen. I want to serve this little town well, just as many of you do." She smiled at Francisco and Sheldon, George and Mercy in the doorway, Lewis, Carlo poking his head into the window from the porch outside. "I don't know how to tell you just how much I love living here," she met Ed's eyes then, and was a little shaken by the scowl on his face, but she looked away again and took a deep breath. "But I hope you make the Aveline Café your second home. Thank you to all of you who helped me, and most of all, to Sam Grant, the grand renovator." She swept her hand around to Sam and smiled at him. Everyone applauded, and Katie grinned so wide she thought her face would break. "I won't keep you from your dessert any longer. We open for business in exactly one week. Enjoy!"

Wild cheers and stomping followed her speech, led by Frankie and Sam in the doorway. She gave a little bow and went to speak with her guests again. The band picked up their instruments again and played with a little more gusto. Katie saw Juanita and Mercy dancing with Dorothy and grinned. She was wandering around, watching the dancing and saying hello to people she hadn't greeted yet, when she felt a hand on her elbow. Ed stood very close to her with a tight grip on her arm. She frowned and pulled away from him.

"I need to talk to you," he said. "Alone."

She looked at him levelly. "Okay," she said. "For a minute."

She led him out to a bench in the garden and sank onto it, waiting for him to speak. She thought she should let him get whatever this was off his chest before she told him that he wasn't welcome in her life anymore.

"I'm hurt, Katie," he said, pacing, "that you wouldn't consult with me before making such a huge decision."

"I'm sorry?" she said, heat rushing to her face.

"Don't you remember our plans?" he asked, turning to her. "To start our own company if we ever had the chance?"

She had vague memories, she supposed, of dreaming of their own insurance company. It seemed remarkably fuzzy now.

"Whatever we thought up," she said, "That was before you left me, Ed. You told me I embarrassed you. That you couldn't drag me around anymore." He didn't deny it. He looked up, nodding.

"That's the other thing, Katie baby, why would you think you can handle something like this? After what happened? You don't know who to believe or what to believe. You don't know when to push and when to leave things. How can you have employees? You don't know who to trust! People could be stealing from you, and you wouldn't even know it. What about that contractor guy? Does he have access to your accounts?"

Katie had been sitting with her head down, listening to him list her exact fears. She was still confused about what had happened in the weeks and months leading up to the court case. She knew she had misjudged people, but not in the way Ed thought. Even the reminder, though, even the sound of his voice, brought the shame back. She rubbed at her arm, reliving the hate. When she heard what he said about Sam, though, she looked up with a laugh.

"Now you're being ridiculous," she said. "I trust Sam completely. I would trust him with my life."

"It's not too late for us Katie," Ed said, sitting close to her. He grabbed her hand and stroked it with his thumb. She felt herself reacting to the familiarity of his smell, his eyes. They had been together for so long. He told her he would marry her, just as soon as he made the next promotion. It stretched out to the promotion after that. She didn't want to feel softness toward him, but she knew him so well. He kept talking. "You could sell this place; you'd make a load of cash, now that you've renovated it. And then we'll start our business."

She stared at him. He smiled at her, so sure she would fall in line, the way she always had. He had always used her—she saw that clearly now. He had ridden on her success, using it for his own benefit in the company, dropping her name when he was in trouble for not bringing enough sales in or slacking on the job. And now he wanted to use her money. He was barely even pretending this was about love.

"I think you should leave, Ed," she said. It took him a minute to realize what she had said, and then he jerked back, looking shocked. She felt a glimmer of satisfaction. "You're welcome to take some of the cookies home with you. I made gift bags. They should be out already. It's a long drive back to L.A."

"You're not serious," he said.

"I'm very serious."

She sat for a moment after he stormed to his car. He hadn't taken a gift bag, and she shook her head. He was missing out. The cookies were delicious. She looked out at the garden and the tall trees of the park beyond, remembering sunny mornings when they had stayed in bed, the kitchen a mess from her cooking. Ed had never encouraged any pursuit that wasn't directly related to his career success. He had taken everything she gave as though it was his due. There were good memories, but now she could see his presumption and indifference to her as a person woven like a string through them all. She looked at the stars glowing through the branches of the tree above her, sprinkled through the sky. God was utterly extravagant with the amount of beauty he tossed around. The world was full of it. Katie's heart felt light with the thought of mornings stretching into the future, nights into infinity, all of them without Ed, without the feeling of not being enough that seemed to follow her when he was around. The stars were very clear and the music sweet and lilting into the night, mingling with the sounds of laughter.

Katie was absorbed in her thoughts, and jumped when someone sat beside her. When she saw it was Sam, she laid her head on his shoulder. They sat in silence for a while.

"I have a confession," he said finally.

She sighed. "Not you too."

"My confession is that I was eavesdropping shamelessly. And I'm thankful for your trust because I'm planning to take you for all you're worth."

She burst out laughing. Sam put one hand on her face, planting a kiss on top of her head. And a small, wounded corner of her heart began to heal.

CHAPTER THIRTY-THREE

In the week after the party, Sam found reasons to show up at Katie's house every day. He claimed he needed to get stuff done before the café opened, but Sam knew he just wanted to be close to Katie. He found useful things to do, though, rebuilding the inside stairs while she cleaned the front bedroom.

"I think I might actually move in here one day," Katie said, sounding skeptical even as she said it.

Sam looked at her. She stood at the top of the stairs, looking down at where he was working, halfway down the stairwell. She was in a cleaning outfit of a pair of cutoff shorts and a halter top. Her hair was tied up under a scarf, and she looked like an adorable cartoon of someone cleaning a house. Except that a cartoon character would invariably be small, and Katie was a tall, golden painting of a woman.

"What do you mean, might?" he asked. "This is your house, Katie. You should be in the master bedroom."

She went back into the bedroom and emerged after a

moment with a pile of dresses in her arms, dropping them in the hallway. She sighed and wiped her forehead, leaving a gray smudge on her skin.

"I know," she said. "But it still feels wrong. As though I'm taking Nana's room, even though she's not here anymore." She looked around. "What was Carlo thinking? He told the movers to put everything back in the house, like I would want all my grandmother's clothes back in her old room. I get it, he wanted to put it back as it was, but a little creativity would have helped him think it through."

"I don't think it has anything to do with that," Sam said.

"What? Creativity?"

"No," Sam said, carefully brushing glue on a spindle and placing it back in the railing. "I don't think taking your grandmother's room has anything to do with why you haven't moved in there. I think the truth is you think you don't deserve this house. You're sharing the whole bottom floor with the town. This floor should be fully yours. You're still hiding, Katie, and the tiny back bedroom is a perfect hiding spot."

Katie crossed her arms. "Sam!" she exclaimed. "What are you talking about?"

"Think about it. You act as though it's just some miracle that you've managed to create a restaurant in a number of months, like you don't know how it happened."

"You created a restaurant," she said.

"That's what I'm talking about," he said. "I'm your contractor. That's what people do, Katie, they don't build their own restaurants, they hire people to do it for them, like you did. And then you sourced your ingredients and designed a kitchen and created a menu and course-corrected when you felt you'd gone in the wrong direction. Because you're amazing. And I still don't know what happened to you in L.A., but that jerk of an ex has you thinking you deserve nothing, that this is all luck, that you haven't done anything great." He swallowed, brushing glue onto another spindle. "You should be in that master bedroom. You should take up all the space on this floor. That's all."

He heard footsteps and looked up to see her walking down the stairs toward him. Then her soft lips were on his cheek, and he inhaled and moved so he could kiss her back. She tasted like mint and strawberries. He put a hand on her face, then ran it down her neck, moving closer to her when she sighed.

"Sam! Help!" It was Maddie, calling from the front room.

Sam broke away and looked at Katie, his head fuzzy. He sighed and walked down to the front room, where Maddie sat curled up on the couch with her new laptop.

"Help?" he said, eyebrows at his hairline. "You seem fine."

"The periodic table is confusing me," she said. "I need help."

As much as Sam loved Maddie, and he had come to love his niece much more than he would ever have foreseen, she was driving him crazy. Her charter homeschooling was going well; she was mostly pretty disciplined, and he only had to check in with her now and again, but she couldn't have been more of an interruption in the romance blooming between Sam and Katie if she tried.

He looked at her with narrowed eyes for a moment,

before sitting next to her and taking a look at the screen. A few minutes and explanations later, he caught sight of Katie traipsing down the stairs and out toward the pickup, a pile of dresses in her arms. She flashed him a rueful smile as she went by. Their moment was over.

CHAPTER THIRTY-FOUR

The late summer weather was so balmy and perfect that Sam made a plan to whisk Katie away to the lake, just the two of them. At the last minute, though, Maddie told him tearfully that she didn't want to go to her grandmother's house, so Sam brought her along. They met Katie, who was holding an enormous picnic basket, on the corner in front of the park, and Sam was glad he had texted Katie in advance about Maddie's emotional state. He took the picnic basket when Katie held it out to him, and watched as she threw her arms around Maddie. After a hug, they started walking, arms slung around each other. Sam followed. He could hear them talking in low voices, but he caught only snatches of what they said.

"...Missing your mom?..."

"... She's not doing so well..."

Sam was thankful for Katie's help with Maddie, but— he tipped his head back and looked at the white, fluffy clouds—his dream of a day at the lake with the woman he loved had turned into a therapy session for a fourteen-year-old.

The day improved from there, though. The three of them went out on Sam's neglected little speedboat. The summer had been so busy that he hadn't taken it out even once, and it felt great to be out on the water again. They sped around the lake, Katie's hair a glorious, coppery mess around her face, Maddie for once not wearing the baggy black coat. Katie and Maddie turned their faces to the sun while Sam raced along, trailing a shimmery spray of water. He tried to impress Katie with his skills, making sharp turns and throwing the little boat around the lake. She laughed and shrieked until Maddie started to turn green and Sam slowed the boat to a gentle drift. They bobbed along, soaking in the breeze and sunshine. Sam felt contentment soaking into his bones. He thought of the way he usually came out here alone, or with Frankie or Sheldon, and realized he'd rather be here with Katie and Maddie. Thank you, God, he thought. I've been stupid.

He took them to his favorite cove—a little rocky beach with firs and oaks sheltering it, secreted away on the other side of the lake. They sat in the shade, headachy and tired from the sun, though the air was slightly too cool under the dense canopy of the trees. Maddie put the coat back on, and Katie pulled on a sweater. Sam stayed as he was in his T-shirt. He'd take the cold after such a hot summer.

Katie opened the picnic basket to reveal grilled eggplant and prosciutto sandwiches, a thermos of cold hibiscus tea and another of coffee. They ate until they were full, then sipped at hot coffee. Maddie went for a walk along the beach to collect rocks while Katie and Sam sat. He reached out and looped his pinky around hers, and she met his eyes dead on, sending a shiver straight through him. He could feel her warmth, smell her sun-warmed skin mixed with roses, and he longed to kiss her. They still hadn't told Maddie about their relationship, though, and the day's beginning had already been full of tension. He could see the fourteen-year-old on the other end of the cove where she sat, combing through rocks with her fingers. He smiled into Katie's green eyes.

"So," he said.

"So," she answered.

"When are you going to tell me about what happened in L.A.?"

Her face paled, and she pulled her hand away from his.

"I'm not," she said.

"Katie?" he asked, dipping his head so he could see her face after she turned away slightly. She was frowning at a rock in her hand. "Is that fair?"

"You haven't told me what happened in college," she said. "That's not fair either."

"Okay, then. A story for a story. I want to know what could possibly make you feel so bad about yourself that the slugly Ed only says a few words and you wither up on the proudest night of your life."

She looked at him, smiling slightly. "Slugly?"

"It describes him perfectly." He captured her hand again, and she squeezed his fingers and didn't pull away. "He's a slimeball."

"You first," she whispered.

"Oh, it's really not a big deal. I'm sure whatever Lucy's told you is mostly accurate." He smiled at her guilty look of surprise. "I can always count on her to tell all the stories I'd rather forget. I fell for a girl, a funny, beautiful girl who loved my adoration and lived on it until she fell in love with someone else, then she left me, but not before she'd been cheating on me for some time. I don't think I'd ever realized that her humor was the hurtful kind, until the messy scene with me like a big-eyed Bambi, crying in the cafeteria when I heard she'd been cheating. She left, seeming to feel no regret, but she came back pregnant. I wanted to help her, though it wasn't my baby, but her parents whisked her away, and I lost her a second time. She's married now. Wildly successful. And I'm a carpenter in a small town. She made me realize women were going to be my downfall if I didn't swear off them completely."

"That seems drastic," Katie said.

"Well, public heartbreak is drastic."

"I'm really sorry," she said, holding his hand between both of hers. The water was very still, so clear he could see the rocks on the bottom.

"Thanks," he said. "Your turn."

She took a deep breath. "Okay, so I was head of human resources in an insurance company. I was known for being the best in my field, and different branches of our company flew me out to train their departments. I was that good. New York wanted me to transfer there, but I stayed where I was because of Ed."

She took a shaky breath, looking at Sam's hand in hers. "I had a crush on him for a long time before he noticed me. But I don't think he knew I existed until a meeting when the CEO talked about what an incredible asset to the company I was. They put me on a pedestal, really. The employee who couldn't fail, who always worked late, who could always be counted on. It was inevitable, now that I think about it. I had to fall. Or maybe they were grooming me."

She played with his hand, almost like she didn't know it was still in her lap, rubbing one fingertip over the lines on his knuckles until he almost couldn't breathe. He longed to make her sadness disappear.

"The manager of my branch was smart, handsome and funny. He was a perfect gentleman to me, and I knew his family well. He was one of my biggest fans. So I didn't believe the first reports of sexual harassment that came in. I did the thing, Sam, where I tried to sweep it away because I couldn't believe it. It was the third woman who convinced me, and she convinced me with hard evidence. She'd recorded a conversation where he threatened to fire her if she didn't sleep with him." She swallowed. "Those women that I'd brushed off...it was as though my eyes were opened. I saw how every woman in his department was young and attractive. I saw how cold he was with his wife. I went from feeling like a part of their family to seeing straight through this whole charade I had been coddled into. They treated me well so I wouldn't kick back if something came to the surface. I started talking to more women, discovering how widespread it was, to my absolute horror, and how people had been trying to hint about this to me for years." Her voice broke.

"Katie," Sam said, scooting closer to her so that he could put an arm around her. "You didn't know."

"I didn't know, and it was my fault. Far from being the star of human resources, I was a carefully groomed lap dog,

Sam! So I collected as much evidence as I could and helped three employees press charges. That switched things around quickly. I had been gathering evidence quietly, so it was a surprise when I announced that we were pressing charges. Overnight, I became the black sheep, and I wasn't prepared for that level of hatred. It was covered in the papers, all over the Internet, and his wife hated me. I wasn't ready for that. I thought she would be glad to be rid of him, but she was preserving a carefully constructed lie all along. She knew!" Katie was staring out at the lake, lost in her thoughts. "Because I was the key witness in the company, they skewered me. They ran over my reputation, my credentials. They accosted me walking home. They threatened and slandered me. I held up mostly but fell apart on the witness stand. They accused me of ungratefulness and disloyalty. I hate the idea of being ungrateful or disloyal. It was so confusing."

They were silent for a while, sitting there.

"Does it make you feel better that you were right?" Sam asked finally. He didn't know what to say, but he knew she needed to keep talking, to tell him all of it.

"Not really," she said, slowly, "because it took me so long to listen. My world turned inside out, so it was as though nothing I had believed had been real. And Philip got slapped with fines and kept his job. Nothing changed. Those women... they were dragged through the mud along with me. I thought I could count on Ed, but he tried to convince me to drop it all because 'This is just all part of this kind of life, baby.' I couldn't believe it. He left me immediately when I refused. I was no longer the rising star he could hitch his chariot to. I got dumped and fired and cross-examined, and everything I had worked for was gone. Then my Nana died, and I found that I had forgotten how to exist, how to get out of bed or be okay inside." She took a deep, shaky breath. "And then I got the letter from Jackson & Jackson, telling me about the house." She smiled at him, her eyes sad and tired. "You know the rest."

They sat in silence for a minute, Sam's hand still captured between Katie's. She frowned out across the water, a tiny line between her eyebrows. Finally, he spoke.

"Phew," he said.

"What?" she asked, startled.

"You talked so much about this horrible thing you had done back in the city that for a moment I thought it really might have been something bad. Murder, or something."

She laughed, but it fizzled into a sad sound that caught at his heart.

"But this sounds like a hero story, Katie," he said. "Even if you made a mistake and did the wrong thing at first by not listening to those women, it sounds like you more than made up for it."

She looked at him, her face drawn into a tired, unhappy downward curve.

"Pretty big mistake," she said. "It's a moral lapse, isn't it, not being able to be a good judge of human character?"

"You seem to be forgetting who was the real wrongdoer in the situation. It was your boss. You got caught in the crossfire."

"They made me feel like I was the one doing something wrong. Like I was ruining Philip's life by telling the truth. It was so confusing, and there was so much guilt from every side. And then—this is the worst thing, Sam—his wife at the trial, she found me in the lobby and screamed at me. She told me that he couldn't sleep anymore, that his blood pressure was going through the roof, that I had ruined their lives. She had this knife in her hand. I thought she was going to try to kill me, but eventually, she just threw it at me and walked away. I felt as though she had spit at me."

"Again, he ruined their lives. Telling the truth is not what ruined their lives; it was living a lie that did that."

She picked up a rock and turned it over in her hands.

"I'm trying to believe that," she said. "I think it would be easier if the punishment had fit the crime, if everything hadn't just gone back to normal, with Philip getting to keep his job. It felt like we were the ones who suffered. The women he had hurt. And me, trying to tell the truth. It makes trying to do the right thing feel futile."

"You should talk to Mercy about that," Sam said quietly. "She might have a few things to say."

Katie nodded, and they sat in silence again for a while. Then she looked at him, her heart and feelings all rising into her eyes. "Thank you for being so kind, Sam. You can see now why I had to do something completely different."

"Yeah, plus working at an insurance company—no offense —sounds like a soul-sucking nightmare." She laughed, but he wasn't done. "Don't believe any lies, Katie. God sees your rightness. And your mistakes. And he forgives the mistakes and honors the right things you did. Don't drag lies around with you, about your inability to judge character, or blame for what happened. Look at me, thinking that it was women who caused all the pain in the world, and I should just avoid them. And then you came."

She laughed and shook her head. "You didn't think that, really."

"No, but you know what I mean."

She took a deep breath. "Okay, new topic—" but Sam caught her mouth in a kiss, and he tried to put his belief, his craziness for her, his compassion and desire and admiration, all into the moment of his mouth on hers. It went on for quite some time, and when he pulled away, she was staring at him hazily.

"Whoa," she whispered.

He laughed and sat back, then looked up to see Maddie down the beach, standing and staring at them. She looked away quickly when he looked at her. He sighed.

"I need to go talk to my niece," he said, nodding toward Maddie.

"Let's go together," Katie said.

CHAPTER THIRTY-FIVE

As Sam walked down the beach with Katie, their feet made shushing sounds on the tiny pebbles. They didn't hold hands, but they did brush wrists. When they reached Maddie, Sam sat down beside his niece. She had gathered a large pile of pebbles, making a little hammock for them with her T-shirt. The expression on her face was bleak. Sam felt a sharp twinge of love and pity.

"Hey," he said.

"Hey," she answered, not looking at him. She picked up another stone and looked at it. "Have you ever noticed how pebbles are deceptive?" she asked. "They look so glamorous when they're wet, but you get them home, and they become just a bunch of rocks, and you're like, why did I even pick these, and you have to toss them in the trash."

Sam wasn't sure how to respond to that, but Katie sat down on the other side of Maddie and began running her hands through the pebbles.

"The trick is to get the ones that will be beautiful no matter if they're wet or dry," she said. "Like this one."

She handed Maddie a smooth white stone. Maddie took it and added it to her collection. "The other thing is to remember why they were beautiful to you and not get rid of them, just let them be secretly beautiful, in a jar or glass somewhere."

"Or keep them underwater," Sam added, then, when Katie cocked an eyebrow, went on. "What? Like in a fish tank or something." She shook her head at him and went back to sorting through pebbles.

Maddie turned to look at Sam. "Do you think she's ever coming back for me?" she said, and her voice reminded Sam of Katie's moments before, when she was talking about the trial. Bleak and sad and full of self-blame.

"She'll come," he said. "I know my sister. She couldn't keep herself away from you. No one could."

Tears welled up in her eyes as she looked at him, but she smiled. "I'm okay with it, by the way," she said, pushing her chin out. "Whatever's going on between the two of you. Not that anyone cares what I think."

Sam smiled at the irony. Here he was, sneaking around like a teenager, not openly declaring how he felt about Katie because he was worried about how Maddie would take it, and she believed that no one cared what she thought. He glanced at Katie, and she gave him a warning frown, so he sat up straighter.

"Thanks, Maddie," he said. "That means a lot." He reached out and messed up her hair, and she smiled into the stones on her lap.

He dropped by Green's later that evening, since he and Maddie were out of cereal, milk, and just about everything else. His carefully kept lists had disappeared long ago. He pushed his cart through the store, collecting things he thought Maddie might like; stuff he never would have bought before, like three kinds of granola, crackers made of black beans, and pomegranate juice.

He was muttering to himself about why there needed to be so many kinds of yogurt when he walked over to Sheldon's office door. Inside, his friend was sitting in the beach chair with a glass of rum on ice beside him. Uh oh.

"Hey buddy," he said, walking into the room.

"Don't you hey buddy me," Sheldon said. "Traitor. I know what you've done; it's written all over you."

"I haven't done anything," Sam said.

"I mean your heart. It's fine, bro. You deserve it. Consider yourself officially released."

Sam didn't know what to say to that.

"I talked to Theresa the other day, you know," he said, instead of responding.

Sheldon looked up at him quickly, and Sam shrank from the look in his eyes. Sheldon looked, sad, angry, and frustrated.

"You know," he said, "I have quite cheerfully waited for her to come back without a lot of anger in my heart, but I'm finding that anger is surfacing. Not because of the reasons you think," he added, as Sam nodded.

"Oh? What are your reasons?"

"That niece of yours is very sad," Sheldon said. "How could Theresa be so selfish?"

Sam shrugged. "She's always been a bit selfish."

"No, she hasn't. There's a difference between selfish and struggling. But she seems to be crossing some line, lately."

"Hard to tell when she's not here. Maddie always defends her. She talks about how great her mom is."

"That's what I mean," Sheldon said. Sam turned to go, not sure what to do with his friend when he was locked in this kind of melancholy. Sheldon took a sip of his drink, then spoke just as Sam was leaving the room.

"I've been having trouble with theft," he said. "A lot of things have been missing lately."

"The students are back," Sam said.

"Yeah, I'm sure that's it," Sheldon said. "Just so you know to be extra careful with your stock."

"Thanks, bud," Sam said, then pushed his cart away to check his groceries out.

CHAPTER THIRTY-SIX

At the next women's gathering, Katie shared the same story she had told Sam. She was shaky but felt a little bolder after sharing it once already. She told them everything, watching the women who sat clustered in Mercy's living room, marveling a little that she had opened up. Just a few months ago, Katie had barely been able to walk into Mercy's kitchen, and here she was, sharing her most painful secrets.

Mercy sat at her kitchen island with a glass of wine in one hand. She had removed her earrings and draped them over a candle holder that sat on the island, playing with the beads absent-mindedly. Juanita was curled up in a large armchair, teasing Mercy's cat with a piece of yarn, but also paying close attention to Katie's story. Faith was with them that evening, cross-legged on the floor, her head cocked to one side, her lovely face open and concerned. Dorothy and Lucy sat side by side on the couch, and Zoe and Ingrid were in chairs at the table. Zoe's face looked as though she was going to cry.

"The court case was horrifying," Katie said, "and I couldn't stop crying on the witness stand. They used it as evidence of me being an unreliable witness. In the end, Philip paid a minor settlement to the women, and I left L.A. after falling apart completely."

She looked at her hands, open on her lap. Her stomach tightened with anxiety as she imagined the disgust of the women in the room toward her tepid reaction and lack of power. "Now you know my sordid past," she said.

Mercy snorted. Katie looked up.

"Sounds like someone else's sordid past," Mercy said. "Not yours."

"Yeah," Zoe added. "I guess I'm trying to understand what part of this is yours to own."

"I didn't believe them soon enough," Katie said. "I was trying hard not to be biased because of something that happened when I was younger, but I ended up doing something worse, which was not listening to the victims of sexual assault. I worry about my judgment."

"Katie," Dorothy said, her voice clear. "What did you do once you knew the facts?"

"I helped them press charges," Katie answered after a moment.

"Then that's all there is," Mercy said. "The repercussions of seeking truth can be difficult because people often would rather stay in their fantasies." She looked at her daughter. "Seeking justice for Zion has been a nightmare in some ways. People say we should stop harassing the police, that we're trying to ruin the life of an officer. People who don't know him call our son a thug. It happens again and again in cases like ours. I'm sure that people tried to say the women you helped were asking for it."

Katie nodded, transfixed by the older woman's words.

"We have to ask, are we telling the truth?" Faith said. "It's not our job to make the truth pretty or to bolster the fantasy that all is well in the world when it isn't. You didn't ruin anyone's life. They ruined their own lives when they chose to act wrongly. It's a false narrative that consequences shouldn't come to people who consider themselves above the law."

"In other words," Lucy said. "You did good, Katie. Stop beating yourself up."

"You'll need to be tough if you're going to tell the truth. It's a hard thing, staying soft and being tough at the same time. I think Jesus showed us how to do that, though," Mercy said.

Katie sipped her wine and played with her hair. She felt a weight leaving her as the effects of confession loosened the tight ache around her heart. She watched Juanita playing with the cat, half-mesmerized by the yarn flipping over the cat's paws while he tried to catch it, and was startled when Ingrid called her for dinner.

"You okay?" Ingrid asked softly.

Katie nodded. "We're eating at the table today?"

Ingrid nodded. "Yes. Zoe made lasagne and Mercy says we don't want to see what happens if we get sauce on her couches."

Katie smiled, running a hand over the white couch. "Fair enough."

She joined the women at the table, feeling weak, as though she had been crying. She thought that if she had these women as her friends when the incident had happened, she might not have fallen apart so completely.

"How's the troublesome student, Zoe?" Mercy asked, after they were all seated with glasses of wine and plates of lasagne in front of them.

"Are you asking me if I was anger-cooking again?" Zoe asked, raising an eyebrow.

Katie smiled. "Anger-cooking?"

"We eat well if Zoe's mad," Lucy said.

"Maybe it was anger-cooking, maybe not. But he is still being a punk."

"What's he doing?" Faith asked. "I think I missed this."

"Just the usual." Zoe and Faith exchanged a look, but Katie still felt in the dark. She looked around to see if the others understood.

"He's making trouble because she's black," Lucy told her. Katie frowned.

"What kind of trouble?" Katie asked.

"Reporting me for what he calls unfair grades, telling the dean that I'm biased. Asking for another professor, but I'm the only psychology professor right now."

"And damn good at it," Faith said. "She was my professor," she added, for Katie's benefit.

"I'm going to deal with it," Zoe said. "I don't want to waste any more breath on this stupid guy. Katie..."

Katie looked up.

"What's happening with you and Sam?" Zoe asked.

Katie felt her face burning up. "What do you mean?" she asked, remembering his desire that they wait to talk about it.

"It's possible that Larry saw you two kissing at the party,

and possible that he told me," Lucy confessed. "And possible that I told all of them. And a lot of other people."

"Well," Katie said. She couldn't keep a smile from spreading across her face. "It sounds like you don't need me to tell you what's happening with Sam."

The squeals that met her statement made her smile even more.

CHAPTER THIRTY-SEVEN

The café opened as planned, on a Sunday morning in late September. By the end of the first two days, Katie had reason to remind herself of everything she knew about transitions. She fell into bed, utterly exhausted, every single night. At her old job, Katie had often given new employees a pamphlet detailing the effects of switching to a new job, so she knew all the symptoms in theory, but real life was a shock. She wrestled with dizziness, tiredness, and confusion as her brain tried its best to absorb so many new things.

She and Lucy held daily meetings on café management, with Katie doing her best to communicate her vision of family and warmth down to every last staff member. Lucy would handle the front end of the café: the servers and cash register. Katie was kitchen manager: orders, food prep, cooking, chefs in training, and dishwashers were all in her section. Katie daily thanked God for Lucy, fervently. Lucy was a machine, working tirelessly, guiding the servers through their paces, correcting their mistakes, praising them when they accomplished orders without a glitch. With Lucy's help, Katie had hired Maddie and two college students as servers. Maddie became Lucy's right-hand woman, and Lucy raved about Maddie's head for numbers as the teen helped her figure out the complicated pricing scheme and shift schedule.

And there it was. Katie owned a café.

Lewis brought armfuls of produce from his farm, and whatever Lewis didn't have, Katie ordered from Sheldon. The first day Sheldon delivered something in person, Katie's jaw dropped. He had sauntered into the kitchen in a newsboy delivery cap and suspenders.

"My delivery uniform," he told her as she cleared space for him to set the box down. "You're welcome."

She grinned at him. "Thank you."

Katie made soup, supervised sandwiches, and prepared her own mayonnaise, sauces and dressings, pasta sauces, and hollandaise sauce. She made every kind of salad she loved; rice noodle salads, green, potato, and pasta salad. Every day the café made all day breakfast, with sandwich choices and a soup and salad special. And customers came. They sat on the porch under the bougainvillea, and they praised Katie's food and pies. The café began to show signs of being a success. More than a success. It was almost always full, and on Saturdays, a line stretched out the door.

Katie was exhausted by closing time at four, and she was often curled up with a book in her pajamas by the time Sam came over in the evenings. He was renovating the second floor now, but slowly, in his spare time, after the customers were gone and his own store closed.

"I don't know how you do it," Katie said to him one

evening, watching him work from the couch they had moved into her grandmother's room. She still slept in the tiny back room, but Sam was adamant that she would move into the front bedroom once he was finished. Katie still wasn't sure. Sam had stripped the floors back to a smooth, polished hardwood, and their warm colors made the room inviting. She could imagine one of those beautiful Turkish rugs from the flea market on the floor, her café anniversary present, as she told herself.

She couldn't imagine herself a year from now—what would be happening between her and Sam? She lost herself, thinking about it, and blinked when Sam answered her.

"Do what?" he asked, glancing over at her from where he fitted the corner moldings together on one of the windows. It took Katie a moment to remember what she had said.

"Work at your shop all day and then come here and work some more."

He raised his eyebrows at her. "Your job is a lot more exhausting than mine. I'm not on my feet cooking all day."

"Speaking of which, I need to start the yogurt," she said, rising to her feet with a groan. "The milk's probably cool enough. Be right back." She made homemade yogurt for the fruit-granola-yogurt breakfast, popular with the college kids. She was still working out what to make ahead, what to make in the moment, and how to avoid waste, getting used to the little rhythms and schedules that made things easier. It was complicated, but she was getting there. Soon the café would be a well-oiled machine.

She loved seeing Maddie smiling shyly at customers and joking around with the other server staff. The deal was that

Maddie had to finish homeschool before she could work the second shift each day. She often helped Lucy close the café, putting the chairs up and sweeping, flipping the sign on the door to "closed," a happy task that Katie sometimes did too, always with a sigh of happiness. Katie also loved to see Lucy shining in her new job. She had a feeling that she and Lucy would be working together for a very long time. Already, Katie couldn't imagine doing it without Lucy. She watched Lucy moving between customers, bossing them around, telling them what they should eat, and felt proud to have her. Larry was proud of his mother too, especially now that she was working in a different building, on a different street, even. Katie scooped some of the last batch of yogurt into the pot of warm milk and poured it into glass containers. She wrapped them in towels and set them on the counter close to the oven so that the yogurt would be ready by morning. She yawned and stretched, walking slowly back upstairs to flop back onto the couch. Sam was on the phone.

"Okay, right. Sure. Yeah. No problem," he said, then stared at the screen on his phone for a moment before slipping it back into the pocket of his jeans. "That was odd," he said.

"What?" Katie asked, sitting up and crossing her legs.

"That was Sheldon. He sounded... weird. He wanted us to come and see him at Green's."

"Both of us? At this time of night?"

Sam grinned. "Katie. It's eight o'clock."

"Well, I've been up since five," she said.

"You'll get used to it," he said. "I did." He turned and

started packing his tools away. "I suppose we'd better go down there."

"Did he sound good weird? Or bad weird?"

"I honestly couldn't tell, which makes me nervous. I've known Sheldon for so long that I almost always know what's going on with him." He pulled his jacket on, looking at her as if to say, "Well?"

She groaned, then smiled up at him. "You really want me to come? Don't you want to stay here and make out for a while?"

"Katie. Come on, you lovely thing, we should go. Sheldon's my best friend."

Katie felt her face suddenly fall into serious lines because she had become very fond of Sheldon as well. She tromped down the hallway to her room and found a coat to throw on over her pajamas.

"Do you think he's getting married?" she called back to Sam.

"I highly doubt it," he said.

"Maybe she's a secret girl," she said when she rejoined him in the hallway.

"No. I'm absolutely certain that's not it," he said.

"How can you be so sure?" she asked. She locked the front door, and they walked down the porch stairs to the street, falling into step as they walked toward Green's. Sam caught Katie's hand in his, and she shivered. Her thin pajama pants weren't warm enough for the fall air.

"Trust me," Sam said. "He's not over...he was engaged to my sister."

"Your sister?" Katie was shocked. Her hand flew to her mouth. "Maddie's mom?"

"The one and only. Having Maddie around has made him a bit melancholy. At one time he thought he was going to be Maddie's father, and now she's back in town and doesn't even remember him."

"He's not—he's not Maddie's father?" She dropped his hand and looped her arm through his. He pulled her close, and she was glad for his warmth. The stars were very bright.

"No. He would have liked to be her adoptive father, though."

Katie had about a million more questions, but they were already at the store. Sam pulled the door open, and she breathed the familiar wave of smells: essential oils, baking, and spices. She loved this store. But then she noted the eerie silence. The cashier stared at them, then glanced away as they got closer.

"Sheldon in his office?" Sam asked. The cashier only nodded.

Sam led the way, flashing Katie an alarmed look just before he opened the door.

CHAPTER THIRTY-EIGHT

K atie wasn't prepared for what she saw in Sheldon's office, and for quite a few moments, she couldn't comprehend what was happening. Maddie was in the office. She should have been at Sam's house, reading, but there she was, sitting on the little couch, her face streaked with tears and eyeliner. Beside her was a little pile of spice bottles. Sheldon was in his office chair, on the phone. He was speaking urgently, in a low voice, with words almost too quiet to hear.

"I don't understand. No, of course, I haven't been...it's not...you have no idea. You're miles away..." When he caught sight of Katie and Sam in the doorway, he leaped up and thrust the phone in Sam's face. "Here," he said. "You talk to her. She's impossible."

Sam looked utterly bewildered, but he took the phone and left the office.

"What's going on?" Katie asked, feeling like her knees

were going to buckle. Had Maddie been attacked? Had she received bad news about her mom while she was shopping? What was she doing here?

"I caught Maddie shoplifting this evening," Sheldon said, and Katie's hand flew up to her mouth.

"Oh Maddie, what?" she asked. She went to Maddie and sat on the couch beside her, putting her arms around her. Maddie stared at the floor. She didn't give any sign that she felt Katie beside her.

Sam came back into the room, silently handing the phone to Sheldon. He took a seat on Sheldon's beach chair, the only available chair in the room. It made him seem at odds with himself, his body relaxed, and his face tense.

"Well?" Sheldon demanded.

"We agreed to talk tomorrow," Sam said. "I can't talk to her when she gets like this. Maddie—shoplifting?"

"You should have left her out of it!" Maddie shouted, coming out of her trance. "She sent me here because she can't deal with things like this. Why did you call her?" She glared at Sheldon.

"Because she should be here," he said.

"This isn't the first time, Maddie?" Katie asked softly.

"Oh no," Sheldon said. "In fact, this is the seventh time I caught her stealing in my store."

Both Katie and Sam stared at Sheldon with open mouths and Maddie burst into tears.

"Shel! Why wouldn't you do something sooner?" Sam said. "This isn't a game—you're playing with a girl's life."

"I'm not playing," Sheldon said. "I wanted to see what

kind of problem it was. Was it a little bit of light-fingered lipstick taking? Or something more compulsive? I think, as you can see from what I found her with today," he indicated the spice bottles next to Maddie, and his voice became very soft, "it's something more compulsive."

Maddie sobbed into her hands, and Katie absently stroked the girl's back, but her mind was reeling. Maddie had been everywhere in her home. She was a compulsive thief? Wait, she'd been working with Lucy for the café. Katie's heart dropped into her stomach. She felt like she had been punched.

She stood. "I need to go," she said. Sam widened his eyes at her, and she saw clearly that he wanted her to stay, that he didn't know what to do, and he needed her help. "I'm sorry," she said to him, to Sheldon, to the room. "I have to check something."

Maddie shuddered, and for one moment, she lifted her head, and her eyes pleaded with Katie, but Katie turned and nearly ran out of the claustrophobic room.

SHE WALKED SWIFTLY through the store and out into the cool night, shivering. She pulled out her phone as she walked.

"Lucy? Hi."

"Do you know what time it is?" Lucy asked.

"Yeah, sorry," Katie said, checking her watch. It was only nine, but they were on café time now. Nine o'clock was like midnight.

Lucy heaved a sigh. "I guess it's okay. What's up?"

"I need to know if Maddie has been around the cash."

"Around the cash? Sure. Of course. I've been having her balance the register at night. That girl is a whiz with numbers."

"Lucy," Katie said, closing her eyes. "She's fourteen."

"So? I was holding down a full-time job by the time I was fourteen. Two full-time jobs."

Katie didn't know what to say to that. "Okay, Luce, I'll talk to you later."

She stuck her phone back in her jacket pocket and walked home quickly, balling her hands into fists and banging them on her thighs as she walked. She tried to talk reason to herself. Even if money was missing, it was just a problem with a troubled teen. No big deal. But she could feel her heart starting to thud in her chest, and by the time she unlocked her front door, she was shaking violently. She walked through the darkened café rooms, back to the lockbox in the kitchen, and opened it with the key on her chain. She stared at the contents, then began trying to balance the cash inside. It took her an hour and four tries, but in the end, it was apparent that $200 was missing, give or take a few dollars. She sighed, slumped over on the counter, her head in her hands.

The doorbell rang, and Katie knew who it was. She didn't want to talk to him, didn't even want to see him. But she answered the door anyway, and there was Sam, standing in front of her, his face frustrated, his hair standing on end. She knew he'd been running his hands through it. She let him into the house, and he turned to her as soon as he was inside.

"How could you leave me back there?" he asked. Katie

stiffened. She had come back to see if Maddie had stolen from her. How could he not know that?

"I needed to check on my café."

"That's what you're thinking about?"

"Two hundred dollars are missing," she said.

He shook his head. "Unbelievable," he said. "That's really what you came home to do. Maddie's in trouble, Katie! I'm sure things are missing from my store. But it doesn't matter when a girl is in trouble."

Katie felt a hot rush of anger wash over her. "She's not my niece!" she said loudly, too loudly. "And it matters to me! I trusted her! I trusted you! I hired her and let her into my business. It hasn't even had a chance. I just wanted it to have a chance." She crossed her arms over her chest, trying not to cry. "This was supposed to be starting over. And I'm back in the same mess."

He shook his head again and took a step back. "What are you even talking about? I came over to talk to you and hopefully get some wisdom for Maddie. But I see I'm on my own because you're completely wrapped up in your own story. Good luck with that."

He left, closing the door softly behind him. He wasn't a door slammer. You could say that for him.

Katie collapsed on the floor, rocking back and forth, her arms around her knees. Familiar waves of panic and shame rolled over her, and she felt as though she had moved back through time to the days after the court case when she could barely even breathe. She had that feeling of being in a different universe, as though she had thought she knew the rules, but everyone was playing a different game, and nothing was in its right place. She began to weep and couldn't stop. Eventually, she pulled herself upstairs and into her bed, finally falling into a dead sleep.

CHAPTER THIRTY-NINE

Katie woke with a massive headache. For a moment, she couldn't locate the reason for her sense of dread, but then the events of the night before crashed over her. She curled up into a ball on her bed, putting a pillow over her head. Everything had come back, all the shame, the panic, the racing heart, and shortness of breath. After a moment, a thought made Katie sit bolt upright. The café would open soon unless she did something to stop it, and Katie knew without a doubt that she couldn't open her restaurant today. Facing people was impossible. Her stomach hurt from just the thought of it. She padded quickly downstairs, opening a drawer to retrieve paper and a Sharpie, and wrote a note for the front door: "Closed for Family Emergency."

Katie hoped it would be enough to deter Lucy and the others. She stood in her front hallway, thinking, then shook her head. Lucy would pound down the door to find out what the family emergency was, and Katie couldn't talk to anyone in this state. She would go to pieces. She shivered and ran back upstairs, throwing toiletries and clothes into a duffel bag. She found the leash and some dog food, hauling it all down to the car and throwing it in the hatchback. She squatted down in front of Sirius and buried her face in his fur. His whole back end was wagging.

"Yes, we're going on a drive, boy," she told him, her voice muffled. She could barely breathe as memories came to her from the night before, shouting at Sam the way she had, his scorn for her. She glanced at her watch. She had time before anyone would turn up, and he deserved a note as well. Overhead, the leaves shook with a breeze. What could she say? Her head was a mess of fears and thoughts and shame. In the end, all she wrote was, "I'm sorry," and then signed it, "Your —uh—best friend."

Food...she needed food, but her heart thudded with the need to get away. She ran back to the kitchen and filled an old produce box with milk, cheese, eggs, fruit, bread, and a few vegetables. She took the spinach and some of the mushrooms that had just come in yesterday. She had been planning to cook them into a quiche for today's special. She stared at the box, regret and pain mingling inside her. *Oh, Katie,* she thought. *You shouldn't have tried something this big. You should have known you would mess it up.*

Her breath caught as panic washed over her in waves. She was hot, then cold. She put spices and herbs in the box, then carried it to the car and pushed it inside, closing the hatch with a bang.

She heard the rumble of a car and her whole body tensed as she turned to look. It was Lucy, who parked and got out of the car slowly. She looked at Katie, then at the sign on the front door, then back at Katie.

"I heard," she said. "Sam told me about the missing money." Her voice was uncharacteristically soft, and her response was so different from what Katie had expected that tears pushed at the backs of her eyes and her throat ached. She pushed her fists into her eyes and gulped deep breaths, trying to regain control. Sirius whined at her feet. Lucy walked to stand beside her.

"You need to get away?" Lucy asked, rubbing her back with one strong hand.

Katie nodded, her eyes still shut tight.

"I get it. Just come back to us, okay? This café is one of the best things that ever happened to this town."

Katie nodded again, though she didn't think there was any way she could ever come back. "Thank you," she said.

"I'm sorry for the part I played in losing the money," Lucy said.

"Oh, Lucy, it's not the money."

"I know that, Katie. Trusting people is hard, and it's a beautiful thing to do. It's not your fault, you know."

Katie shook her head quickly, glancing down at her friend, who looked up at her with an open, earnest face. Katie thought of a picture of the two of them from the opening party, now taped to one of the fridges in the kitchen, Katie tall, pale, freckled, and orange haired, towering over Lucy, who was short, plump, and Asian, with silvery hair, both of them grinning and squeezing each other tight. She didn't believe Lucy when she said it wasn't Katie's fault, but she loved her. She gave her friend a fierce hug and then walked to the house to lock the front door. Lucy stood on the grass and watched as Katie got into the Subaru and drove away.

The door to Grant's Hardware was still closed and locked, the downstairs lights not yet on. Katie could see a light on upstairs, and she was very quiet as she tiptoed up to the front step and shoved her note under the door. Hopefully, it would be enough to keep him from being mad at her forever. She thought of his hair, how soft it was under her hand, of the perfect width of his shoulders, the space between his neck and his shoulder where her head fit perfectly. She thought of his smell as she sat in her car with her hands on the wheel. With a deep breath, she turned the car on and drove away, nearly blind with tears.

CHAPTER FORTY

At the cabin, Sirius ran to visit all his favorite spots outside, and Katie threw the windows open to flush the musty smell out of the rooms. She lugged everything from the car into the house, put the perishables in the fridge and stood in her kitchen, empty-handed and unsure. What now? She turned to look at the vast, turquoise lake through the window. Tiny lights sparkling on ripples called to her, so she walked down to the shore and sat on the stony beach.

She remembered the hope she'd felt the last time she sat here, and felt a wave of sadness and loss. She felt so different right now, as though her brief reverie had been blown out, like a candle. A verse from the Bible came to her, one they had read at the last women's group.

Hope deferred makes the heart sick. A proverb. It was true. Why had Katie allowed herself to hope?

She had walked straight back into the same trap, thinking she knew who and what to believe.

For once, she sank into the memories, allowing them to

wash over her. The day the corporate bosses of her company called her into the head office to stand in front of a panel of men, livid that Katie had helped the women press charges. Their faces. She closed her eyes. They accused her of betraying the family who had taken her in. They treated her like she was stupid.

Katie had been sure that she was doing the right thing. Men who broke the law and hurt women should pay for it. But her bosses told her that she was tearing a family apart, that she was subjecting Philip, a good man, to shame and scandal. Katie had tried to stand up for herself, but in front of the power in that room, she felt like a child. It became hard to tell up from down, what was real from what was a lie. She shrank into a small, accused, shamed version of herself, unable to eat or sleep.

When she spoke with the three women who Philip had harassed against their will, everything seemed clear. He had coerced and threatened them. It wasn't right. But when Philip's wife screamed at her in court, she grew confused again.

Part of the problem was that Katie had believed the lies Philip had told her. He was like a father figure to her, and she had basked in the attention his family gave her, the way they treated her as though she was special. Unknown to her, it was preparation for her to fall in line in case any of his "indiscretions" popped up. But Katie hadn't fallen in line.

At first, she had, it was true. She hadn't believed the notes, emails, and hints the women in her office had given her until it was almost too late. Although only three women pressed charges, many more told her eventually that they would work anywhere but that office if they could. Sexual harassment was a crime. Katie knew that the right thing was to report it, to help the women pursue their rights. But that panel of men thought otherwise. Katie had poked the beast. She knew that beast already.

She buried her face in her hands as she tried to block out the other memories, from way, way back, earlier than her career in human resources. But she was too far gone in shame to protect herself, and memories flooded her from long ago, in culinary school. Katie had always wanted to be a chef and had entered culinary school with the full heart of someone who had been loved and protected her whole life. She had less than one fateful year in school before she walked away from that dream. *Hope deferred makes the heart sick.*

The head chef and teacher had picked her as soon as he laid eyes on her. She was the student he wanted to sleep with that year, or so she had heard from students who had been at the culinary arts college longer. He was handsome, and she was flattered, but Katie would never get involved with someone who was married. She had turned him down, fully believing she had every right to do it.

So he made life hell for her, shouting at Katie more than anyone else, failing her unfairly on tasks she knew she did well. When she went to administration and complained, they brought him in, and he sat in the office talking over her, expertly flipping the script. She'd had a crush on him all year, he said, and wasn't taking rejection well. The accusations of unfairness were part of a childish fit she was having. "You're very pretty," he said, laughing at her, "but I'm married. I'm not looking for an affair."

It was his word against Katie's, and she was not the star chef of the school. She felt humiliated. Not long after, she withdrew from the college, forfeiting the tuition she had already paid and entering a field that was the farthest thing from cooking she could find—human resources in the insurance industry.

The memory of her sorrow and confusion dug at her. She went from feeling that life was fair, that wrong could be exposed and punished, to being very confused about how the world worked. She thought of what Mercy had told her about their work. She and George tried to bring justice to police officers who wrongly targeted innocent black people, and their efforts were frustrated again and again. And yet, they kept on.

Since the day with the chef, Katie had seen more and more of how the world tipped toward the powerful and denied justice to those who had been wronged. But did that mean she was wrong in trying? Were Mercy and George wrong to keep going? Were they "ruining the lives" of the officers they attempted to hold accountable? Never. Had she? *Was it her fault?* Was it her fault that she had believed her boss to be a man of integrity? What about the hours she had spent with his family? Was she wrong to turn against him for what he had done? Was she disloyal? She thought of another teacher at the culinary school.

"Look," the teacher had said. "We all know about Frank. He's kind of nasty. But you won't get this chance again. Can't you just go along with what he wants?"

Was it her fault for not going along with the way things worked?

Katie leaped to her feet and walked the length of the beach, throwing a stick for Sirius, while he retrieved it for her, his whole body wriggling in ecstasy at having her all to himself to play for an entire day. The day passed that way. Katie walked the beach and followed trails, trying to sweat the panic out of her lungs and heart. She couldn't face what had happened with Maddie yet. She needed to sort out the old stuff, going over it again in her head, finding all the shame that had sunk into the cracks.

Why did the world work this way? Why had they not believed her at school? Why had she not believed the women who came to her? Was there any way to truly be objective? Did everyone make choices based on their false beliefs and biases? If so, the world was a very unfair place. And she was part of it. She knew one thing, though. George and Mercy were not wrong in pursuing justice. Maybe, in that space, she could find that she hadn't been wrong, either.

When dusk was falling, and her stomach was hollow with hunger, she went back to the cabin, flicking on every light to send the shadows flying. She breathed in the old fir fragrance of the cabin, the comfort of it, then she cracked eggs and made herself an enormous spinach and mushroom omelet, slicing through the mushrooms cleanly with her chef's knife, adding swiss cheese when the eggs were firm in the pan. She ground sea salt and pepper over the finished omelet and poured herself a glass of wine, then sat in front of the TV, which still was connected to a DVD player. She looked through the box of old DVDs and picked "You've Got Mail." She watched in a stupor, taking small, heavenly bites of the omelet and giving her mind a break from thinking everything through.

She shut the movie off before it was over, padding to the front room to fall asleep on the big bed there. She was both physically achy and heartsore, tired enough that she fell asleep before she had time to obsess about her questions again.

CHAPTER FORTY-ONE

The next morning, Katie woke with pain still in her heart. She went to the kitchen to retrieve the bag of her favorite coffee, inhaling the scent of the grounds, then scooping some into the paper filter in the ceramic drip cone. She poured the hot water from the blue enamelware kettle over the grounds, watching the way they bloomed, breathing in their scent.

Tears came to her eyes suddenly, and she felt her hands trembling as she began to cry. *Just keep moving, girl*, Katie told herself. *Just get some food into you.* She sliced fruit into a bowl, then spooned in the yogurt, weeping. She fixed her coffee with brown sugar and half-and-half, then took her coffee and fruit salad to the little breakfast nook in the corner of the kitchen. She held her face over the coffee and took deep, slow breaths until her tears slowed and she could take a sip. She was shaking.

It was Sam. The disgust in his face. He had always looked at her with such admiration—for how she planned out the menus, for her cooking, for the way she decorated and dreamed and planned. But that look, the way he had seemed to feel such contempt. She'd seen that look before, from other men, ones who had dismissed and condemned her as a troublemaker. She was certain she could never face that look again.

She got up to wash her dishes, then changed into jeans and a T-shirt and called Sirius, who was sniffing around the tall firs in the forest just beyond the cabin.

"We're walking again, boy," she said. "Find a stick!"

At the word stick, he bounded off joyfully. Katie rubbed at her arms, walking to get a water bottle from the car. She hiked swiftly, hoping the sun would warm her soon. She followed a path that meandered around the lake and then up a mountain for a spectacular view. Katie allowed herself to drift, to simply exist, sitting when she felt tired, standing when she was ready to go again. When Katie sat, Sirius flopped beside her, taking short naps while she collected her thoughts, shuffling through them as though if she just got them in the right order, she could understand what had happened to her. Why had she plunged back into such sadness? Why had the past surrounded her again just when she seemed to be able to find a path out of it?

Katie didn't feel angry with Maddie. She felt mad at herself, for the way she couldn't make sense of the world and her lack of clear judgment. What Ed called her willingness to be sloppy. Oh, God, what would she do now? She prayed silently but without hope. She knew she couldn't return to running the café. It had been glorious, but Katie had proved that she still couldn't judge character accurately. She had failed. She flinched as the thought stung her painfully. She stood and kept climbing, unable to sit still. Hunger pinched at her but she ignored it for the moment. Better to keep moving.

The sky was a brilliant blue on the beautiful fall day. Everything was clean and sparkling, and she couldn't help smiling at Sirius's failed attempts to chase crows. Should she take Ed up on his business idea? He wanted her back, and she wasn't sure if Sam wanted her anymore. She thought about what it would mean. Offices. The city. Ed finding a thousand ways to make her feel small, all with a smile on his face. Scolding her for dreaming. She shuddered. No, she would never do that.

What did she want? She knew what she wanted. Desire was as close to her as breathing, she could see her longing clearly. She wanted the last weeks back. She wanted the weeks before she knew that the girl who handled her cash had been pocketing it. That someone she had loved and cared about had betrayed her. Again.

Katie wanted the café life back, waking at dawn to get ready, asleep on her feet by eight. She wanted Sam in her house, fixing things or puttering around muttering about molding and wainscoting. She wanted Sam with the soft look he got when she touched his face. Not the bad look he had given her. *You can't have it,* Katie told herself. *Better not to think about it.*

She wanted her belief that the world was fair. She certainly couldn't have that. The last years had been like a gradual waking to an unwanted reality, a reality that many people had lived their entire lives. Whether or not she wanted her fairytale reality back, it had never been real.

Hunger finally drove her back to the cabin. Katie rummaged through her food and came up with something for a light pasta sauce. As she boiled water and chopped basil, she thought about Maddie, really thought about her, for the first time. What kind of pain must the girl be in to be stealing bottles of spices? She had known there was pain in Maddie, but she hadn't realized just how deep that hurt went, that she would risk so much. And Sam? How was he handling it? With his quirky mom and his absent sister, what was he doing for Maddie? Could he see that stealing was about more than just taking? That it was about control, much the way that Katie's refusal to leave her apartment had been about control when she had been chased by panic so often.

Maybe Maddie was anxious, like Katie, and as Katie remembered her hunched shoulders, her little pale, pinched face, she knew the answer: Of course she was anxious, and maybe taking things made her feel a bit better. She thought about how Maddie always protected her mother. Even when she was in trouble for stealing, she had leaped to defend her mom.

Katie bowed her head, feeling pity wash over her. No wonder Sam had looked at her that way. When she thought back, she saw it wasn't the same look her bosses had given her. It was simple disappointment. Sam was disappointed that Katie had left her young friend, that she hadn't been there to lean on, which was what Maddie needed.

Katie took her food to the couch and ate slowly, still thinking. Katie had behaved as though Maddie's stealing was all about her, unable to get through her own pain to reach her young friend. In a flash of insight, she saw that they had all blindly trusted, except, perhaps Sheldon, who had his eyes open. How could they have known? A tiny burden lifted from her shoulders. It was impossible to know everything.

But Katie knew she could never return to running the café. Her old fears had invaded her new life, and she had lost the flame of hope for a better, less fearful life, one where she wouldn't be shamed for making wrong decisions. Katie had thought that Aveline would heal her and give her a reason for living. She had hoped that maybe the reason included the man named Sam, this boy she had known when she was young, one of the brave kids who jumped off the dock with his eyes wide open, his bony shoulder blades like little wings.

She had found safety in her dreams here, but that shelter was damaged now, and Katie was sure it could never be repaired. And she had broken Sam's trust. She sat in the dark for a long time, mourning that trust.

MADDIE COULDN'T SLEEP after Sheldon caught her and called Sam and Katie to the store. Maddie had made Katie run away. It was what Maddie always did. She was too much. Her heart hurt. She was still tossing and turning at dawn. She wanted to go for a walk and think, maybe go down to the lake, maybe throw herself in. No, just kidding—she wouldn't have the guts. Her eyes felt swollen and sore. She avoided the mirror, knowing how bad she probably looked. She always got a pink nose and red eyes like a rabbit when she cried.

Finally, Maddie eased downstairs on tiptoe. Just before she opened the front door, she saw a piece of paper on the ground and picked it up. It was addressed to her uncle, but Maddie opened it anyway. She was a criminal already, no use pretending. It only had a few words scrawled on it.

"I'm sorry,

Your—uh—best friend."

Maddie opened the door, putting the note in her pocket. She jogged the two blocks to Katie's house, breathing heavily by the time she got there. There was a note on the door, and Katie's car was gone. From the sidewalk, Maddie squinted to read what it said, and finally, after taking a few steps closer, saw that it read, "Closed for Family Emergency." She knew what that meant. Family Emergency was what her mother told people when she got up to leave and knew she would never come back. It was what she said when she dropped Maddie off at the bus station by herself, never planning, it seemed, to retrieve her daughter. Maddie sat on the sidewalk and cried. She knew she wouldn't give Sam the note. He didn't need to see that Katie had put him in the friend zone before she left without even saying goodbye. After a while, she rubbed at her eyes and walked back to the store with a heart heavier than anything she could ever fit in the pockets of her jacket.

CHAPTER FORTY-TWO

S am peeked into Maddie's room and saw her asleep on
her bed, her eyes shut tight, blankets wound all around
her. He didn't wake her. The past two days had been hard on
her. Hard on everyone. He went to the kitchen and scooped
coffee into the coffee maker, turning it on and pulling out his
bowl to pour his cereal, a ritual he never had to think about.
But the box came up light in his hand, and when he looked
inside, he saw only a few spare cornflakes dusting the bottom
of the bag. Maddie had eaten the last of them. He stood there
looking into the empty box for a moment, then reached for
some of her granola and sliced a banana over it, adding milk
and taking the bowl to his counter in front of the window.

Fall had come, and though it was after six in the morning,
the sky was still dark. The paperboy rode his bicycle down
the street, throwing papers by the glow of the streetlight. The
last days had been terrible, and Sam felt the ache of them still
sitting inside his ribcage. Two nights ago Sheldon had called
them in. Then Sam had said stupid things and hurt Katie,

and the next day, Lucy had come barreling over to his house and told him that Katie was gone. She'd packed up her car and left. Sam had gone over and read the sign on her door. He had stood there feeling hollowed out, as though his insides were missing.

He took a bite of granola and pulled out his phone to read the news, but it couldn't hold his attention. He shifted, feeling itchy and irritable. Nothing satisfied him like it used to. When he ate the food he made for himself, he wondered what Katie would do to make it taste better. When he sat with his books, working on figures and balanced columns, he thought about how Katie would have music playing, and he wished he was at a table in her café, working while she sang in the kitchen. Life had become bland when she wasn't around.

He closed his eyes, seeing all six feet of her in his mind: golden skin and freckles, red hair falling around her or twisted up so that her lovely neck was visible, her wide-set green eyes, the tiny gap between her two front teeth, the way she bit her bottom lip when she was worried. The way she stared off into the distance when she tasted her cooking. He stood, pushing his chair back. The coffee was ready. He poured himself a cup.

Yesterday had been like a bad dream. Katie was gone, but Sam also had to deal with Sheldon, and talk things out with Maddie, who cried the whole day. Sam talked to his sister on the phone—she cried, too—and explained things to his mother, who didn't understand, apparently, why Sam hadn't seen that something was going on with Maddie.

He had learned that Maddie had been arrested and done

community time for theft before Theresa sent her to live with them. Sam felt angry and betrayed by his sister, how could she send Maddie to them after such a thing, without even telling them what to expect? He was mad at pretty much everyone.

Nothing hurt more, though, than when Katie stood up and left Sheldon's office, looking out for herself before anyone else in the room.

She hadn't been there for him or Maddie. He couldn't believe she would leave like that, thinking only of herself. And she was still gone. She hadn't even called or texted to see how he was doing.

He gulped his coffee down, nearly scalding his mouth, then pulled on track pants and shoes and went outside. Sam had been meeting Frankie weekly to run but couldn't wait for their day. He'd been so busy with both Maddie and Katie that he had become a little off balance. The air was clear and crisp, smelling of autumn. He breathed it in and started to jog, feeling the familiar burn in his chest as he warmed up. He headed to the path by the lake. Memories were everywhere. He, Katie, and Maddie at the lake. He tried to push the thoughts away, but they wouldn't leave.

He had a sinking feeling in his stomach as a single thought slowly dawned on him. He'd been too harsh with Katie. He was actually angry at Maddie and his sister, but he had taken it out on Katie because she was the only one he could rely on—not his mother, his sister, or his niece. He had become used to his family being full of people he couldn't count on. Katie had burst in as a welcome change. She thought about him. She made him food or left a glass of ice water on the stairs when he was working on the porch. Beyond all that, she was intelligent and big-hearted. But then, in a crisis, she had let him down, despite how badly he needed her.

But was Sam being fair? What could he expect of people? The answers eluded him. This was the real reason he had wanted to stay separate from other people. He never knew what expectations to hold, and it seemed that he always came out a fool.

The sky grew brilliant with the sunrise. Sam was in the rhythm of running now, his feet pounding the path, flying along. Birds called overhead, and the lake water made whispery sounds on the rocks beside him. Sam had known that Katie was hurt, that she had gone through trauma and was having a hard time just getting through the days. He had become her friend knowing that, he had started to love her knowing that, yet he had expected more of her than she could offer. Maybe Sam wasn't as blameless as he had imagined, yesterday and this morning. He finished his run at five kilometers and walked it off, heading home. He needed to talk to someone.

CHAPTER FORTY-THREE

After he showered and changed, Sam walked to the church. He checked his watch. It was eight o'clock. Time for his store to open. He texted Larry:

Need a moment.

Open, please?

He got a thumbs up and walked into the cool, wood-smelling church. He stood for a moment in the old sanctuary, soaking in the quiet that always seemed to center him, then strode back to the little room that Francisco used as an office. He knocked lightly, though the door was ajar.

"Come in," he heard. Frankie was sitting at his desk, writing in a journal. He wore jeans and a T-shirt. No clerical collar. He turned as the door swung open.

"Hey, Sam," he said, his face changing as he noticed the look on Sam's face. "Whoa, friend, what's going on?"

"Do you have a minute to talk?"

"Always," Frankie said. He pointed at his armchair. "Have a seat."

Sam sank into the old chair and looked at his friend.

"I need to run a scenario by you, and you need to tell me if I'm the good guy or the bad guy in this scenario."

Frankie looked at him for a few heartbeats, then sat back and crossed his arms. He smiled. "I suspect that if you have to ask, you know the answer."

"Humor me, Reverend."

"Go ahead—I'm listening."

"Okay," Sam said, running his hands along his thighs. "Imagine that you went through something really big and you needed a friend to stand by you. But the really big thing made her feel panicky, and she ran away rather than standing by you. So then you went and berated her for running away, and you made her feel worse, and then she disappeared." He paused. "Are you the good guy or the bad guy?"

"Sam."

"I know, I know, there is no good guy and no bad guy. But do you think I did the wrong thing?"

"I wasn't going to say there is no good guy or bad guy. I was going to say you're obviously the bad guy in that scenario." Frankie laughed.

"You're only partly kidding, I'm guessing," Sam said. His stomach hurt.

"Only partly." Frankie was silent for a few minutes, watching Sam. "I assume you're talking about Katie and the situation with Maddie?" he finally asked. "Sheldon told me," he said, at Sam's look of surprise.

Sam only nodded.

"Aren't you in a relationship with Katie?"

"Yes," he said. "Well. I think so."

"I think so too. Let me run another version of the story by you. My wife used to tell me that every woman needs something different from a man. Seems like Katie needs to feel safe. When you got mad at her, it only emphasized that she wasn't safe. Even though I was joking about being the bad guy, there isn't really a right or a wrong in that situation. It's relationship stuff. Neither of you got what you needed when you needed it. She needed to feel safe. You needed her to stand by you. But that's people. We can't always deliver." Frankie took a sip of coffee from a cup on his desk, leaning back in his chair and looking at the ceiling. "It's like Jesus asking the disciples to pray with him before he died. And they just kept falling asleep." He looked at Sam and smiled, the familiar smile lines fanning out from his eyes. "We're in good company."

Sam put his elbows on his knees and dropped his head into his hands.

"You always make so much sense," he mumbled. He had needed to feel that Katie was there for him. When she disappointed him, he made her feel worse about what she was going through. Maybe it was understandable, but he still felt like a total jerk. "What do I do now?"

"Do you want Katie in your life?" Francisco asked.

He nodded, his heart aching.

"Excellent. Finally, you're being honest. Okay, Monkman. You need to repair it. Let her know she's safe with you. She loves you—it's obvious—and you'd be an idiot to let her get away. You are sometimes quite an idiot so I wouldn't put it past you. But you don't have to lose her. Find a way to reassure her. You know what she needs, and you care. That's all you can do."

"But she left."

"Do you know where she is?"

As soon as Frankie asked, Sam realized that he knew exactly where she was. She had gone looking for safety.

"Yes, actually, I think I do."

"So, go to her. Take the first step."

Sam stood. "Thanks, man," he said.

"Always," Frankie answered.

Sam turned at the door. "By the way," he said. "What about you?"

Frankie looked up from where he had gone back to his writing.

"What about me?"

"What about love for you?" Sam asked.

"I had love," Frankie said. "It was enough for a lifetime."

Sam wasn't sure about that, as he left Frankie sitting alone at his desk. But he soon forgot about Frankie's life as he climbed into his truck, his heart nearly bursting as he threw it in gear and drove back toward town. *Repair things,* he thought. It wasn't nearly as complicated as he thought. But he needed to work on repairing things with Maddie first. Maybe then he would know what to do about Katie.

MADDIE SLIPPED into the therapist's room silently, closing the door behind her, so quietly that it took the therapist a moment to notice Maddie was there. After a minute, the woman looked up. Maddie, in the meantime, had been watching her. She was tall, with dark brown skin and short, curly hair, shaved on one side. The therapist was beautiful—and familiar. She stood and walked over to Maddie, holding out a hand.

"I'm Faith," she said. "Maybe you know my parents, George and Mercy?"

Maddie shrugged. "I think I met them at Katie's opening. You too, maybe?"

"I think so. It's nice to meet you again, Maddie." She gestured with one hand. "Let's sit on the couches."

"Is it a coincidence that you're my therapist?" Maddie asked, hanging back.

"No, your uncle asked me if I would be willing to take on a new client and I told him, of course I would. I've known him and your grandma since I was a kid."

"How old are you?" Maddie asked, sitting on one of the couches while Faith settled herself on the other.

"I'm twenty-four," Faith said. "But...we're here to talk about you. And specifically, what you've been up to."

Maddie clenched her hands and put them under her legs. She didn't want to talk about it.

"First of all—have you stolen since you got caught?"

Maddie's heart beat wildly as she hesitated, then gave a slow nod.

"What was it? And from where?"

Maddie reached into her pocket and pulled out a duck-shaped paperweight. She held it out to Faith, her palm flat so that the duck sort of rocked on her hand for a minute before becoming still.

"You stole that from the receptionist's desk?" Faith asked. She blinked, then seemed to realize her mouth was hanging open. She closed it and leaned back in her chair, looking at Maddie.

"Aren't you going to take it?"

"No, I'm not. Put it on the table for a minute. What was it about that duck that made you steal it?"

Maddie sat up a little straighter. No one had ever asked her that question—not her mother or Sheldon, not the police, not Sam.

"What do you mean?" she asked.

"Well, I'm guessing you don't need a duck. Or several bottles of spices. Or soup stock. So what is it?"

Maddie mumbled something.

Faith cupped a hand behind her ear. She had silver bracelets and long beautiful hands. Maddie felt small and plain beside her. She spoke a little louder. "The way they feel when I hold them. The weight, the size, the roundness."

Faith smiled. "Now we're getting somewhere. Okay. I'm going to teach you something called changing the channel. Here's what we're going to do..."

A WHILE LATER, Maddie left Faith's office with a tear-stained face and, for the first time in ages, hope in her heart. She walked to the receptionist's desk slowly but with determination, and when she reached it, she held out her hand again, palm flat, the duck balancing on it. The woman looked up. She had gray hair and a shirt with dancing kittens on it.

"I took this earlier," Maddie said, reciting the words that

Faith had told her to say. "I'm sorry that I took something that belonged to you." The woman smiled, and her eyes were kind as she took the duck back from Maddie.

"Thanks," she said. "My granddaughter gave that to me. I would have been very sad to lose it."

Maddie felt sadness and happiness at the same time as she made her way out to Sam's truck. He sat in the driver's seat, reading something on his phone.

"How'd it go?" he asked, as she let herself into the truck.

"It was okay," she said. "You didn't tell me you knew my therapist."

He shrugged. "It's a lot harder to find a person I don't know in this town than to find someone I know. Faith is great. She helped your grandma after Grandpa died."

"She gave me homework," Maddie said.

"She did? Is it hard?"

Maddie nodded. "Very hard. I have to start now." She reached into her back pocket and pulled out the wrinkled piece of folded paper. "Here," she said. "I took this. I'm sorry I took something that belonged to you."

Sam unfolded the paper and looked at it, staring at the words. Maddie knew what it said:

"I'm sorry,

Your—uh—best friend."

To Maddie's surprise, a huge grin split Sam's face.

He put a hand on her shoulder, still smiling. "Thanks," he said.

"Don't say thanks yet," she said, her voice glum. "There's a lot more coming."

CHAPTER FORTY-FOUR

Air rushed into the open windows of Sam's truck as he drove along the curving lakeside road. Glimpses of late afternoon sunlight lit the interior of the truck from between the trees. All afternoon he had thought he would never get away from the store, but finally, he made a break for it, apologizing to Larry a hundred times for making him open and close on the same day.

Larry only grinned. "As long as you don't hire my mother again, we're fine."

Sam rounded a sharp corner a little too fast, then forced himself to slow down. It wouldn't do anyone any good if he crashed into a tree. For a moment, he considered the possibility that he was wrong about where Katie had gone. But Sam knew his friend. He knew what spoke to her and healed her. He didn't think she would have gone anywhere else.

It wasn't long before he saw he had guessed right. He pulled into the little parking lot in front of the cluster of lakeside cottages and right away he spotted her car parked under the firs in front of one of the cabins. It was the one beside the A-frame, just as she had told him. Sam's heart thudded and he jumped out, walking around the truck to retrieve a box from the passenger seat. He knocked on the door of the cabin, shifting the box to hold it under one arm. He waited but didn't hear anything, not even Sirius jumping up to investigate.

After a moment, he turned the handle and opened the door. "Katie?" he called. Silence.

It was a small space, perfectly neat, with bright open windows on the lake side of the house. Something smelled heavenly, and he walked back to the kitchen, leaning over the stove to breathe in the fragrance of the sauce simmering in a bright steel pot. He turned, and his heart started pounding in earnest as he caught a glimpse of Katie through the open window. She was on the lakeshore with her dog.

He set the box gently on the dining room table and went to her, loping down the stairs of the back deck, and onto the stones of the beach. She hadn't seen him yet. Her back was turned to him, and she was throwing a stick for Sirius, her arm arcing over her head. She glanced up as he approached, and froze. She stared at him for a long moment, all the color drained from her face, and then he opened his arms, and she walked right into them.

He held her and smelled fresh air, sun-warmed skin, and that faint scent of roses. She pressed her face into his neck, and he felt waves of gratitude because he hadn't lost her—she wanted him, and they were standing together on a pebble-strewn shore with the sun sparking along the water.

When she pulled back enough to look up at him, his arms

tightened. Her eyelashes were spiky and wet with tears, but she smiled.

"You found me," she said, and then he kissed her, tasting her mouth and her face, covering her with kisses, trying with everything in him to tell her how much she meant to him. The world was lips and warmth and breath. He felt as though he was drowning in her. But then she pulled away, suddenly, and in the hollowness she left, he thought he would cave in on himself. She was so beautiful, her loose cinnamon hair swirling around her arms, brilliant, tall, golden. She stood looking at him, Sirius nudging the stick in her hand and whining. With a smooth motion, she threw the stick for the dog. Then she sighed and spoke.

"Oh, Sam...we need to talk."

He nodded. He still hadn't said a word. Katie spoke again.

"Come up to the cabin with me," she said. She walked in front of Sam, but he caught up to her and held her hand, weaving his fingers between hers. They went back into the kitchen through the patio door, the way he had come out, and she paused for a heartbeat to look at the box of things on the table.

"I see you identified which house was mine," she said, smiling at him.

He cleared his throat, unsure that his words would come out right.

"I figured you wouldn't mind," he said. "I've been in and out of your house in town for months now."

A cloud crossed her lovely face, and he wondered if she

was thinking about the trust she had offered to him and by default, to Maddie. How was he going to fix this?

"What did you bring?" she asked, standing by the stove to stir the sauce. She lifted the wooden spoon to her mouth and tasted the sauce, looking off into the distance in that dreamy way she had, needing to sense whether the flavors were right. She added salt and ground some pepper in, then tasted it again, nodding to herself.

Sam went to the box. There was an envelope on top addressed to Katie. Sam took it out and placed it to one side.

"Peace gifts," he said. "Parmesan, olive oil, grapes, dark chocolate, three more kinds of cheese..." He trailed off as he looked up to see her looking at him, leaning against the stove, a small smile on her face and her arms crossed in front of her.

"Well done. Some men would just bring flowers," she said.

"There are flowers in here, too," he said. "Katie, I'm so sorry for what I said. I'm sorry for not understanding."

She stared at him, her face intent. A breeze lifted the curtain beside her, snapping it out like a sail.

"It was how you looked at me, Sam. Like you couldn't bear to be in the same place as me. Like you despised me."

"I don't deal well with not getting what I feel I need," he said. "It's a major fault. But I could never despise you, Katie."

Her eyes burned into him. Suddenly she turned back to the stove and stirred the sauce again. "I've thought a lot about what happened, too," she said. And I'm really sorry that I walked out on Maddie. She needed me. You needed me. But the things that happened to me before I came to Aveline are still so fresh. I'm not sure how to get over the fear."

He watched her as she stood at the stove, her shoulders hitched up, stirring the sauce longer than she needed to. He went to her and turned her slowly around, taking the spoon from her and laying it on the counter, where it splashed a cheerful tomato smear across the tiles. He pulled her close to him and held her gently.

"I love you, Katie Grace." He heard her breath catch in her throat. "And I will love you when you are weak and when you are reigning in your café, when you have to run away and when you spend hours helping a young girl find clothes because her clueless uncle didn't realize she didn't have any. You are a wonder. I'm so sorry that you were hurt, and I'm sorry that I hurt you again. I love you no matter what, I—" but he didn't get any more words out because she leaned forward and caught his mouth with hers and he tasted tomato sauce and relaxed into the way she seemed to surround him completely.

CHAPTER FORTY-FIVE

Later, Katie scooped each of them a swirl of spaghetti noodles and added a large spoonful of the red sauce, topping the dishes with shavings of parmesan and fresh basil. Sam carried the heavy ceramic bowls to the patio. The salad was already on the table, along with a candle that wavered in the slight breeze of the evening. The lake was still, the last violets and indigos of the day sky reflecting on its surface, the trees like brushes against the sky. They sat and looked at each other.

"Silent prayer?" Katie asked. Sam nodded and closed his eyes, feeling gratitude wash over him again. He heard an owl calling in the distance, and his heart reached out to God, offering trust, asking for peace. He opened his eyes.

"Bon appetit," Katie said, before she took a forkful of pasta, lifting it to her mouth. Sam did the same, sighing as the flavors exploded on his tongue—the richness of tomatoes that had been simmering all day, the faint tang of the cheese, and the herbs, zingy and mellow in perfect balance.

"I don't know how you do this," he said. "But I know that your café is the best thing that has happened to Aveline in a long time."

He glanced up at her as he said it, smiling, and was startled to see her face fall and crumple, as though she might cry. She took a shaky breath and put her fork down.

"Yeah," she said, her voice cracking, "about that. I'm really sorry, Sam, but I'm not sure that I can go back to running the café. I might need to sell it."

He felt her words like a fist in his gut, leaving him breathless. Sell it? All the time he had put into the house, into the restaurant and the kitchen and her bedroom. All for her. And she would sell his work? But he had made the mistake of reacting too quickly the other day, lashing out at her. He kept quiet and ate, slowly, savoring every bit of the pasta until he had scraped his bowl clean. He scooped himself some salad and ate that too, thinking all the while. He loved this woman, but he didn't know how to help her.

When he finished eating, he finally looked up. Katie sat watching him with her face resting on her hands, elbows on the table, a small, sad smile on her face. Her freckles stood out in the candlelight, and the flickering glow did something strange to the color of her eyes, turning them golden instead of green. He reached across the table and touched her face, and she caught his hand and kissed it, sending tremors through him.

"You can't sell the café," he said.

Her face fell. "I guessed you would think that way," she said. "But I've thought it through. I was wrong to imagine I could do it."

"Katie. What do you mean? You love that café. You're radiant there." He felt a bit of desperation, wanting to convince her. She seemed so decided.

"I do love it. But I have a fatal flaw. I can't be trusted with something like this."

"You're still listening to your sorry excuse of an ex-boyfriend," he said, trying to keep the snarl out of his voice. Not succeeding.

She sat back in her chair. Her eyes were sad and very serious. "I don't want to talk about this if you won't listen," she said.

He sighed and ran a hand through his hair. "Okay. I'll listen. But after you're done, will you give me a chance to respond? Can I try to change your mind?"

She smiled and leaned across the table, grabbing his hand.

"Yes," she said, "but I want to be comfortable. Let's get ice cream and sit on the couch." She gestured to the outdoor couch that faced the lake.

"You have ice cream? How did you get it out here without it melting?" he asked.

"A cooler," she said, disappearing into the house. Her voice trailed out from the kitchen. "With ice. I knew I was going to need ice cream at some point. I may have run away, but I didn't run without being prepared."

She reappeared, holding two bowls heaped with ice cream. Sam's eyes widened at the size of the servings.

"I've been doing nothing but walking since I got here," she said. "I figure I can eat a little ice cream."

"I can't say the same for myself," he said. "Lately I've been eating and then eating more. Someone beautiful has been feeding me." He took a bowl and sank into the couch, gazing at the stars that were slowly appearing over the lake. A faint whispering came from the water lapping onto the stones on the shore. It was beautiful. "I'm definitely going to have to keep running with Frankie in the mornings if you're going to keep feeding me."

"Oh, I'm going to feed you," she said. "I just don't know if I'm going to feed the town." She sat down sideways on the other end of the couch, leaning against the armrest with a pillow behind her, stretching her legs to put her feet in his lap.

Sam took a bite of his ice cream—vanilla, with bits of chocolate and caramel scattered throughout. The sky was dark now, the stars brilliant against the blackness. A chilly breeze blew up from the lake and Katie shivered. Sam pulled a blanket off the back of the couch and arranged it around them.

"Okay, go," he said. "Try to tell me why it's a good idea for you to sell the restaurant."

She took a deep breath. "So...I told you about what happened at my old job. I listened to the wrong person, believing the perpetrator, doing too little too late to stop him." Sam started to shake his head, but she put a hand up to stop him. "Something is missing in me. I have some fatal lack of judgment. I misjudged Ed, my old bosses—all of them really, not just Philip—and now, no offense, Maddie."

"No offense taken."

"I really thought they were all going to do their best by me. But they were all deceiving me, Sam. Do you know how that feels? Maybe you do. I don't know why I trust people so hard, and then I get so wholly spun around when they're false. I'm completely shocked every time." She gazed out at the lake, her face so sad that Sam wanted to pull her into his arms. But he had promised to listen, and this was important. He took another bite of ice cream as she went on. "So I think that someone like me shouldn't be running a café. I have staff, and customers, and the person in charge of all that needs to have clear sight when it comes to people, don't you think? I owe it to them." She let out a shaky sigh. "And then there's what it does inside of me, how I shrivel when I find out I've believed the wrong person. It tears me up inside. Yesterday I was thinking about this proverb: 'A hope deferred makes the heart sick.' That's how I feel. Heartsick. I think I'm done with hoping. I need to find something I can do that doesn't involve staff, or customers, or people at all."

Sam thought carefully as he scraped the last drops of ice cream from the bottom of his bowl. He was relieved. If she had said that she hated cooking or didn't want to be in charge of making meals for so many people, there was nothing he could do about that. But this was about confidence and mistakes. This was about a story she told herself. He thought this was fixable. He believed, he knew the Aveline Café was right for her. Now, all he needed was to get through to her.

"Did you read the second part of that proverb?" he asked.

She shook her head. "I don't remember," she said.

"Okay, wait," Sam said. "First things first. Back in a sec." He carefully moved her feet off his lap and went to the kitchen to retrieve the envelope he had left there. He sat down again and put her feet back on his lap, arranging the blanket around them. Then he gave her the envelope and a small clay bird.

"Oh!" Katie exclaimed. "My bird! I haven't been able to find it. What's this?"

"Open and see. It's from Maddie."

Her eyes filled with sorrow as he said Maddie's name, and she looked down at the envelope in her hand for a long moment. She settled the bird on the blanket and opened the envelope carefully, pulling out a folded piece of paper. A wad of cash fell into Katie's lap as she unfolded the paper, and she touched it lightly with her fingertips. From where Sam sat, he could see that the notes were twenties. Katie drew a breath and began to read the letter out loud.

"Dear Katie, I took these things from you. I'm sorry that I took something that didn't belong to me." Katie sat in silence for a few heartbeats, then went on. "I've never loved doing anything as much as I loved working for you. I'm so sorry. I've been sick, and I've done a lot of wrong things, but I'm getting help now. Love, Maddie. PS. Please come back."

There was a pause, and Sam looked at Katie's face and then at the stars over the lake. "I can see why you love it here," he said.

"Yes," she whispered. "It's beautiful, isn't it?"

"She is getting help. She's seeing Faith for therapy, and this letter is just one example of what she's been doing all over town, only in person. Faith said she could write you a letter because you were away. She seems... lighter... than she has in a long time."

"Is this your turn?" Katie asked.

"No, that was Maddie's turn. This is my turn."

He looked at her, sitting wrapped in a blanket, her hair tied up in a messy bun, her eyes on his face, her dark eyebrows, so startling on a redhead.

"The whole proverb goes like this," he said. "'Hope deferred makes the heart sick, but a longing fulfilled is a tree of life.' Everyone makes mistakes and trusts the wrong people, Katie. Your jerk of an ex-boyfriend made you believe it's a character flaw particular to you, but I was fooled by Maddie, too. The truth is, the truth that you taught me..." she looked up suddenly, her lovely face startled, and put a hand on her chest as if to say, "me?" He nodded. "The truth that you taught me is that a clean and orderly life without disappointment is a small life. And if you want to live a big life it's going to be messy, and that's good, that's okay because messy means that you're living! I understand if you don't want to come back to work in your café, but only if you don't like it anymore. Because I think you seemed right at home there, and trusting people isn't wrong. If you trust people and they let you down, it's because you have *people*, people with failings, in your life, and that's what a big life is. I wanted a life for God only, a monk life. But I'm learning to love him through loving people, even with every horrible messy thing that comes along with it. Like my niece stealing from my best friend, which causes the love of my life to run away after I mess up and shout at her." He smiled at the look on her face. "You're just learning about this love from God. You're absolved, Katie. From making the wrong call, believing the wrong person. You don't need to hang onto it anymore. You can cook food and feed people freely, from love, because I think that's who God made you to be."

She stared at him.

"That's a pretty good argument," she said, slowly, and he gazed back at her for several long moments before he leaned in to kiss her, the stars and the lake gleaming, the black outlines of the tallest trees making slashes in the sky all around them.

CHAPTER FORTY-SIX

After Sam left, Katie spent two more days at the cabin, thinking, dreaming, and deciding.

She walked for miles, throwing a stick for Sirius until her arms burned. She cooked and ate slowly, on the patio, savoring every flavor. She tried new recipes of her own invention. She spent time with her journal, writing lists: things she loved to do, things that scared her, things that gave her life, things that felt like they sucked the life straight out of her.

The list of things that gave her life included: Nana's house, walking and dreaming, cooking, serving food to friends or strangers, Sam, Sirius, gardening with Maddie, women's circle, visiting farms or the farmer's market, and thinking up new recipes. After she finished with her list, she could see a clear picture of her new life at the Aveline Café, as though God had led her straight here, waiting for her to get sick of a life without reverie in her old career in the city.

The Aveline Café was perfect for Katie, and it became obvious that she shouldn't leave. She spent hours in the sunshine, at the table with a cup of coffee or tea, drawing in her journal, and thinking about what had triggered such a strong response in her heart. In the end, Katie knew she couldn't listen to the fear. The trauma was in her past. She had been badly hurt before, but the fear was out of proportion in her life in the present, especially with Maddie, who was just a kid after all, also hurt and bound to fail sometimes.

Katie called Mercy and asked if she could host women's circle out at the lake.

"I want to cook for all of you," she told her new friend.

"Are you sure?" Mercy asked. "Lucy told us what happened. Are you ready to host a group of rowdy women?"

"I would love to make something special for you, and I think I need company." Katie paused, trying to ratchet up her courage. "I need my new friends," she finally got out.

"We're more than friends," Mercy told her, her voice soft. "We're your sisters. I'll talk to the others and see what they think. But speaking for myself, I would love any chance to eat your food." She got back by text a little later.

It's on, the text read. Get ready.

Katie smiled and started to prepare.

While she cooked for the women, Katie thought about how hard it had been to ask them to come, how non-intuitive it was for her to try to draw close. She had assumed they would want to be far from her when she was in her worst moments. Why was that? Why did she pull away when others were drawing close? The questions tugged at her. She didn't have answers, but she thought she was starting to see clearly.

She cooked risotto and salmon and filled the cabin with

candles. When her friends arrived, they flowed into the house, exclaiming over the beautifully lit cabin and large back deck.

"We need to have women's circle here at least once a month," Lucy declared.

"That's fine," Katie said, grinning. "Except for the months when my parents stay here, or there are renters."

"As often as we can," Lucy amended.

Faith and Dorothy weren't able to make it that night, so only Mercy, Ingrid, Lucy, and Zoe had come. They all ate at a table on the back deck, watching the stars over the lake. Katie closed her eyes as she tasted the risotto, flavors of rosemary and thyme mixed with cream that mellowed and softened the flavors. The salmon was perfectly grilled and zesty with lemon, sharp with pepper. The women moaned over their food and praised it. Katie waved off their praise but was filled with the happy feeling she had when people liked her food, like a perfect fit. When the air grew chilly, they cleared the table and brought their glasses of wine to the couches inside the cabin. Mercy pulled an afghan over herself. Ingrid tucked her feet up, showing off her striped socks.

"So tell us," Zoe said. "What's going on?"

"What did Lucy tell you?" Katie asked. Lucy shifted, looking around the room. "As much as I know," she confessed. "I was worried about you and wanted to ask them to pray."

"So... you know about my past already. And you know I have a hard time with people breaking my trust. I think the revelation that Maddie had stolen from me felt like something I couldn't overcome. I wanted to be a brand new person in Aveline. But my pain followed me, and when I discovered the theft, I felt like I was in a loop, trusting the wrong people, again and again. I thought I would have to sell the café."

"What?" Lucy said. "No!"

"You think that because you don't always know who to trust, that your judgment can't be trusted," Mercy said. "Is that right?"

"Yes," Katie said, grateful for the understanding.

"It's a load of crap," Mercy added.

"What?" Katie asked, shocked at the quick turnaround. Zoe, Ingrid, and Lucy were nodding in agreement. Mercy went on.

"Ask me how many lawyers I have trusted who turned their backs on me when I was making waves with my push for police accountability. They don't want to rock the boat. I can't blame them, in a way, but I have no choice but to rock the boat hard. It's been rocked for me."

There was silence for a few minutes. Once again, Katie took in the gravity of what Mercy was doing with her life. The Aveline Café was easy in comparison.

"I've trusted the wrong people too," Ingrid said after a while. "Mostly men."

"People are complex," Lucy said.

"True," Mercy added. "Some people are trustworthy in some ways but not in others. You're not in some special category, Katie."

"Unless it's the category of women who have caught the eye of Sam Grant," Lucy said. The other women burst out laughing while Katie felt a fierce blush rise to her face. "That man was blind to any female until the very first day you came to town."

"He was my first kiss," Katie admitted. They all stared at her. "Back when I was eleven," she amended, and the room exploded in noise as they laughed. After a while, things calmed down again. "Well, thanks for being honest," Katie said. "You'll be happy to know that I already decided to keep the café open. And to keep things open between Sam and me." She smiled, shyly, as the women started exclaiming, and things grew loud again.

Mercy grabbed Katie's hand as the women were leaving, just before she went out the door. "Don't forget that broken people are worth it, even when they break your trust. And Maddie's young. Young people are always worth it."

Katie nodded. "I know," she said. "Thank you." Mercy nodded and left, slinging an arm around Lucy as they walked out to the van together.

CHAPTER FORTY-SEVEN

Katie woke to soft morning light filtering through dancing tree branches. She stretched and smiled, turning onto her side to gaze through the big bay windows in her new room. The beauty of the old oak outside made her heart soar. Sam was right about this room. It was Katie's—she could feel it now. Nana had given it to her and it was okay for her to take it. Katie ran a hand over her soft new set of sheets, and for a moment allowed herself to sink into the warm, sweet-smelling bed, perfectly happy.

But it was past time to get up. Today was the day of the café's reopening. Ten days ago, Maddie had got caught stealing and Katie had run. Eight days ago, Sam had argued for Katie to keep the café. And six days ago, Mercy had told Katie that young people were always worth it.

Katie had carried Mercy's words with her, all the way back to Aveline. When she saw Maddie again, she saw the desperation in her eyes to be accepted, to not be written off.

Katie remembered the feeling of being rejected by Philip and his family and by Ed, and how badly it hurt.

Maddie had failed to be honest with Katie, but people did that, living life with others pretty much assured pain at times. Katie had opened her arms to Maddie, tucked her under her chin the way she wished people had done for her. And standing there, holding Maddie, Katie had a moment of truth. This. This girl getting a second chance. This was how God would turn things around. It wasn't in Katie getting what she wanted, or being safe from hurt. It was the open-handed offering of love, even when it wasn't deserved.

Contrary to everything she had imagined, she hired Maddie back on probation as kitchen staff. Maddie wouldn't have the responsibility of closing the café or working with money much, at least not at first. And Katie had decided, as the one capitulation to her fear—which still choked her at times—that Katie herself would reconcile the cash and close the café in the late afternoons. She was good with numbers and would be able to spot any discrepancies right away. It would be more work for Katie, but more work was a small price for being able to give someone she loved another chance.

Katie knew she needed to get up, but took a few more moments to gaze at the beautiful molding Sam had installed in the ceiling corners. She had dreamed about him, back at her parent's cabin, and thoughts of him had invaded every waking moment until she knew she had to come home to him, back to her beautiful house and café, back to life with her new friends.

When she arrived, late one evening, she had unlocked

her house, and walked slowly up the stairs to find a note on the door to her grandmother's room. "Look in here," the note said, and when Katie did, she found, to her utter shock, that the room was finished. The lamps were polished, the bed was made, the windows sparkled, and there were roses on the pillow. She ran all the way to Sam's house, jumping at him when he opened the door, kissing him all over his face until he pulled away, laughing and protesting that he couldn't even see if it was really her.

Then she went to work. She restocked, cleaned and supervised the cleaning team. She made yogurt and spent time walking with Lewis on his farm.

Today was the day. She *really* needed to get herself out of bed. It was past time to put the bread in the oven. It had been rising all night in the pans and would overflow if she wasn't careful. She sat up and stretched, then froze. There were voices downstairs. She glanced at her clock. It was only ten to seven. And then the yeasty smell of bread baking came to her. Who on earth was here?

She dressed quickly, throwing on a blue polka dot dress and tying her hair up in a bun. She put a little eye makeup on and brushed her teeth in her luxurious ensuite bathroom—Sam's next project was to install a shower—dabbing rose oil behind her ears. She looked at herself in the mirror—red gold hair, green eyes under long dark eyebrows, a few new creases fanning from her eyes. She nodded at herself. "I live in a life of love," she said, using her new phrase to start the day. "It may be messy and unexpected, but it will always be full."

She could hear music playing faintly in the kitchen as she skipped down the stairs, and she opened the door to find not one, but three people in there. Maddie stood at the oven, watching the timer that counted down the minutes before the bread was done, ready to pull it out in golden, crispy perfection. Sam was chopping fruit for the morning's fruit salads and smoothies, and Lucy was busy organizing the prep station.

"Wow," Katie said, leaning against the door. "This is unexpected."

Maddie turned away from the oven. "Happy re-opening day!" she said, and broke into applause. She stopped after a moment when no one joined her, shrugging and turning back to the timer. Lucy's arms were loaded down as she carried containers of chopped mushrooms, peppers, and grated cheese that Katie had prepped the night before. Sam was just staring at her, his hands covered in mango juice.

"You look so beautiful," he said. "You're the most beautiful woman in the world."

She rounded her eyes at him.

"No more secrets," he said, walking around the counter to kiss her gently, keeping his hands away from her clean dress.

"Okay," she said, happiness welling up in her. No more secrets.

Lucy snorted. "It's not like you were fooling anyone anyway," she said.

"I love you, Katie Grace," Sam said, as though Lucy wasn't there.

Katie looked back into Sam's face, his blue eyes fringed by dark eyelashes, that dimple, the beard that was growing back, his disobedient hair sticking up, the crinkles around his eyes. He was so lovely to her, so strong and yet gentle, the one who had carefully built her a home in a new place. A spacious place.

"I love you, too," she said, leaning in for another kiss. She stood back after a moment and looked around at the bright, warm kitchen, walking out to the dining rooms, pausing to straighten a tablecloth or center a little jar of sugar. The house glowed with sunlight that came from the windows, and the smell of eucalyptus drifted from the lake. Roses nodded against the windows. The wood floors glowed. The house was perfect. She walked to the door and opened it to meet the day.

To learn when the next Aveline book is out, sign up here!

What is the most important ingredient for a book's success? Besides, of course, the book itself?

It's what you, the Reader, says about it. Social proof. Reviews.

When people are out there, in the wilderness of the book jungle, looking for something to read, the main question they ask is, "Have other people read this? Did they like it?"

So if this book is your kind of book, and you think it might be someone else's kind of book, I will be over the moon if you leave a review on whatever site feeds you your books. Reviews can be the key to a book's success. Thank you!

ACKNOWLEDGMENTS

Thank you dear reader, for taking a chance on a new book!

Thank you to all my Journey Mama readers who have followed me over to my Rae Walsh adventures, and thanks to my unicorn readers group.

Kathleen Andersen, Jessie Benkert, Molly, Donia Goodman, Rose Anderson, Erin Smith, Teresa Q., Amanda Friese, Jessie John, Tj and Mark, Annie Laurie Nichols, Stephanie Donnelly, Ro Keyzer, Erin Yeatman, Diane Brodeur, Alicia Wiggin, Brittani Truby, Karen Engel, and Elisha Pettit, I am thankful for you with great gusting winds of thankfulness, you have no idea. You are all radiant wondrous people.

Thank you beautiful Shekina Community. I love you!

Thanks, Chinua, for believing in a new endeavor, for playing basketball with me, and for always singing and playing.

And thanks to my kids, Kai, Kenya, Leafy, Solomon, and Isaac, for hugs, fun, sarcasm, silly evenings around the table, and endless inspiration.

ABOUT THE AUTHOR

Newsletter

If you want to join Rae Walsh's Newsletter and learn about books and new releases, sign up here. Your address will never be shared!

~

Bio

Rae Walsh is the women's fiction/inspirational romance pen name of Rachel Devenish Ford. Rae is the wife of one Superstar Husband and the mother of five incredible children. Originally from British Columbia, Canada, she spent seven years working with street youth in California before moving to India to help start a meditation center in the Christian tradition. She can be found eating street food or smelling flowers in many cities in Asia. She currently lives in Northern Thailand, inhaling books, morning air, and seasonal fruit.

~

Works by Rae Walsh:

    The Lost Art of Reverie: Aveline Book 1

Works by Rachel Devenish Ford:

The Eve Tree

    A Traveler's Guide to Belonging

Trees Tall As Mountains: The Journey Mama Writings- Book One

    Oceans Bright With Stars: The Journey Mama Writings- Book Two

    A Home as Wide as the Earth: The Journey Mama Writings: Book Three

    World Whisperer : World Whisperer Book 1

    Guardian of Dawn : World Whisperer Book 2

    Shaper's Daughter: World Whisperer Book 3

Reviews

Recommendations and reviews are such an important part of the success of a book. If you enjoyed this book, please take the time to leave a review.

Don't be afraid of leaving a short review! Even a couple lines will help and will overwhelm the author with waves of gratitude.

Contact

Email: raewalshauthor@gmail.com
    Blog: http://journeymama.com
    Facebook: http://www.facebook.com/rae.walsh.author
    Twitter: http://www.twitter.com/journeymama
    Instagram: http://instagram.com/journeymama

CPSIA information can be obtained
at www.ICGtesting.com
Printed in the USA
LVHW042303221119
638197LV00003B/232/P